LOVE IS DANGER

CLUB AEGIS

Christie Adams

Blue Topaz Books

UNITED KINGDOM

Blue Topaz Books
Suite 12678, PO Box 4336
Manchester, United Kingdom, M61 0BW
www.bluetopazbooks.com

Publisher's Note: This is a work of fiction. Names, characters, places, and incidents are a product of the author's imagination. Locales and public names are sometimes used for atmospheric purposes. Any resemblance to actual people, living or dead, or to businesses, companies, events, institutions, or locales is completely coincidental.

Edited by **Julie Naughton**
Cover by **Syneca Featherstone**
Book Layout © 2017 **BookDesignTemplates.com**

Love Is Danger / Christie Adams—3rd ed.
ISBN 978-1-910791-53-0

CLUB AEGIS

Aegis—the shield of Zeus, and by extension, a means of protection. The men and women who are members of Club Aegis have all played their part in protecting their country. They work hard... and they play hard. Their lives are not always easy—and sometimes they have to put their lives on the line, not just for their country but for those they love.

CHAPTER ONE

Stacie Matheson hated driving in the rain. She hated driving in the dark too. Even so, those two things, combined as they were now, wouldn't normally be enough to tear her nerves to shreds. However, once she factored in the rude awakening she'd had in the early hours, it was hardly surprising that she felt on the verge of unfamiliar tears—there was only so much a person could take in one day.

As if that weren't enough, she was in what felt like the middle of nowhere. She could no longer deny the simple fact that she was lost. She was supposed to be heading for a village in the Berkshire countryside, but she suspected that she was no longer even in the right county.

Get a grip, Stacie.

Why had she chosen yesterday of all days to update the sat nav? She'd forgotten to pick it up before leaving for work that morning—the damn thing was still sitting on the table in her apartment, when it should have been helping her to get this wreck of a car to the small hotel where she was supposed to be spending the next couple of nights. On the internet, it had appeared to be the ideal location to put some distance between herself and the selfish, womanising bastard she'd been sleeping with for the last six months—not to mention calling down every curse she could think of on his worthless, no-good head.

Thank God she'd never actually fallen in love with him. Her stomach churned sickeningly at the very idea.

A spontaneous early morning visit to Jonty's apartment two days ago had given her a surprise she hadn't bargained for—and exclusive entrance to relationship hell. Things had been going downhill ever since. After finding him in bed with a bimbo—and judging by the contemptuous sneer the bimbo gave her and the familiar way in which she was draped around Jonty, this wasn't the first time they'd been together—she'd had to endure a barrage of phone calls and aggressive texts from the two-timing creep.

The grand finale of this abuse had arrived with his uninvited visit to her apartment just after two o'clock that morning. Either he'd charmed his way into the building or more likely tailgated one of the other residents—he certainly hadn't used her intercom. God, if she'd been besotted enough to give him a set of keys… it didn't bear thinking about.

Stacie had never been more grateful that she'd had the great good sense to resist Jonty's precipitous attempts to move her in with him—all she'd had to do, to extricate herself from his life, had been to leave the keys to his place on the hall table as she'd stormed out. She'd never wanted the blasted things in the first place, but he'd insisted.

What she hadn't anticipated, though, was how badly he'd react to her ending their relationship. The accusation at the time had been bad enough—apparently his involvement with another woman was all Stacie's fault for not moving in with him. She'd had no idea that he would take it as far as he did.

At one point that morning, while he was delivering his pre-dawn tirade of verbal abuse from the other side of her front door, he'd hammered on it so hard that she'd feared he might break it down. A rather extreme reaction, she'd thought, given the relative brevity of their liaison, and one that had made her wonder if he was as high as a kite on drink. She shuddered—given that it seemed she barely knew the man after all, was it alcohol, or could it have been some other kind of substance abuse? Either way, she considered that she'd had a lucky escape.

Unable to sleep after he'd finally left, she'd thrown some clothes and other essentials into a couple of bags, ready to stow them in the boot of her car before leaving for work.

On arriving at the office, she'd asked her manager for a few days off—she'd been prepared to beg, if necessary, but fortunately it hadn't come to that. A search on the internet at lunchtime had enabled her to find a suitable hotel, and at the end of the day she'd fled the city just as fast as she could, unable to face the weekend at home with the possibility of another scintillating encounter with Jonty.

Stacie glanced at the temperature gauge on the dashboard. Just lately it seemed to have been reading a little higher than normal. She hoped that it was just a figment of her imagination, because the last thing she needed was for the car to break down. Not just because she had no idea where she was—she'd never got around to renewing her breakdown coverage. The reason for that oversight was the stress of coping with Jonty's suspect behaviour over the last few weeks, the prelude to the grand finale that had played out over the last couple of days.

So where on earth was she? The country lane was winding on forever, not a road sign to be seen. It wasn't especially late, but at this time of year it was already dark. If she could just find a village with a pub where she could ask for directions to a hotel or a bed and breakfast, she'd feel a whole lot better. As it was, all she could see was the road ahead—as far as the next bend—and the trees and bushes that lined it.

Stacie huffed; this was proving to be a really stupid idea. She should never have left her apartment. If Jonty had come back again, she could have just ignored him—running off like this was letting him win. Maybe she should just turn the car around and see if she could find her way back to the motorway and go home.

"Oh God, not now!"

All of a sudden, the engine temperature shot off the

top of the scale, attributable no doubt to the steam billowing out from under the bonnet. At least, Stacie hoped it was steam. She guided the car to the side of the road, came to a halt and switched the engine off… and couldn't stop the stupid, useless tears that wouldn't get her anywhere.

After the last few days, this was all she needed. What the *hell* was she going to do now?

Cam Fraser guided his Jaguar off the motorway and onto the exit road. It had been a shit week, he was running late, and it was pissing down with rain. Again. *Bloody brilliant.* He tried to console himself with the fact that within half an hour—maybe less, if he was lucky—he'd be getting intimately acquainted with a single malt, in the company of his old friend Alex Lombard and Alex's gorgeous wife Beth. The weekend away from the manic pressure of London was going to be a long one, the highlight of which would be the party Beth was hosting to celebrate the imminent publication of her second novel.

He was also going to explore with Alex the possibility of the other man returning to Spectrum Security, the company they'd started together when they'd left the military. His friend had been avoiding this discussion for far too long. Cam reckoned that Alex had been resting on his laurels for long enough after selling his own business for a not-so-small fortune—it was high time he got back into some gainful employment, did something useful, and stopped basking in the glow of his wife's well-deserved success.

Cam was a frequent visitor to the Lombards' stylish home, a large spacious property in rural Hampshire. He'd known Alex for around half his life and Beth for well over four years now, ever since Alex had taken her on as his executive assistant. After a rather fraught situation about a year ago, when the repercussions of an incident in Alex's distant past had been in danger of costing him his life, Cam's relationship with the couple had grown considerably closer. Earlier that year, in spring, he'd been the best man at their wedding.

Consequently, Cam knew the route to their house with his eyes closed, but it was just as well that he was concentrating. When he rounded the next bend, the sweep of the Jaguar's headlights revealed a car pulled up at the side of the road some distance ahead of him. The hazard lights were flashing—the vehicle appeared to be in no state to go any further.

Oh shit. He could feel his Good Samaritan gene kicking in, overruling the clamour of his aching, stress-knotted shoulders. He knew he wasn't going to drive past without stopping—it just wasn't in his nature—but if fate was on his side, he'd find that the driver had already called their breakdown service and was just waiting for a mechanic to arrive.

Cam pulled in ahead of the aged vehicle. The aged *hideous* vehicle. He could probably count on the fingers of one hand the number of orange—*orange*, for Christ's sake!—cars he'd seen in his life. While he was no expert, he didn't like the look of the vapour that was escaping from under the bonnet. Grabbing the flashlight out of the glove compartment, he ducked out of the car, snatched a rag and his fluorescent waterproof jacket from the boot, and ran back to the other car, grimacing against the rain.

The driver was still behind the wheel and looked to be resting their forehead on the rim of it. Cam experienced a glimmer of disquiet, wondering if whoever it was had been taken ill. A sick driver and a sick car—could things get any worse?

Don't answer that!

It didn't do to tempt fate.

As he neared the vehicle, the flashlight illuminated long, rich blonde hair—the driver appeared to be a woman, and she had a white-knuckled death-grip on the steering wheel. He hoped that the lack of a response to the light wasn't a sign of a more serious, possibly health-related issue. After a moment's hesitation he tapped lightly on the window… and was rewarded with an ear-piercing shriek. What the hell was he getting himself into now? Positioning the flashlight so that it would illuminate his face, he motioned to the driver to lower the window. It descended about an inch.

"Are you all right?" he called through the crack. "Do you need any help? It's okay, you can trust me—I was a Boy Scout." He turned on the smile that usually obtained the desired result.

The window descended a little more. Cam angled the flashlight again, so that it shed a little light on the car's occupant without blinding her, and found himself looking into tearful storm-grey eyes. They were set in an absolutely stunning face framed by that tumbling cascade of golden waves. His stomach lurched, as if he'd taken a physical blow.

Grabbing his libido by the scruff of the neck—there was a time and a place for the thoughts that suddenly whizzed through his mind, and this wasn't it—he figured he'd better take control of matters, starting with an introduction. "My name's Cam—Cam Fraser." He dug out his driving license as proof. "Do you need any help?"

If he'd been hoping for a glib reply that would have sent him on his way with a clear conscience, he'd have been sorely disappointed. It was just as well he hadn't set his sights that high, because what he got was the frozen stare of a deer caught in the headlights of a car.

In that instant, Cam realised two things—firstly, he couldn't get much wetter, and secondly, he wasn't going to get dry any time soon. The situation was going to require some finesse. He crouched down, resting one knee on the tarmac, so that he was on a level with her. "It's all right, honey," he said softly, slipping easily into Dom mode and adopting the tone he'd use with a novice sub in need of reassurance. "I won't hurt you, I promise. Have you called anyone to come and take a look at the car?"

This time, she shook her head—progress of a sort, he supposed. He wasn't ready to give up just yet, though. "Would you like to call someone? Your breakdown service? You can use my phone."

"I—I'm sorry," she gulped. "It ran out and I forgot to renew it. Stupid of me, I know –"

"Don't say that." Cam's voice was sterner than he intended, shocking her and surprising himself. Maybe he'd better tone down the orders a bit in favour of ramping up the charm. "Shit happens, but it's nothing we can't deal with. If you open it up, I'll take a look—can't promise anything, though."

Cam lifted the bonnet. It didn't look good—in fact, it reminded him of the time the cylinder head gasket failed on the clapped-out wreck that had been his first car, back in his teenage years. If that was the problem now—and he was pretty damn sure it was—not even a breakdown service could get this vehicle moving tonight. He dropped the bonnet back into place and returned to deliver his verdict.

"This car's not going another foot tonight without serious help," he said. "Now, where were you heading for?" With luck, she was visiting friends or family in the local area who'd be able to help her out in the morning.

Not friends, not family—she was heading for a destination far enough away for a quick bit of mental arithmetic to tell Cam he'd be lucky to make the Lombards' house by midnight, if he were to give her a lift there. This called for an alternative strategy.

Cam came to a decision. He couldn't just leave her stranded there, nor could he find it in himself to dump her at the nearest hotel for the night, leaving her to deal with her car problem alone—that just wasn't his style. To him, the answer was obvious—she was going to accompany him to the Lombards'. Good thing she didn't look like a psychotic murderer—God knows he'd encountered enough of those in his previous military life.

"There's no chance of you getting there tonight—" He broke off, realising that he didn't know her name. He tilted his head, asking her the question with his eyes, curious to see whether she would respond, and respond accurately.

"Stacie," she supplied, without missing a beat. "Stacie Matheson."

The name suited her. "Well, Stacie, I have an idea. I'm on my way to visit some friends of mine. Their house isn't far from here, and they have plenty of room for visitors." Time for the Dom voice again, if this was going to go the way he needed it to. "Why don't you come with me? Have something to eat, get a good night's sleep, and in the morning we'll figure out what to do about your car. You can trust me, Stacie—Scouts' Honour."

A mixture of hope and relief brightened her face briefly, and then it was gone. "I can't," she whispered. "I don't know you."

A good point. "That's right, you don't know me, Stacie, but you can't stay here all night, either. It's already dark, it's going to get colder, and even if you do stay here—which, from a personal safety point of view, I wouldn't advise—you'll still have the same problem in the morning. Let me take care of you, Stacie."

The ball was in her court now. Cam stood up and waited, oblivious to the rain that was now starting to run down the back of his neck in icy rivulets. He'd known worse. His concentration was on Stacie, willing her to agree to his proposition. A couple of seconds later the car door edged open. He took hold of it, slowly pulled it wider, and offered the young woman his hand.

Even in the light cast by the flashlight and with her long hair starting to hang in disorderly rats' tails due to the rain, her grace and the sense of beauty flowing from her left Cam fleetingly stunned. He suppressed the urge to praise her as if she were a sub responding to instruction—instead, he focused on the job at hand. "Give me your keys, Stacie, then go and sit in my car—the door's unlocked. Do you have a bag?"

"In the boot." She pressed the keys into his palm. "Just the small one—it's all I'll need for tonight. And… thank you."

Cam smiled his approval, and through her gentle touch realised that she had allowed herself to relax… even if it was only a little.

A stranger's hand was warming her chilled skin, yet for some unaccountable reason Stacie felt as if her own hand were where it had always belonged.

Although the man's—Cam's—flashlight was quite powerful, she hadn't been able to get much of an impression of him beyond height and breadth, short hair that could have been any shade between brown and blond, and a flash of penetrating blue eyes. And that touch that felt as if it could hold her safely for the rest of her life. She was clearly having some sort of delusion. Stress—it had to be stress. Or maybe anxiety. Something… like that. In the circumstances, who could blame her?

Common sense was screaming at her to snatch back her keys, get back in the car and lock all the doors, but overriding that was something more powerful and elemental—and it had nothing to do with seeking shelter from the weather. She was responding to this man in a way that was all primitive instinct, and although that reaction confused her at a fundamental level, she didn't want it to stop.

As she ran towards his car—a brand-new Jaguar convertible that looked frighteningly expensive—she stopped to glance back, hoping that he wouldn't catch her looking at him, only to find him watching her. The nod he gave her was strangely calming, so she continued to the passenger door of the sleek, dark car with the lighter soft top. She froze in her tracks when she opened it.

The dashboard wouldn't have looked out of place in a state-of-the-art jet, but it was the pristine ivory leather seats staring her in the face that made her draw back, along with grey carpets that were a shade too light for her peace of mind. There was *no way* she was getting in there.

"Stacie, what is it?"

Cam's hand on her arm shattered the spell and turned her attention towards him. How had he sneaked up on her so quietly? "I—I can't!" she stammered. "I'm soaked…" She looked back into the car, the direction of her gaze revealing the cause of her reluctance.

The vehicle's owner made an impatient noise. "And the longer you stand here, the wetter you'll get. Stacie, it's only a damn car! For God's sake, get in! I'll be right back."

Painfully aware of the mess she was liable to make, Stacie slipped off her coat and bundled it up to stuff in the footwell, in the hope of minimising the possibility of causing any damage to the luxurious upholstery. She slid into the passenger seat, jumping slightly when Cam forcefully closed the door behind her. A few moments later, once he'd retrieved her bag, the Jaguar's boot closed with similar intensity and the man himself was taking his place behind the wheel.

The fluorescent yellow jacket was now gone, revealing a frame no less imposing than that first impression. When its owner turned towards her, she hugged her tote bag to her chest, almost using it as a shield.

"Relax, Stacie." His voice started to calm her with only those two words. "Your car's locked up and not going anywhere. We'll be at my friends' house in around twenty minutes, maybe less, and I know you'll be more than welcome. You're safe now."

For no reason that she could name, she believed him. She felt safer with him—with this *stranger*—than she had since the first blow of Jonty's fist on her door that morning. From his reaction, anyone would have thought Jonty had caught her cheating on him, rather than it being the other way around. She'd seen him lose his temper on more than one occasion during their time together, but that morning was the first time she'd been on the receiving end of it. Once was more than enough. Trapped in the memory, she flinched when Cam touched her hand.

"Stacie? What's wrong? You look terrified—I told you, I won't hurt you."

"It's not you."

She heard herself say the words, and all of a sudden common sense reasserted itself. This man was a completely unknown quantity, for heaven's sake—a handsome, confident knight in shining armour with a compelling air of command about him, but it didn't make him any less the stranger. And she'd got into his car with barely a thought for the possible risks in doing so. Had she gone completely insane? "Please… give me my keys and my bag. I can't be here—"

"Stacie!"

Before she knew what was happening, strong arms had reached over the centre console and gone around her, holding her tightly to a broad chest. He smelled of rain, expensive aftershave and all things male, and that and the physical comfort combined to allay the panic that was threatening to overwhelm her. His deep voice had an indefinable quality that helped to soothe her as well. Why wasn't she scared anymore? He was a stranger, she should be scared. Shouldn't she?

"Shh, honey, it's all right," he murmured, stroking her arm. "Trust me. You've had a crap experience, but it's over now. Just a short time from now, we'll both be getting warm and dry again. *Trust me.*"

His voice again—the mesmeric quality of it wrapped around her, comforting her in ways that reminded her of… now she *was* crazy, imagining that this man was like the ones in the novel she was reading. Men like that just didn't exist, no matter how much she might secretly want them to.

Stacie was on her third copy of the book now. She'd lent the first to Jen, her best friend, who'd then passed it on to another friend. The second copy had disappeared somewhere in the office and was no doubt circulating around the entire female contingent. Desperate to read it for—was it really the fourth time?—Stacie had bought another copy just yesterday, and was half a dozen chapters into it. The story was downright addictive.

As the sense of panic receded, so her ability to think calmly began to reassert itself. Slowly she pulled away from her rescuer, a slight case of embarrassment making her cheeks burn. "I'm sorry," she murmured, "it's just that it's been… let's just say it's been a rough couple of days."

"Tell me about it later, Stacie." He reached across her for the seatbelt and snapped it into place. "For now, just relax and get warm. When we get to where we're going, you can tell me all about whatever it is you're running away from."

Thank God they were so close to his destination.

Cam must have been more tired than he thought, for him to have given in to the irrational impulse to take a woman he'd known barely fifteen minutes in his arms and offer her comfort. This wasn't the club. This wasn't the prelude to a negotiation with a sub he'd never met before, and it most certainly wasn't governed by the etiquette and protocol of Domination and submission. What the frickin' hell was it about this woman that was making him go all Dom and protective all of a sudden?

Whatever it was, it was dangerous—especially to a man in Cam's position. After a lifetime of avoiding commitment in relationships, he'd finally admitted to himself not so long ago that he was attracted to the kind of relationship that Alex and Beth shared. Not just attracted—he wanted the whole nine yards, right down to the wedding bells.

He was only just getting used to the idea; what he hadn't expected to happen so soon was meeting a woman whom he could imagine on his arm when those wedding bells rang. And he sure as hell hadn't planned to run into her in the middle of nowhere. His subconscious had kind of assumed he'd meet a suitable sub at Aegis one evening, and he'd take things from there—there was no way he'd bargained on being blindsided in the middle of a storm by a complete stranger.

Or he could just be working too hard and fatigue had robbed him of the capacity to control his imagination. Put a pretty blonde in his path, and his ability to think straight went south. As explanations went, that one was far more feasible. Either way, though, the sooner they got to his destination, the better.

Cam's concentration was on the road ahead, but he risked a sideways glance at his unexpected passenger. He was in a prime position to appreciate the delicate lines of her profile—and to see that she was as taut as the proverbial bowstring. His honest opinion? She was on the verge of panic—second thoughts probably, and entirely understandable, given that she didn't know him and she didn't understand yet that she could trust him.

He wanted her to trust him. He wanted her to kiss him, and he wanted her on her knees in front of him. *Shit!* He was reacting to her just like he would to a sub at Aegis. Again, he wondered what the hell had come over him.

At that point, his head started to take an interest in what his instincts were fantasising about. He reminded himself that after tomorrow morning, when she went on her way, he'd probably never see Stacie Matheson again.

A prospect he found disturbingly unpleasant, when he shouldn't have found it *anything*.

The Jaguar ate up the distance to the Lombards' home, and pretty much at the time he'd predicted he was guiding the car through the huge wrought iron gates. As he pulled up outside the house, he heard Stacie gasp.

"Your friends live here?"

Cam switched off the engine. "It's called Winterleigh. Nice place, and they have plenty of guest accommodation. Don't worry, Stacie—Beth and Alex will make you more than welcome."

"Are you sure, Mr. Fraser? I don't want to impose."

Mr. Fraser. Shit—that made him sound like the father

he'd never known. The sperm donor who'd sired him had been just one of the many men his alcoholic tramp of a mother had slept with, before the booze had taken its toll and left him orphaned at the age of eight. He frowned at the disconcerting thought that the woman beside him might view him as some sort of father figure.

"It's Cam," he reminded her as he got out of the car, then went around to the passenger door to help her out, collecting their bags from the boot on the way. "Come on, let's get inside before the rain starts again."

Viewing him as family rather than just a friend, Beth and Alex had both insisted that he have a set of keys to the house. Cam unlocked the front door, then stood back to let Stacie enter first. He'd barely closed it when he felt the warm familiarity of one of Beth's hugs and heard the single word she whispered in his ear, a word that gave him the welcome he really needed tonight.

"We were starting to think you'd got lost, Cam," she said with her usual radiant smile as she stepped back to look up at his face. "What happened to you?"

He leaned down to kiss her cheek. "I was running late, the weather was lousy and then I found a fair damsel in distress. Beth, let me introduce you to Stacie—Beth Lombard, Stacie Matheson. I told her you wouldn't mind putting her up for the night, while we work out what to do about her car."

Bloody hell.

Standing in the well-lit hall, this was the first opportunity he'd had to take a clear look at the young woman whom he'd assisted. What he saw, through the nervousness and the superficial damage wrought by the storm, cemented that first impression back at the car. Not just beauty, though, but a sweet, innocent loveliness, the like of which a man like him could never even aspire to take as his own, yet every cell in his body screamed to possess her and make her his. Almost in a daze, he held out his hand to her, his mind registering vaguely that she had to be at least a dozen years his junior. "Stacie."

Emerging from the corner into which she'd slipped on entering the hall, she stepped forward—and irrational though it was, pleased him no end with her instant obedience. She took his hand, offering no resistance when he put his arm around her slender shoulders and pulled her against his body, acting on subconscious instincts older than time.

"Dear heaven, Stacie, you look absolutely exhausted!" Beth stated unequivocally, ready to take the other woman under her wing. "Do you have a bag with you?"

Before she could answer, a new voice joined in with another question.

"Where the bloody hell have you been, Fraser?"

Stacie had been in a state close to shock from the second she stepped past her rescuer and into the entrance hall of the stunningly impressive house. Suddenly feeling way out of her depth, she'd sought refuge in the corner by the door, only to realise that the interior, far from being imposing, was as warm and friendly as the smiling woman who had suddenly appeared and flung her arms enthusiastically around Cam Fraser.

She was younger than Stacie had somehow imagined—beautiful in a very natural way, with long, lustrous brown waves framing a face with a flawless complexion, remarkable green eyes behind a classy pair of designer glasses, and an unashamedly voluptuous figure. She was clad in an outfit that was both casual and chic, and around her neck she wore an elaborate heavy gold chain.

However, it was Cam himself who robbed Stacie briefly of the power of speech. Now that she could appreciate the full impact of him, her instinctive reaction was that, for the first time in her life, she'd met a real man and one who made her feel more feminine and alive than she'd ever felt before. With very little effort she could get into trouble. Oh, so much trouble…

He was tall. God, was he tall, well over six feet of solid muscle as far as she could tell, from his dark blond, military-short hair to his expensively booted feet. His clothes spoke of wealth, just as his car did, and they covered broad shoulders that she longed to feel beneath her hands, purely in the interests of confirming whether or not they were as strong as they looked, of course. Absolutely no ulterior motive at all. Cam Fraser was definitely all man and with his arm around her, Stacie found herself reacting to his overwhelming masculinity in a very wet, female way. No wonder she was having trouble keeping her wits about her.

And now another man was joining them—another

equally impressive specimen of manhood, as ridiculously good-looking as Cam, but dark-haired where Cam was blond. When he spoke, all three turned as one in the direction of his voice. As he descended the final tread of the magnificent staircase, his sternly handsome features relaxed into a broad grin. He came to greet his friend with a brief and most definitely masculine hug.

He went on to introduce himself as Alex Lombard. He shook Stacie's hand, and then moved to his wife, drawing her into his side in such a way that all Stacie could do was wonder how it must feel to be the woman who had such a man so blatantly, so deeply in love with her. That was something she herself had never known, yet suddenly found herself wishing for it with an almost physical intensity. Oh yeah, she was tired and overwrought, she had to be.

"Stacie, why don't you come with me?" Beth lifted her arm towards the staircase. "Cam, bring Stacie's bag, would you? You know where you're going—Stacie can have the blue bedroom, two doors down from yours."

Although she was following the other woman, Stacie was more aware of her rescuer just a few steps behind her, all the way up the staircase and along the gallery to the last door on the right. Consequently she was barely listening when Beth showed her into the room and informed her that dinner would be ready in about forty-five minutes. She thanked her hostess and watched the other woman leave.

"You see, honey, I told you everything would be all

right."

CHAPTER TWO

Cam carefully set Stacie's bag down by the dressing table, focusing on the simple act as a means of diverting his attention from the intimacy of the setting. At the same time, he was making a mental note to speak to Alex about his sub's trouble-making tendencies, as he recalled the saucy wink and smile Beth had flashed in his direction as she left the room. The woman was incorrigible—one of her many traits that he loved.

But now he was alone with another exquisite woman and he really should be walking out of there, so that she could relax and freshen up before dinner. The trouble was he found himself a little too attracted to the slightly anxious smile she was giving him.

"That's right, you did," she agreed, a little self-consciously. "Your friends are very kind."

Cam couldn't argue with that assessment. "Yes, that they are. Anyway, I'd better leave you in peace and give you a chance to get cleaned up. Beth and Alex don't stand on ceremony, so don't worry about dressing up for dinner. If you need anything, I'm two doors away in that direction." He nodded to his right. "I'll be back soon to escort you downstairs. See you in a little while, Stacie."

When Cam got to the door of what had become his home away from home over the last few months he paused, debating whether or not to go downstairs first and sedate his errant thoughts with a generous measure of Alex's best Scotch.

"I don't think so," he muttered under his breath, pressing down the door handle. Greeting Stacie with the miasma of alcohol fumes around him wasn't a good idea… and he wasn't about to explain to himself why it wasn't a good idea.

Minutes later he was under the shower, sluicing off the negative feelings that had accompanied him from London and looking forward to the evening ahead—and the night. When Beth had greeted him with that familiar hug a short time ago, the word she'd whispered in his ear—*Trinity*—was the word she'd chosen months ago to avoid the embarrassment of blatantly telling him that he would be welcome to join her and Alex in their suite for a play session… and to spend the night with them.

To his surprise and that of her husband, she'd suggested the idea, but drew the line at spelling it out in so many words. He smiled to himself as he remembered the way she'd blushed at the time, when she'd said that it was the one and only time she was going to describe exactly what she meant. She'd then nominated the word to convey the invitation in future. Although she was no longer embarrassed, she still used their code word as a form of verbal shorthand.

And tonight Cam needed the company and the distraction. Work had been getting to him of late—it was nearly two years since he'd last had a break long enough to recharge his batteries and he was getting to the point where he was running on empty. He hadn't even had the energy and enthusiasm to seek companionship at Club Aegis, not since… oh hell, he couldn't even remember, beyond it being quite some time before his recent three-month stint in the Middle East.

He knew he should be pleased that business was going so well—if it weren't, he wouldn't be in a position to buy toys like the top-of-the-range F-Type Jaguar convertible parked outside. Nor would he have been able to instruct the estate agent to look for a house for him within easy driving distance of this one. Even so, there was still something vital missing from his life.

He knew precisely what it was, and it was something he couldn't buy. A grunt of humourless laughter had him shaking his head. Actually, he *could* buy it, if he wanted to—by the hour, maybe by the night, but it would be a cold, emotionless facsimile of what he'd recently decided he really wanted.

Thinking about relationships and intimacy led him to thinking about Stacie again. It was a connection he had no business making. In addition, he was too tired for his body to be responding the way it was. She was way too *young* for him, he told himself harshly, repeating the y word over and over again as he rinsed away the suds. There was no way she'd want an old man like him in her bed.

And as for anything else…

Back in the bedroom, he pulled out a clean pair of jeans and a white polo shirt and dressed quickly. Time was getting better of him, and he had escort duty to perform. He pushed his bare feet into a pair of loafers, squared his tired shoulders and walked out of the room.

Even if her hosts didn't stand on ceremony, Stacie was glad that she'd packed the smart, cream linen skirt and the classic, cornflower-blue top in the small holdall that had made the journey with her. She'd been able to have a delightful shower in the sumptuously appointed bathroom, found a hairdryer in one of the dressing table drawers and was just finishing off her light makeup with a subtle touch of warm pink lipstick.

Shoes! They were one thing she hadn't put into the smaller bag—the spare couple of pairs she'd brought with her were back in the car, in the larger of her two bags, which left her with only the ones she'd been wearing to travel in. Ridiculously impractical for wet weather, they were still damp and they'd look horribly out of place with her much lighter-toned outfit anyway. What was she going to do now?

A gentle knock at the door put the brakes on her mental panic. That would be Cam, ready to take her down to dinner. Perhaps he'd…

Stacie shook her head. *Hold on, girl.* Why would a stranger she'd only just met know what she should do about a pair of wet shoes? Hoping a smile would mask her embarrassment, she opened the door.

It was… a puzzling moment. Cam was there, mouth open as if he were about to say something but looking as stunned as she felt, after his eyes had swept over her from head to toe and lingered there, as if her bare feet had some strange fascination for him.

As for Stacie, all of a sudden her mouth was dry and her pussy drenched at the sight of a man who was pure sun god. The contrast between his blond hair, tanned skin and white polo shirt—with short sleeves that clung to his well-defined biceps and revealed the bold design of a tribal-style tattoo adorning his upper right arm—was breathtaking, while the clean but faded jeans emphasised long legs and muscular thighs. His feet were shod in tan leather loafers that bore the distinctive hallmark of very expensive quality.

Stacie's gaze returned to his face, her brow creasing in a tiny puzzled frown when she realised he was *still* looking at her feet. Her immaculately pedicured toes scrunched up in automatic reaction, the small movement enough to break the spell.

"Ready?" he prompted, offering his hand.

Stacie smiled awkwardly. "You won't believe this, but I don't have any shoes. The ones I was wearing are still wet, and at the risk of sounding like a drama queen—which I promise I'm not usually—they'd look silly with this anyway." She gestured at her clothes.

He looked her up and down again, then his eyes flicked briefly towards the shoes a few feet away. "You're right, they wouldn't suit your outfit. Don't worry about it."

And then, to her immense surprise he toed off his shoes, revealing long, bony, masculine feet as sun-kissed as the rest of him. "Safety in numbers, Stacie—now you won't be the odd one out. Shall we go?"

With that, he took her hand and tucked it into the crook of his arm.

The muscular forearm made her fingers itch to test its strength—she was equally entranced by the fine golden hair that glinted in the light. And the scent of him—she could get drunk on that alone. Clean, fresh and boldly masculine, he smelled even better than he had in the car, something she wouldn't have believed possible.

"Beth's cooking dinner tonight," he told her as they descended the staircase together. "She said it's nothing special, in view of the party tomorrow."

"Party?"

"To celebrate Beth's latest achievement. She's got caterers coming in tomorrow morning, but—ever the perfectionist—she's been fretting about all the arrangements for the better part of a week. Alex has been telling her all day not to worry about it."

Stacie smiled, wondering at the little pang of disappointment she experienced when she realised she'd be on her way well before the celebration started. It was nothing to do with her, she reminded herself—these people, who appeared to be especially close friends of Cam's, had just been kind enough to offer her their hospitality for the night. Tomorrow she'd be dealing with a car that didn't work and finding the hotel where she was supposed to be avoiding Jonty and getting her act together.

What would it have been like, though, to be the woman having that conversation as Cam's partner, invited to join the festivities with him? She wanted to ask what Beth's achievement was, but she was wary of prying into something that wasn't really any of her business.

The room to which Cam took her was both informal and luxurious, and already inhabited by two people who together made a simply stunning couple. Alex rose to greet them, one dark eyebrow ascending as he took in the sight of two pairs of bare feet.

"Cam, I know we're pretty casual around here—"

"I'm sorry, Mr. Lombard," Stacie interjected, her face colouring with embarrassment. "It's entirely my fault. My shoes are still wet and I only have the one pair with me—the others are back in the car."

"Oh lord." Beth came to join her husband, her eyes on Stacie's feet now as well. "You poor thing. I'd offer you a pair of mine, but I think they'd be about two sizes too big for you. Alex?"

Speechless, Stacie watched the other woman elbow her husband in the ribs at the same time as she slipped off her own shoes. The heels on them were three, maybe even four inches high. Just the thought of trying to walk in shoes like that gave Stacie vertigo. And with Beth now barefoot, Alex became an even more imposing presence in the room.

"That's so much better!" Beth pronounced with a sigh. "I feel like I've had them on all day. It's such a relief to be out of them!"

Stacie tried her best to stifle the chuckle, especially when she caught sight of the resigned expression on Alex Lombard's face as he joined in with everyone else.

"Stacie, please—call me Alex. Won't you sit down and join us in a glass of champagne to celebrate?"

It was all so warm and friendly and comfortable, Stacie thought a few minutes later. She was sitting beside Cam on one of the two big sofas, champagne flute in hand, and still pondering exactly what was being celebrated. Alex and Beth sat together on the other sofa, Beth with her feet tucked up beside her as she curled into her husband's side. His arm was wrapped around her, while her hand was resting on his thigh. They looked so at ease together, two halves of a whole and each the perfect complement to the other.

Stacie wondered how long they'd been married. Alex looked to be about the same age as Cam, slightly taller than him, she thought, with dark hair and dark eyes and a faintly forbidding air about him, until his face broke into a smile. And he was utterly in love with his wife—anyone could see that. There was also something protective to the point of being proprietorial about the way he was holding her.

Jonty would never have looked at her like that. Stacie knew that now—and it hurt. Not because she'd lost him—it was because he simply wasn't that kind of man, and she found herself wanting that kind of man… the kind of man she'd been convinced couldn't exist outside the pages of the steamy romances she read. And if Alex had the look of a romantic hero, then so did Cam. He also had that extra something that was getting her all hot and bothered in a way that was so bad, it was good. Too good.

She struggled to haul her sensible side to the fore. The three people in whose company she sat were way out of her league. All three were stylish, sophisticated and very wealthy, even if they weren't as openly ostentatious about it as those who actively sought the limelight. She was an admin assistant in a large office, and financially she lived from payday to payday. They were worlds apart.

There was something else as well. She had to face up to the one fact she'd been avoiding—that Cam could easily have a significant other who for whatever reason hadn't accompanied him on his visit. Stacie had no choice but to pack her fantasies away and try to forget they'd ever existed.

"Stacie? Are you all right?"

The sound of Cam's concerned voice just inches away brought her out of the depressing gloom of her thoughts. She was tired—that had to be why her mind was wandering all over the place. She plastered a bright smile on her face even though her heart wasn't fully in it. "I'm sorry—it's been a long day."

"And we're not helping by delaying dinner with all this chatter." Beth stood up. "Come on—we're eating in the kitchen tonight. All I can say," she continued with a mischievous smile as she looked down at her wiggling toes, "is thank God for underfloor heating!"

The meal was delicious and yet another reason for Stacie to be envious of her gracious hostess—if Beth hadn't been the kind of person it was impossible not to like. The other woman was bright and charming, and warm and friendly, with a loving streak a mile wide—Stacie saw it in the way she would touch her husband's shoulder as she moved past him and the glances she gave him while they were eating. She didn't know why, but every time she noticed one of the little caring gestures Stacie felt the urge to steal an eyeful of Cam.

But as the meal and the evening progressed, what Stacie also observed was the gradual way that Beth was becoming more and more tense. If it was related to what she was talking about it, it was all to do with the forthcoming party. Nor did it go unnoticed by her husband. Stacie couldn't miss the way he repeatedly looked in her direction. It was quite touching really, but at the same time Stacie felt that there was an odd undertone to the way he was looking at her, his eyes narrowing almost as if he were analysing her behaviour.

After dinner they adjourned to the room—the family room, they called it—where they'd toasted Beth earlier, with the exception of Alex, who excused himself and disappeared. It might have been her imagination, but before he left Stacie thought she saw a look full of hidden meaning flash between the two men, a thought that she dismissed almost as soon as it occurred. She really was developing an overactive imagination. Probably down to too much alcohol, a growing tiredness and all the emotional stress of a very long day.

Over coffee, Stacie found herself relaxing a little more—it was strange but she was starting to feel as if she'd known these people for a lot longer than just a few hours. Against her better judgement she was getting way too comfortable. Another reason why she shouldn't have succumbed to that last glass of wine with dinner. The conversation was in full flow when it was interrupted by a single word.

"Beth."

It was almost a replay of what had happened when she and Cam had first arrived. All three of them looked up to see Alex filling the doorway—he certainly knew how to make an entrance. His expression was neutral but there was something about his voice, the way he spoke his wife's name, that sent a slightly unsettling shiver down Stacie's spine. Appearing to be almost in a trance, Beth stood up and went to her husband.

"Cam, you know where everything is—would you look after Stacie, please? If you'll excuse me, both of you?"

Cam risked a glance at Stacie as she watched his

friends depart, her expression clearly mystified. He was hoping that she wouldn't ask any awkward questions. No such luck—the awkward questions started almost immediately.

"What was all that about? Is she all right?"

To give Stacie her due, she did sound genuinely concerned—Cam liked that, even if he wasn't happy about dodging the verbal bullets coming his way. He knew exactly what his friend was up to and didn't relish the prospect of trying to focus Stacie's attention elsewhere. He sure as hell couldn't tell her the truth. "She's fine," he said dismissively. "Fancy another coffee?"

His companion wasn't about to fall for his diversionary tactics. "He doesn't hit her, does he?"

Now why would she leap to that particular conclusion? Cam took in the frown that accompanied the fierce question, wondering if personal experience was the explanation. His fingers twitched as he curbed the urge to form a fist at the thought of some bastard raising his hand to this lovely young woman.

And how in the name of heaven could he answer the damn question? *Not in the way you mean, Stacie. Only because he has her permission to do it, Stacie. Every stroke is given and received with love, Stacie.*

He had to think fast. This woman wasn't part of the community and unlike Beth, she didn't show any signs of being a sub in the making—when she'd greeted him with bare feet it had been for purely practical reasons, not submissive ones, no matter what his rebellious libido might have wanted.

No, she'd never understand.

"Would a man who laid his life on the line to save his wife's life abuse her?" Cam asked without rancour. "Alex and I were in the forces together—I've known him for over twenty years. I've known Beth since she went to work for him. Don't worry, everything's fine—it's probably just something to do with the party. You know how it is with these things."

It was too much to hope that she wouldn't have picked up on every particular of what he'd just said. She looked at him with eyes wide open—he had a feeling what was coming next.

"Beth's life was in danger? What happened?"

Cam kept the details to a minimum. Even so, the way Stacie's face paled did not escape him as he related an abridged account of the incident. A year down the line, and it still made his blood run cold to recall how a deranged lunatic, bent on revenge for his brother's demise, had threatened both Beth and Alex. All so unnecessary. If only his arsehole of a sibling had followed Alex's orders and not gone rushing into that booby-trapped building, then Alex wouldn't have been injured while trying to rescue him. Nor would Beth have been subjected to a terrifying ordeal and the sight of her now-husband fighting for both their lives.

"And Alex was wounded in the process of rescuing her. He's fine now, though."

She nodded slowly. "What happened to the man—

Underwood?"

The threat was neutralised. He doubted that Stacie would take the news well, however he broke it to her. "You have to understand—he was playing for keeps. As far as we can tell, he planned it to be double murder/suicide. Alex had no choice, if he was to save Beth."

He watched her put two and two together, saw the way she came to the correct conclusion. "It was self-defence, Stacie. He was going to kill both of them—me too."

"You were there?"

Cam nodded. "I was still searching outside the house when Alex came back to check the interior and make sure Beth was all right. He found Underwood had taken her as his hostage—not that he had any intention of releasing her, his goal was to torture Alex. I'd just returned to the house when I heard the fight and then the gun shot. Underwood was going to use explosives to kill both of them and himself—I'd have been collateral damage."

"Oh my God." Horror turned her voice into a whisper.

"It's *over*," Cam countered forcefully. He hadn't expected the story to affect her the way it clearly had. "It's been over for a long time. Don't think about it."

Her expression slowly changed from one of shock to one of reflection. "You said Beth works for Alex?"

"Until Alex sold his business late last year, she was his executive assistant. Since then, he's been supporting Beth in her new career."

"She's lucky," Stacie said after a telling pause, during which her eyes paid a brief visit to a past that wasn't the happiest. Cam detected an almost wistful quality in her voice. "What does she do now?"

"Given that the party tomorrow is to celebrate the publication of her second novel a few days from now, I think we can all comfortably start calling her a writer," Cam replied. Although she wasn't his, Cam still felt very proud of his friend's wife and what she'd accomplished in such a relatively short space of time. "We probably won't see them again until tomorrow."

And that was another lie. Cam knew full well he'd see them both a little later on, after Stacie was safely tucked up in bed for the night. "Now—about that coffee. Give me a few minutes and you can tell me all about what you're running away from."

While making the drinks, Cam mulled over his interest in Stacie Matheson and whatever it was that had put her to flight. Common sense dictated that he mind his own business and leave well alone, but for reasons he didn't want to delve into too deeply he wanted to make sure she was all right. Sending her on her way—even with her transport problem solved—had a sense of unfinished business about it.

Returning with two mugs, he paused in the doorway, wanting to get a good look at Stacie with her guard down. What he saw was a young woman with the kind of beauty that hit him like a physical blow and an air of vulnerable preoccupation that struck him as being way out of proportion with the inconvenience of broken-down vehicle. No, she was troubled by a lot more than that heap of a car, and

Cam found himself not just wanting to know all about it, but to do something about it as well.

"Here you go." He held out one of the mugs as he approached, noting with interest the way her smile returned and for a moment covered all traces of her anxiety.

"Thanks." She took the mug in both hands and pursed her lips for a cautious sip of the steaming brew. "Mm, that's good—thank you."

"You're welcome." Cam took a moment to dim the lights, creating a more intimate environment in which he hoped she might find it easier to divulge what was bothering her so much. The question as to why he was so interested, he parked at the back of his mind. He set his mug down on the coffee table and sat beside her, leaning back into the corner of the sofa so that he had a better view of his unexpected but very welcome companion.

For a few seconds he simply looked at her, finding a somewhat perverse pleasure in the way she began to fidget under his silent, assessing gaze. Her features settled in an expression that was a curious mix of smile and frown.

"Why… What is it? Why are you looking at me like that? Do I have broccoli stuck between my teeth?"

She looked like she was about to give in to a nervous giggle. Cam, on the other hand, had never felt less like laughing in his life—leaving aside the times he'd seen his closest friend, Alex Lombard, at death's door. And the reason he'd never felt less like laughing was that what he saw in Stacie was attracting him like a moth to a flame. He wanted her. In the space of just those few seconds, mild interest had transformed into powerful desire. It felt as if whatever had been missing from his life had just slotted into place.

Which was utterly *crazy*.

He reached to touch Stacie's face but paused just before he made contact. He didn't have the right to do what instinct cried out for him to do. "May I?"

After a moment's hesitation, she nodded. He continued, gently stroking her hair away from the beautifully sculpted curve of her cheekbone. It was probably wishful thinking on his part, but he could have sworn she wanted to press her cheek against his hand—instead, a soft flush lent a delicate bloom to her creamy skin.

"Tell me what's happened, Stacie," he commanded gently, injecting a little of his Dom tone into his voice. "It's not just your car, is it? Something far more significant is bothering you."

Another tentative nod, and then she was looking away from him.

"It's silly," she said. "Stuff like this happens all the time. Relationships end."

And she hadn't wanted it to end. Cam pushed aside the totally bizarre sense of jealousy he felt in that instant, only realising he'd given voice to his thoughts when Stacie spoke again.

"No, I finished with him." Her eyes locked on to a bad memory. "I'd had my suspicions for a while, that something wasn't quite right. A couple of days ago, when I somewhat impulsively acted on those suspicions, I found him in bed with another woman. Enough was enough."

She took a fortifying sip of her coffee. When the tip of her tongue, pink and kitten-like, swept over her lips, Cam shifted uncomfortably in his seat—his cock was taking way too much notice of that innocent little gesture.

Suddenly she gave a nervous, self-conscious little laugh. "Why on earth am I telling you all this? I'm sorry—I must be boring you to death."

"Not at all. I get the feeling that it's something you need to get off your chest." *And don't look at her chest!*

Stacie's expression turned into a grateful smile. "Maybe so. Well, since I found them together, he's bombarded me with phone calls and text messages, until the early hours of this morning when he came to my apartment, banged on the door and demanded to see me. There was no way I was letting him in. He yelled through the door, said he wanted me back—he said he still wanted me to move in with him, and no one else could have me. He was so angry. And drunk." She sighed. "I assumed he was drunk, anyway. I suppose it could have been something else. With this happening, it makes me wonder what else he might have been hiding from me."

Cam was ready to string the bastard up for so many reasons. "Did you call the police?"

She shook her head. "Perhaps I should have done, but I just wanted him to go. I didn't want any trouble. When I got to work, I asked my boss for some time off."

"You needed to get away for a few days?"

She nodded. "I didn't want to be there in case he came

back. Except I forgot to pick up the sat nav when I left home this morning. I got lost when I left the motorway, and then with all that rain, and it being dark, and to top it all off, the car…"

Christ, no wonder she was so distressed. Cam couldn't help himself this time—he laid his hand gently against her cheek, his thumb stroking her incredibly soft skin. If only she'd been a submissive—then he could have taken care of her the best way a Dom could take care of a sub.

"Stacie, your ex is a piece of shit and not worth your tears," he said bluntly, more than a little distracted by the way she was letting her cheek rest against his hand. "We'll deal with everything else tomorrow. Right now, you need to get some sleep." He glanced at his watch, mildly taken aback by the lateness of the hour. "We have an early start ahead of us to get you on your way again."

He watched her draw in a deep breath and let it out on a sigh.

"You're right, Cam. Thank you for everything you've done for me tonight. I'd probably still be sitting in the car if it weren't for you and the Lombards—if you hadn't come along when you did. I'm sorry, I'm not normally like this, but like I said, it's been a very long day, and I do feel very tired."

"Stacie, I want you to stop apologising. You've done nothing you need to apologise for. Come with me—it's time for me to escort you to your room and let you get some sleep."

He offered her his arm, savouring the moment when

she took it and fell into step beside him. It felt *right*. He kept his place slow and deliberate, all the time wanting the staircase to be longer, her suite to be further away, anything to delay leaving her at the door to her room.

The inevitable could only be delayed for so long. With deep reluctance he opened that door and guided her through it. When she turned to face him, looking up at him with such a guileless expression, he knew he had no choice.

With a sense of wonder, he touched his fingertips to her jaw, exerted just enough pressure to coax her face into the right position for him to lower his head and caress her lips with his. He wasn't what she'd need or want, he knew that, but for those precious seconds, maybe he could do something to help.

"Sleep well, Stacie," he murmured. "And don't worry—we'll work it out."

As he stripped off in his own room, Cam wondered precisely what he'd meant by that—exactly what *it* had he been talking about? Her car? The bastard who'd terrified her? Or how he could have a relationship with someone so sweet, so beautiful, so young?

Oh, no. No, that wasn't on the table, it couldn't be. Whatever he'd thought earlier, about Stacie filling the empty space in his life… it couldn't be right. That was just the combined effect of a very attractive woman and intimate lighting at the end of a long, tiring day on a man with a high sex drive who hadn't had any in a while.

Cam tossed the thoughts aside and freshened up quickly, before changing into pyjamas—his usual leathers would have been too difficult to explain, should Stacie happen to wander about while he was moving between rooms.

He headed out of the door, unable to resist a brief glance down the hall to the room where she'd be sleeping, hopefully peacefully. Then he turned in the opposite direction, his destination the master bedroom. He knocked softly on the door and entered.

Alex looked up at his friend. "Sorry, Cam, she couldn't wait. She's been unreasonably worried about the party tomorrow night, as you know, and I needed to get her to relax."

"No problem." Cam pulled off his pyjama jacket, leaving the pants in place. "How is she now?"

The other man grinned. "Relaxed."

Cam looked at the woman splayed face down on the huge bed. From the hot colour of her backside, it had been a truly intensive session—little wonder then that the endorphins had kicked in and sent her soaring. "Need a hand with aftercare?"

He knew that Alex was perfectly capable of looking after his wife during her return from subspace. Alongside their visits to Aegis, all three of them had discovered a liking for sharing the intimacy of D/s as a private group—hence Cam's regular weekends in Hampshire.

As Alex released his sub from her bonds, Cam glanced over at him, a question in his eyes. The other man nodded his permission, so Cam moved closer to Beth, helping to warm her as she returned to normality while her husband lovingly applied a soothing cream to her reddened skin.

Beth shifted slightly and gave a contented sigh. Again with her husband's consent, Cam laid a gentle hand between her shoulder blades. She stilled immediately, responding to the familiar touch of the only other Dom allowed near her.

Beth had come so far in the last year. In the bedroom and the playroom, she'd truly embraced her submissive nature and there was no doubt in either his mind or her husband's that that was the reason why her first novel had proved so popular.

"So what's with you and Miss Matheson?"

Cam looked at his old friend and gave a casual shrug. "Nothing. I've known her half an hour longer than you have."

"But you like her."

Cam went still. "What's Beth been saying?"

Her husband laughed quietly, so as not to disturb his drowsy wife, and glanced tellingly towards her backside. "Don't worry, I put her straight about leaving the matchmaking alone, although I don't suppose for one moment she'll take any notice. You know what she's like. So—what are you going to do about Stacie?"

"There's nothing I can do. I'll help her with her car in the morning, get her on her way… end of story."

"You do realise she's interested in you?"

Cam shook his head. "Don't think I'm not tempted, but whether that's the case or not, I'm too old for her." He caught his friend's change of expression. "What?"

Alex rolled his eyes. "She couldn't keep her eyes off you over dinner. She noticed whenever Beth touched me, she saw how Beth kept looking at me, and every time, she immediately looked at you. She's interested. And so are you."

Cam wouldn't let himself believe it—he couldn't. "Didn't you hear what I said? I'm too old for her. Besides, she's only just split up with her boyfriend. Even if… Just don't, Alex. It's not going anywhere. It's not even starting. Apart from anything else, I need a sub and she isn't one. And I'm not ready for this."

CHAPTER THREE

Cam closed the door to Beth and Alex's suite behind him. Even though the click was too soft to be heard, he stopped and held his breath. He doubted that Stacie would be awake at just gone four o'clock in the morning, but it didn't do to take that for granted. One thing was certain, though—waiting a couple of hours would significantly increase the risk of an accidental encounter that could arouse her suspicions and make things awkward for everyone.

Finally rid of the pyjamas, Cam slipped between the sheets—he needed another couple of hours' sleep before he'd be ready to face Stacie over breakfast, but as he lay on his side, his head pillowed on his arm while his free hand stroked his hardening cock, he knew that sleep wasn't going to come. Not while he was mentally replaying his friend's observations regarding the woman who was just a few yards away.

"I'm not ready for this. It's too soon," he grumbled, repeating the words he'd said to Alex a short time ago while Beth was deeply asleep.

You are *ready, Cam. More than you realise. You've already admitted you like the idea of settling down.*

No, not yet, Alex. I've been alone a long time. I need—

Stop hiding from the truth. You're every bit as damaged as I was, just in a different way.

I've never denied it, but I can't inflict that on Stacie. She doesn't need a man like me. Besides, I'm too old—

Give the age crap a rest, Cam. It's just numbers and they aren't worth shit. Have you considered that you might need a woman like her? She could be the antidote to loneliness that you're looking for.

Since when had he and Alex got so touchy-feely? Cam groaned again. Since Beth had dragged them forcibly out of their individual man-caves—for a sub, she could be an almighty pain in a Dom's backside. A half-smile twitched at the corner of his mouth. A beautiful pain, granted.

His thoughts went back to Alex's words. Loneliness and being alone. Two quite different concepts, and Cam had known plenty of both during his life—far too well. They had become a way of life nearly forty years ago, when he was just a child. He'd learned very quickly to push the loneliness into the shadowy corners of his life. Being alone was simply a physical state that came and went.

Although he'd been very much a part of Beth and Alex's life together—his regular weekend visits to Winterleigh had always included an invitation from Beth, as the sub in the mix, to join them for a mutually agreeable play session each night—just recently, he'd started to find it more difficult to keep the loneliness at bay. More and more, he'd found himself wanting what his friends had. The closeness they shared meant that neither of them would ever feel lonely again.

What they had was special and because of that he'd started to distance himself from the couple as well—he didn't want to intrude. Hence his recent extended trip to the Middle East.

He didn't begrudge Alex the luck of having Beth in his life—he'd just wondered if he could be as fortunate, or if he was doomed to the disappointment of failing to achieve the perfection he saw in their relationship.

But now he'd met Stacie and what had started out as a simple act of goodwill towards a stranded traveller was becoming more complicated with each passing hour. He was attracted to her in a way he hadn't been attracted to any woman for a long time, but she was too young, he was too old, and he had needs that were very… specific.

And still he wanted her.

Cam thought of the unattached subs he knew at the club, the ones who knew what he needed from them and what he could give them in return. Those were purely transactional relationships, a temporary exchange of power resulting in an evening's pleasure for both parties. None of them stirred him the way Stacie did, a woman he'd known for a matter of hours and who knew nothing of the public and private worlds he inhabited.

His professional life, both in the service of Her Majesty and in the private sector, had shown him the horrors mankind was capable of inflicting on guilty and innocent alike. As for his personal life… not everyone would or could understand the significance of D/s when it came to what made him the man he was.

Cam found himself craving sleep, the kind of deep dreamless sleep that would vanquish the images playing across his mind. One in particular persisted—Stacie at the club, tied with silk ropes chosen to compliment her colouring, trusting him to take her to the heights of pleasure, where he would send her soaring into subspace, set her free to fly wherever her desires would take her, and be there to catch her and care for her when she returned to earth.

With his hand still on his cock, he rolled onto his back. Thighs tensed, his grip became firmer as his fist moved up and down. In his mind, however, it wasn't his hand that sheathed his cock but Stacie's body as she rode him and took her pleasure. Tight and heavy, his balls drew up and all of a sudden, in an orgasm that almost shattered his spine, his hips made one final thrust upwards and he came, his seed spattering messily across his abdomen and chest.

When he could move again Cam headed for the bathroom. He leaned on the edge of the basin, looking at his reflection with disgust as he rubbed at the sticky white streaks smeared across his belly. Was he really reduced to this?

He closed his eyes, mouth briefly curved into a grimace at the direction his thoughts were taking. He didn't want to imagine what it might be like to hear a soft voice speak his name, feel a gentle hand on his arm, the curves of a body that was all woman beside him… see storm-grey eyes looking at him with passion and desire… tenderness and love…

Stacie woke early. She grabbed her watch from the bedside table and groaned when she saw just how early. Were there really two six o'clocks in one day? It would seem so.

Given the circumstances, she shouldn't have been surprised to wake at this ungodly hour. It was probably more than a little foolish for her to have hoped that things would look better after a good night's sleep. For one thing, she hadn't exactly had a good night's sleep to begin with. The reason for that made her stomach churn again—when she'd checked her mobile phone before going to bed, there'd been another batch of messages from her ex, each more abusive than the last. Only a day ago that sort of behaviour had sent her scurrying out of town—today it just pissed her off, and when she got back home, she wasn't going to let him get away with it again.

And then there was her car. That was a far more pressing problem than Jonty. What on earth was she going to do about that if it couldn't be fixed?

"No use borrowing trouble," she muttered. Cam could

easily have been wrong about it. For all she knew, all it needed was some new part or other and a little—okay, maybe a lot of sweet-talking from an experienced mechanic.

Stacie stretched, using the time to collect what remained of her thoughts. There wasn't much and most of that seemed to have something to do with Cam Fraser. She hadn't been able to get the man out of her mind or out of her dreams. Not after the kiss he'd given her before saying goodnight. Just as well she'd soon be on her way and he'd be nothing more than a memory.

What the hell was wrong with her? This obsession with someone she'd only just met was stupid, but the more she tried to rationalise it away, the more she felt drawn to the tattooed mountain of a man who'd made her feel more cared for in a few hours than Jonty had at any point in their relationship.

Even now, she couldn't stop thinking about Cam—the sound of his voice, the colour of his eyes, the way his mouth tasted. How could an obsession start so quickly and still burn so fiercely?

And why couldn't she stop wondering if he'd send her on her way with one last kiss?

"Stacie doesn't know it yet, but she is going to do me a massive favour and get *both* of you out from under my feet, because even though I'm quite sure that all she needs is a lift to her car, you are *both* going with her to make sure everything's all right. Stan's on his way from the village, so I suggest that the two of you get your arses into gear and go. *Now!*"

Having enjoyed one of Beth's delicious cooked breakfasts, Cam watched with barely stifled amusement as Alex opened his mouth to object, only to shut it abruptly when his wife raised a chastising finger, a look of sheer menace in her bewitching eyes. "A pussy-whipped Dom," he murmured under his breath with a grin, knowing it would irritate Alex no end. "Who'd have thought it? Now I've seen it all."

"And you can stop smirking, Cam Fraser! You heard what I said—I want both of you out of here. I have things to do before the caterers get here, and I need to get changed!"

"And fifteen-all," Alex shot back at his friend, adding darkly, "Oh, she is *not* getting away with that."

Cam knew exactly what his friend was planning by way of retribution—it would involve Alex's hand coming into repeated contact with his wife's curvaceous rear. "I wouldn't bother," he advised as they both exited the kitchen. "You know she'll only enjoy it."

"Remind me again why I married her."

As if he needed reminding. "Because you'd go to hell and back for her," Cam said, all trace of humour gone from his voice. "Correction—you *went* to hell and back for her, and you know you'd do it all over again."

While Alex went to get the Range Rover out of the garage located at the rear of the house, Cam headed off to find Stacie—it appeared that she was still in her room, having excused herself after breakfast so that she could gather her belongings together. He was about to knock on the bedroom door when it opened. She smiled in greeting but the smile didn't quite reach her lovely eyes.

He kept his tone light and easy. "Ready to go?"

She glanced around. Beyond her, Cam could see that the bed was neatly made—the room didn't even look as if it had been occupied. She stooped to pick up the bag at her feet, which Cam promptly took from her.

"I think so. It was good of your friends to let a stranger stay overnight. I'm sure Beth will be glad to have me out of her hair while she prepares for the party."

Cam smiled. "If I know Beth, she'd be happy to have you stay for as long as you needed. Anyway, Alex is taking us to your car, and we're both going to wait with you until you're safely on your way again."

The very idea seemed to horrify her. "You can't possibly do that. Cam, I'm very grateful, but the car's my problem. I can't impose on you and the Lombards for any longer than is really necessary—I can't. You've all been so generous already."

"You seriously think we'd leave you in the middle of nowhere without any definite plan of action?" All at once, Cam found himself wanting to put her over his knee, no matter how absurd a reaction that might be. "No way this side of hell, Stacie. And when you get to where you're going, I want to know you've arrived safely. Is that clear?"

He would tolerate nothing less. There was something about this woman that was drawing out every last protective instinct he possessed. It even came out in the hand he plastered to the small of her back as they descended the staircase and went out to join Alex in his 4x4. Beth was there too, waiting to bid Stacie farewell, which she did with a hug and a kiss on the cheek, and a point-blank refusal to accept any thanks.

"It's been our pleasure, Stacie, honestly. It's been lovely to meet you, and please stop by and say hello if you're ever in this area again. You will, won't you?"

"You'd better, honey," Cam said, with a wry grin, "or we'll never hear the end of it."

He stashed Stacie's bag on the back seat of Alex's car, then helped the bag's owner into the front passenger seat. He sat behind her, trying not to fixate on the fact that his time in her company was now on a final countdown. She was going to be given his mobile phone number, whether she liked it or not, and he fully intended to reiterate the point he'd already made about calling him on arrival.

What he hadn't quite figured out, though, was whether he was going to do what he should and leave it at that, or obey the clamour of his instincts and his body, and ensure that he would see her again.

Stan, the mechanic, dropped the bonnet of Stacie's car and wiped his hands on the rag he took from the pocket of his overalls. He then proceeded to remove his cap, wipe his sleeve over his brow and slap the cap back on his balding head. He looked at Cam and gave a faint shake of his head, as if to confirm what Cam already suspected about the wreck of a car.

"It's the head gasket all right, and if I were you, love," he looked squarely at Stacie, "I'd give serious consideration to scrapping it rather than repairing it—it's likely to cost more than the car's worth."

Cam turned his attention to the car's owner. Stacie looked as if the universe had just dumped its latest and biggest pile of crap on her. He wasn't sure she even realised that the mechanic was waiting for her decision.

"Stacie?"

She looked up at him, her expression blank. "Sorry—what did you say?"

"He wants to know what you want to do with the car."

"I can take it back to the garage for you, take another look and give you an estimate, or if you want rid of it I can haul it to my nephew's scrapyard," Stan expounded. "There's still some value in it broken up."

Cam debated for a moment, and then put a firm arm around Stacie's slender shoulders. She really seemed to be struggling with the decision she was being called upon to make. In a split second, the space between two heartbeats, he made a choice—and it wasn't to remain distant and resigned to letting this woman walk out of his life. "Give us a moment to empty it and then take it to the scrapyard. It's so old, it's a bloody death trap anyway."

At that point, Stacie found her voice—it was a study in

irate indignation.

"Just a minute!" She placed herself between the men and her vehicle. "This is *my* car—who do you think *you* are," she prodded Cam in the chest, "telling *him* to scrap *my* car?"

Her question was clearly aimed with deadly force at Cam. The verbal grenade was the last thing he was expecting. He glanced at Alex, standing a few feet away with his arms folded across his chest. Helpful as ever, Alex raised both hands in a gesture of surrender. "Hey, leave me out of it, Cam. You're running this op."

With an irritated grunt, Cam took a step closer to Stacie, leaning one hand on the edge of the car roof, almost trapping her between the car and his body. "Didn't you hear what I said, Stacie? The bloody thing's a death trap. It's over twelve years old and it's worth fuck-all. Give me a few days, and I can source a decent replacement for you."

Which will give me the opportunity to stay in touch with you. It was heaven-sent. The impulsive offer was the opening he needed to justify maintaining contact with Stacie. Common sense had fought the flare of desire… and lost. He didn't want a quick liaison with this woman—he wanted a real relationship with her.

"I can't *afford* to replace it!" She gulped back a sob, all the wind suddenly gone from her sails. "I can't afford to repair it either, not if it's going to be that much," she added quietly, almost as if she were thinking out loud.

"Stacie, listen to me. Even without the head gasket going, this car's on its way out. Making that repair will cost hundreds, take my word for it." It might have been a long time ago, but he still recalled the pain of the bill he'd received for something similar—he'd even ended up working some of the debt off. "And even if you do get it fixed, it'll only be a matter of time before something else major goes wrong with it, given its age—I know from experience. I'd much rather you let me replace it for you—I can afford it. And if you really feel the need to pay me back," he continued sternly, quelling her imminent protest, "we can make a financial arrangement that you *can* afford."

"Of course I'd pay you back!" She looked horrified, as if the thought of doing anything other than that was completely intolerable. "You'd do that? Lend me the money for a car? But I'm a stranger. You don't know me—"

"I'm an excellent judge of character," Cam interrupted her. Then he smiled. "And besides, I like you. Come on, let's get your things into Alex's car." He glanced at the man in question, who nodded reassuringly at the young woman but somehow also managed to give Cam a look that said he was clearly insane.

"Stacie, it looks like you might be staying with us for a few days after all. You're more than welcome to join the party tonight—you can keep an eye on this old reprobate." He jerked a thumb in Cam's direction.

"Hey, less of the old, *old man*," Cam countered, with plenty of emphasis on the nickname.

Together the three of them cleared Stacie's belongings

out of her car. Alex took the large bag to the 4x4. Cam was helping Stacie with her personal bits and pieces when his eyes locked onto the almost-new paperback she was about to drop into her tote bag. It was the first time he'd seen it in the hands of someone outside their circle, and although he knew exactly how popular the novel was, it was still like a punch to the solar plexus to see an outsider with it.

"What's that?" He hoped his voice wasn't really as gruff as it sounded to him.

To his surprise, she gave a slightly embarrassed grin. "It's nothing, just a bit of light reading. It's a really popular romance—one of my friends recommended it."

It was a romance, all right—one Cam had in part witnessed firsthand. The book she was holding was a copy of Beth Lombard's first novel, published under a pseudonym, and Cam knew for a fact that Beth had based sections of it on her own experience. He'd been lucky enough to read one of the advance copies.

"I think that's the one some of my female friends have been reading—cover looks familiar. What do you think of it?" He was trying for casual—from the look on Alex's face as he returned to see what the hold-up was, he was making a pretty poor job of it.

Her smile was amazing. "I love it—it's the best thing I've read in ages. I know it sounds crazy, because this stuff just doesn't exist in real life, but there are times when I wish I could meet a—"

She broke off as colour flamed in her cheeks. "Sorry,"

she apologised, shoving the book and a pack of wipes into her bag. "Too much information. And I really shouldn't keep the poor man waiting." She glanced towards the mechanic.

No, not *enough* information and she was keeping *him* waiting, Cam thought in frustration.

Did he dare push her into completing the statement? Not right now, that would be showing an undue amount of interest, but maybe he could finesse her into doing just that over the course of the next few hours—before the party started and the cat was let out of the bag with a vengeance.

He felt his balls clench as unbidden thoughts entered his mind, filling in the blanks in what she'd started to say. *Meet a what? A Dom?* Enjoying Beth's book didn't automatically mean she was submissive. He couldn't be that lucky.

Could he?

When they returned to the house a short while later, Alex watched his old friend escort their unexpected houseguest back to her room, the two of them carrying the personal belongings they'd retrieved from her car.

He shook his head—and Cam *didn't* think he had it bad? He'd only just met the woman, but he'd offered to finance a car for her, for God's sake! And now he'd taken it upon himself to keep her entertained while he, Alex, went in search of his wife. His assumption, that she would probably be getting ready to deal with the catering company and the four-piece band that would be providing the entertainment that evening, proved to be correct.

He found her in the bedroom.

"Back already?" She smiled over her shoulder as she rummaged through a drawer full of scarves and other accessories. "That was quick. Is Stacie's car back on the road now? She was nice, I really liked her. You know, we should have asked her to stay for the party."

Alex leaned his shoulder against the door frame, arms folded, patiently waiting for his wife to let him get a word in edgeways. He loved the way she'd blossomed over the last few months. He loved *her*, even if he didn't quite understand why she felt the need to change into something smart to greet the caterers. He'd long since come to the conclusion that there were some things about her that he simply wasn't meant to understand—it was all part of her primal mystery.

"Then you'll be glad to know, my sweet, that she's back. Her car was terminal, so she's going to stay with us for a few days until Cam gets her back on the road again. And get this—he's going to finance a car for her. I know he's interested in her, but a *car*? It's now official—Cam Fraser has lost it. He is certifiably wacko."

Very slowly, Beth straightened up and turned to her husband. The expression on her face spoke volumes about her doubts regarding *his* sanity. "*What?* Are you *sure* that's what he meant? What did he say, exactly?"

Alex sighed, and then repeated his friend's words. He

didn't then expect his wife to smile and give a little chuckle.

"Well, that's one way of staying in touch with her. I mean, if she's going to pay him back for the car, they'll be in regular contact, won't they?"

He could see where this was heading—time to get serious. "No matchmaking, Beth. I mean it. Do we have to go over it again?"

His darling wife feigned innocence. "I'm sure I don't know what you mean. I'm just saying… if she's going to pay him back for the car, they'll be in touch."

What he needed to do was to divert her focus elsewhere… and Alex knew exactly what would grab her attention. "There's something else—our unexpected houseguest is a fan."

"What?"

Alex grinned—objective achieved. "Stacie has your book. *Now* do you believe I didn't buy up every copy and bury them in the grounds?" He made a grab for his wife and started nuzzling her neck.

"Oh God. Alex, stop that!" She slapped his arm and then froze. "Oh shit."

"Potty mouth," he scolded placidly. "What now?"

"The party. She's going to know who I am. Alex, will you stop that? I'm trying to think! *She's going to know I wrote that book!*"

Alex shrugged, unable to see the problem. "Just like everyone else will. You knew that would happen when we decided to have the party. So she's one of your adoring public. Just make sure you have your autographing arm at the ready."

His wife was not to be placated. "She may not be adoring."

Oh, he was so tempted to hold back what he knew, but only for a moment. "What was it she said? 'I love it—it's the best thing I've read in ages.'"

"Don't joke! This is serious!"

"I'm not joking, sweetheart. Those were her exact words." He held her a little closer. "We don't have to have the party, you know—we could always cancel. Or we have the party and say nothing. You don't have to tell anyone outside those of our friends who already know." The option had been at the back of Alex's mind all along. It was always useful to have a backup plan.

"No." All of a sudden, Beth became very calm, finding the inner strength that had helped him to deal with the demons from his past. "I said I was going to do this, and I'm not backing out now."

A familiar pride flowed through him. "That's my girl. Now, why don't you finish changing and we'll go and meet the caterers."

Stacie flopped down onto the bed in the room she'd vacated just a short time ago. What on earth was she going to do? This was not how she had been planning to spend this weekend—she was supposed to be fifty miles away, in a little bed and breakfast, avoiding Jonty, and wallowing in chocolate and erotic romance.

She was not supposed to be in a luxurious suite in a beautiful house, just a few feet away from a man so tasty that he made her want to overindulge in all the naughtiest things imaginable. She glanced over at Cam, who seemed to be watching her with an unusual intensity from his almost sentinel-like position by the door. He appeared to be waiting for something.

"I'm sorry," she finally muttered, figuring that he must have been expecting an apology for her outburst at the car—after all, he'd shown her nothing but care and concern and the sort of generosity that came along once in a lifetime. Not that—now she'd had time to think about it—she had any intention of taking up *that* offer. She'd manage… somehow.

"What are you apologising for, honey?"

Stacie looked at her feet. The bed was so high that they couldn't reach the floor, and all of a sudden she felt about seven years old again. "Back at the car." She sighed. "I shouldn't have poked you."

"Oh, that." Cam lifted an eyebrow as he considered the action in question. "Trust me, I'll recover. I'm not quite the fragile blossom I appear to be."

Stacie pressed her lips together in an attempt to stifle an involuntary snigger—he was so far removed from a fragile blossom, it was untrue. Cam Fraser was more like the sturdiest of English oaks.

"I don't suppose you happened to bring your party animal outfit with you?" he continued, studying her with his head canted slightly to one side as if he were imagining her in said outfit.

She shook her head. "I wasn't planning on attending any formal social events this weekend," she said with a shrug. "It's all right, I can stay up here and read, I don't mind—"

"I do." His voice cut ruthlessly across hers, startling her. The sudden fierceness of his expression also threw her. "You've been invited to the party, Cinderella, so you're not staying up here while we're dancing the night away downstairs. Besides," he continued, his face relaxing into an almost little-boy grin, "I need a dance partner."

Her head shot up at that comment. "Don't you already have—?"

"Nope, so you're it. I already have my party frock, so you and I need to go on a little shopping expedition—dress, shoes, the works. And I know just where we can get them." He held out his hand. "Come on—we have work to do."

CHAPTER FOUR

Cam was in deep trouble and falling in deeper by the minute. Not that he was complaining.

He'd realised, much to his chagrin, that based on their initial encounter he'd made several assumptions about the woman seated beside him, and the one about her being quiet and shy was at best only half-true. Even now, as they drove into town on a mission to find her a suitable outfit for the evening, there was an undercurrent of vivacity about her that was putting him even further under her spell.

"So, Stacie Matheson, are you going to tell me some more about yourself?" Cam said at length. He tried to make the enquiry sound casual, when the truth was it was anything but casual. Suddenly, everything about this woman had assumed a level of importance that was growing exponentially. He had a feeling that the Stacie he'd met the day before was not the real Stacie at all, and that *she* was now venturing out to play.

And he liked her—more than was probably good for his peace of mind, but in his line of business, he was used to dealing with the unexpected.

"What do you want to know?"

Concentrating on driving conditions, he could only afford a quick glance in her direction. Cold, hard facts were one thing, but what Cam wanted to know was far more intimate. There was one question, though, that might kill two interesting birds with one stone.

"Favourite author."

She laughed—and Cam felt his body react as if he were seventeen again.

"I wasn't expecting that! Let me see… that's easy." She named the author of the book she'd slipped into her bag when they'd emptied her car—a lady who also went by the name of Beth Lombard.

Cam grinned, silently and somewhat smugly congratulating himself on being a master of manipulation. "And what do you like about her writing?"

"Oh my God! You know what her book's about—I can't possibly tell you. That would be too much information!"

He would have sworn he could feel the heat of her blush. "Of course you can. I'm interested to know what you think—if you tell me, I'll tell you why."

"Well, I've only read the one book of hers—I think it's actually her first—but it's really well-written, for a start. She uses her words to paint these wonderful pictures, and then there's the way she describes the emotions of both the male and female characters. I swear I've fallen in love with one of the men."

At that, Cam felt his stomach lurch. The two leading male characters were loosely modelled on Alex and him. It had caused both of them a great deal of amusement at the time, much to Beth's delightful embarrassment. And Stacie had fallen for one of them. If it was the one based on Alex… Cam didn't even want to *think* about the possible repercussions of that.

"Sorry, I missed what you just said." Wrapped up in his thoughts, Cam realised that she'd carried on talking.

"Oh, I was just admitting how silly I can be, falling for a character in a book," she confessed. "I mean, it's not as if they're real, right? Most of my friends who've read the book fancy the dark, moody Dom, but if I had my choice, it would be the blond one. He has this great sense of humour, but in the scenes where he's with a sub…" Her voice trailed off and she started to fan herself, a mischievously suggestive grin lighting up her face.

At which comment Cam nearly drove into the back of the vehicle that had just pulled up in front of them. Why the hell had he decided to have this conversation while they were in the damn car? Still… it was a golden opportunity.

"Suppose you met a man like that and he asked you out—what would you say?"

She let out her breath on a long sigh.

"Good question. I mean, when he asked me out, I

wouldn't necessarily know he was a man like that, would I? I don't imagine it's something that would come out in a conversation between two strangers. But then, it wouldn't really happen in the first place, would it? I mean… I've read a lot of romances with D/s themes, but it doesn't happen for real. And even if it did, a man like that wouldn't be interested in someone like me."

Don't bet on it, honey. In Cam's opinion, a man would have to be gay or dead not to be interested in her. He couldn't imagine any man not being attracted to Stacie, but then again… if the idiot she'd been dating had two-timed her and she'd not been snapped up by any of his predecessors, he wouldn't have her by his side right now, would he?

Cam had fully intended to break it to Stacie that Beth was the writer behind the novel of the moment, but given her response to his question, he changed his mind—there was way more to be said than could be covered adequately in the car. On the other hand, though, if he left it too late… the last thing he wanted was to risk letting her think that he was trying to make a fool of her.

He really needed to address these issues before the party, but it wasn't going to happen right now—they were almost at their destination.

The boutique to which he was taking Stacie was definitely high-end. Cam knew the owner and was pretty confident that she would be able to supply exactly the right outfit for his companion. However, it was Cam himself, just browsing the racks, who found a gown that would be absolutely perfect—a stunning confection in black lace and silk, perfect for the evening ahead… and perfect for the woman who would wear it.

She emerged from the changing room… and took his breath away. Spaghetti-thin straps snaked over her shoulders, while the sheath-like form of the dress clung to her like second skin, all the way down to a couple of inches above the knee, from where it flared out in a stunning fishtail. However, as beautiful as the gown was, it was dull and drab in comparison with the woman wearing it. He could tell immediately that Stacie loved it, but then he had to watch her face fall as she caught sight of the price tag on the hanger he was still holding.

"Stacie?"

"It's lovely, Cam, it really is, but… I can't afford this." She looked around the shop, with its stylish clothes and glittering accessories, then looked down at her hands, clasped nervously in front of her. "I can't afford any of this. Can we go somewhere else, please?"

She really thought he was expecting her to pay for this? Cam swiped his fingers through his hair, grimacing at its shorter-than-usual length. "Perhaps I didn't make myself clear, Stacie. This—all of it—is on me. You're not paying for a thing."

Stacie put the finishing touches to her makeup. Even though she was perhaps running a little late, given that some of the guests had already started to arrive for the party, if a job was worth doing, it was worth doing well. Besides… when she saw Cam again, she wanted to hit him with the full arsenal at her disposal. Her normal cosmetic routine was designed to look light and natural, but for a formal event like this, she was pulling out all the stops. And as she examined the results in the dressing table mirror, she was glad to see that she'd achieved her desired result.

And thanks to Beth's hairstylist, who had allowed himself to be persuaded to put Stacie's hair up as well during his visit to the house that afternoon, even her crowning glory was behaving itself. The hairstylist had also been accompanied by a beautician from the same salon, who had given both her and Beth mani-pedis to die for. Sequestered in one of the spare bedrooms for the pampering session, with the two men given strict instructions not to interrupt, she and Beth had got on like the proverbial house on fire. And the results of the pampering spoke for themselves.

Okay—let's see what you make of me now, Mr. Fraser.

It had been a totally crazy day—a crazy weekend, so far. Now she knew how Dorothy felt—this was about as far away from the Kansas of her normal life as it was possible to get. Her time in this glittering variation on the Land of Oz might be severely limited, but she was going to make the most of it. When she left work a little over twenty-four hours earlier, she'd envisaged something totally different—certainly nothing like spending time with a man like Cam Fraser.

Stacie let out a big whoosh of breath at the mere thought of Cam and what he might look like for the party. Her palms were sweating at the image that came to mind, of those broad shoulders encased in formal evening attire. She'd always been a sucker for a smartly dressed man.

"Down, girl!" she muttered to herself, wiping her hands with a tissue. "He might turn up in jeans, for all you know. And just because he bought you *this*," she added, rising to go and look at herself in the full-length mirror, "and he doesn't have a girlfriend, it doesn't mean he's interested in *you*."

The trouble was, she *wanted* him to be interested, and that was in direct opposition not just to her sense of reality but also to what her sense of propriety demanded. She'd only just broken up with Jonty—fact. Her sense of propriety dictated that she spend a suitable amount of time getting over that relationship—it conveniently chose to ignore the fact that the bust-up three days earlier had been the end point of a relationship that had probably started to unravel at the same time as her suspicions about his extracurricular activities had started to form.

And if that was the case, why shouldn't she be interested in another man?

You're a woman, over the age of consent and breathing—if Cam shows an interest in you, even if it's only for this evening, why not?

Regardless, she still needed to focus on the evening ahead and not making a fool of herself in such gracious company. Although she'd been to a few parties in her time, none of them had been anything like this… and she'd never worn anything as exquisite as the dress Cam had bought for her. She just hoped that she could negotiate the staircase without getting tangled up in the skirt.

She was, however, a little self-conscious about being in public without a bra, even though the bodice, which clung to her every curve almost all the way down to her knees, had support built into it. Given that snug fit, though, all she could do was offer up a silent prayer of thanks to the goddess of no-VPL lingerie. Just the thought of going without knickers in Cam's presence… she *so* did not want to go there.

Stacie gave herself another look in the mirror—this was as good as it was going to get. A quick check of the time told her that she should be downstairs already. She slipped her feet into the strappy Jimmy Choos Cam had also bought for her, not that anyone would be able to see them under the eddy of chiffon around her feet. At least they'd enable her to feel slightly less vertically challenged when she stood next to Cam.

And oh, that thought gave her a hot shiver all the way down to her perfectly pedicured toes.

As Stacie descended the staircase, at its foot she saw her hosts and her knight in shining armour clustered in conversation. Beth was facing her, a stunning picture of tasteful shapely elegance in a designer evening gown, her neck encircled by a glittering diamond collar.

A niggle raised its head at the back of Stacie's mind. *Diamond collar*. Why was that phrase, that image, standing out so prominently? Of course—it featured in the novel she was reading so avidly…

Good God above! She looked at the group of three people again, putting two and two together. It couldn't be a coincidence—it just couldn't… could it? No, it *had* to be a coincidence. Her imagination was running riot, making connections that simply couldn't be true. Yet no matter how hard she tried, now that the idea had formed in Stacie's mind, she couldn't shake it free.

This was a party for Beth's second novel, but what of her first? It could easily be the book she was reading for the fourth time, her imagination insisted, and at the foot of the stairs could be the two principals—or at least, the models for them. The heroine with the green eyes could be Beth… the dark brooding hero, her husband. If she was right, did that mean that they were into D/s? If she was and they were, then what about Cam? Was he the blueprint for the Dom with whom she'd fallen a little bit in love? Was it just in appearance… or more?

And then she remembered the way she'd talked about the book just a few short hours ago—and wished that the floor would open up and swallow her whole.

Mortified embarrassment flamed in her cheeks as she recalled the way she'd enthused about the blond Dom to the very man who could be the inspiration for the character. She arrived at the bottom stair so rattled by what she was thinking that she would have stumbled and fallen, had it not been for Cam's swift reactions. She found herself in strong arms, looking up into those remarkable blue eyes narrowed with concern. What must he be thinking of her right at that moment?

"Careful, Stacie, we don't want you having any accidents," he murmured, his eyes never leaving hers. "You all right?"

"Fine… thanks." As he set her back on her feet, she was amazed that her voice didn't come out like a helium-induced squeak. Not only was she locked in mortal combat with the awkward memory of what she'd said earlier, she was also having to contend with the head-on visual assault that was the most gorgeous hunk of manhood she'd ever seen.

In a formal evening suit, he was simply a banquet for appreciative female eyes. The tailoring was superb, made to fit every delicious inch of him—crisp white, sharp black, and every detail made him a tempting morsel good enough to eat… very slowly, so that every delectable mouthful could be tasted and savoured.

Her hands were in no hurry to release him, either. Cam himself didn't seem to regard letting her go as a matter of any urgency—it was only when Beth spoke that the spell holding both of them was broken.

"Stacie, you look gorgeous! I love the gown—where did you find it?"

She felt herself blush. "Cam took me to Isabella's, and you have to give him the credit for choosing the dress. And the shoes."

"Ah, I should have known. Izzy has some beautiful clothes there."

"Cam, I never knew you had it in you!"

This from Beth's husband. In his evening wear, Alex looked almost as delicious as Cam. Stacie risked a quick glance at him—he was looking at Cam, one eyebrow raised in an expression that seemed to be asking a silent question. A flicker of movement, and somehow Stacie instinctively knew it was an answering shrug.

"Never mind them, Stacie." Beth linked her arm through Stacie's. "You come with me, and we'll get a glass of wine while they do that silent communication thing. It used to bug the hell out of me, but now I just leave the big, bad soldiers to it."

For Stacie, the evening was like living in a complete fantasy. Once all the guests had arrived—all of them apparently very close friends of the hosts—it was Alex who stood on the dais first, to announce to everyone that Beth was the writer behind the phenomenally successful novel they'd all been talking about, and that they were here to celebrate the imminent publication of the next instalment.

The disclosure created a buzz of reaction, followed by an enthusiastic round of applause, at which point Beth joined her husband on the dais. She thanked their friends for coming to the party, and then Alex introduced the musicians and the celebrations started properly.

After congratulating her hostess on her success, Stacie headed for the doors that opened up onto the terrace and gardens beyond. Coward that she was, she was taking advantage of Cam's temporary absence at the buffet so that she could collect her thoughts and get ready for whatever damage limitation was necessary. If only she could go back in time and stop herself mouthing off in the car about how much she liked that blond Dom in the book.

Stacie selected a seat on the terrace, close enough to one of the patio heaters not to feel the chill of a late-autumn evening. She took a tiny sip of the exquisite English sparkling wine with which they'd toasted Beth. So, at least one of her assumptions was correct—Beth was indeed the author of her latest favourite book. That made it all the more likely that she, Alex and Cam were the blueprints for the prominent characters, which in turn made it all the more likely that she'd really embarrassed herself in front of Cam that morning.

The overture to her apology was starting to form in Stacie's mind. She was pretty sure Cam would join her soon, and she wanted to be prepared. And maybe she could skulk off to her room with a bottle of wine and get comfortably numb afterwards.

"Whatever you're thinking about, it must be serious."

A half-hearted smile curving her lips, she watched Cam sit down, swapping one plate of delicious-looking nibbles for the glass of wine she'd been holding for him. "Not serious, exactly, but there's something I need to say."

"Oh?" He took a sip of wine, eyebrows rising sharply as he looked at the glass. "I'm going to have to compliment Alex on his choice of wine… or maybe Beth. She's been doing wonders in educating him on how to pair wine with food ever since she took a course for research purposes." He grinned for a moment, then looked back at Stacie, suddenly serious again. "What's the problem?"

"You know I've read Beth's book."

"Several times, if I recall. So have a lot of people, including that lot in there. Beth might actually start believing it soon as well." He gave a short, gentle chuckle.

Stacie took a deep breath. *Now for it.* "I might be putting two and two together here and getting five, but… this morning… the things I said… about the character in Beth's book." She pressed her lips together for a moment. "The descriptions of the two main characters and the male character's friend… they seem awfully like Beth, Alex and you. It's not a coincidence, is it?"

Cam looked at her—she got the feeling he was making a decision of some sort. "No, it's not."

"God, this is so… Anyway, I went on about the friend, and how attractive I found him… and if he's based on you… I'm sorry—I embarrassed both of us."

"No, you didn't." Cam put down his glass and plate, then took Stacie's to do the same. "I did that. No, actually, I did something worse—I put you in an embarrassing position. I should have told you that Beth wrote the book. I was going to, while we were on our way to Isabella's, but the moment passed. What I should have done was make more of an effort to speak to you about it once we got back here… so please accept my apology for not doing that." He sighed. "I'm sorry I didn't tell you the truth."

He really did mean it. Stacie could see it in his expression, in his eyes… hear it in his voice.

"It's all right. I remember how the conversation went and… as you said, the moment passed. And then of course, this afternoon I got waylaid. The thing is…" *Bite the bullet, Stacie!* "Can we just forget what I said? It was a stupid thing to say anyway." She could hope, couldn't she? She fixed her gaze on her clasped hands.

"Do you want to forget?"

"I should. It would be for the best."

"That's not what I asked."

A chill ran down her spine. Something in his voice was compelling her to look at him—she couldn't help herself. Lips suddenly dry, Stacie swallowed hard. No man had ever looked at her with such a direct, penetrating gaze.

Do I want to forget?

Yes.

"No."

Am I insane or do I just have a stupid mouth?

"Nor do I. Look, this isn't exactly the right time to talk about this—how about if we discuss it later?" His expression changed again, and without giving her a chance to answer, he was telling her to eat her food.

Whatever expectations Stacie might have had of the evening, the reality of it was something she'd remember for the rest of her life, no matter what happened with Cam later. Far from being the wallflower she'd half-expected to be—believing that her escort would circulate among any other unattached female guests—she was the partner of one of the two most handsome men there. And he went out of his way to put her at her ease.

An attentive companion and a more than merely competent dancer, Cam remained with her for the entire evening. She was sure it was her imagination, but while they were dancing he seemed to make a point of holding her awfully close—not that she was complaining. She'd never felt anything like this before, and could only wonder how she'd got to the age of thirty-one without finding out what it was like to be held by a man who made her feel so acutely aware of what it was to be a woman. He was simply intoxicating—enough, even, to help her to forget how foolish she'd felt earlier.

A couple of hours into the party, having made a quick trip back to her room to freshen her lipstick and ensure that her hair was still behaving, Stacie was about to descend the staircase again when she saw something that struck her as rather odd. Beth was opening the front door to let in a late arrival. The woman was stunningly attractive—from her vantage point, Stacie could see that she was a couple of inches taller than Beth, with a lissom, well-toned physique and thick, dark-brown waves that just brushed her shoulders. She was attired in a long-sleeved evening gown in midnight blue, the figure-hugging bodice fashioned in lace and the flowing skirt a subtle swirl of satin that fell from the hip.

However, it was Beth's reaction to her that caused Stacie to slow down slightly, a small frown creasing her brow. There was something almost deferential about the way she greeted this latest guest, and though it niggled at Stacie, she decided it must have been the angle from which she was viewing the scene. However, when she heard the opening exchange between the two women, it made her wonder.

"Good evening, Mi—"

"Shh, not here, Beth," the other woman said quickly, with a brief shake of her head and a tiny frown. "I'm so sorry I'm late. Sometimes, very important people have no concept of the passage of time—and not only that, Guy was delayed as well, so he's only just been able to drop me off. I told him I'd get a cab, but he insisted—he says we get so little quality time together these days that every minute counts. He's given me the rest of the weekend off, though, so I'm staying over here with him. Unfortunately, due to pressure of work, he can't come to the party himself—he asked me to convey his apologies." Her lips curved in a wry smile of apology. "He hoped you'd understand, but it's to do with the Royal Household, and in cases like that, the word *no* doesn't exist."

"It's quite all right, Ros. The party's still going strong."

"It sounds like it. Anyway—congratulations, and thank you for inviting us. What you've accomplished—it's an incredible achievement. I, for one, am completely in awe—I can't even imagine where to begin writing a novel."

The two women shared a hug, then Beth turned and caught sight of Stacie as she reached the foot of the stairs.

"Ros, let me introduce you—Ros Edwards, Stacie Matheson. Stacie's Cam's friend and she's staying with us for a few days."

Close up, Ros Edwards was not only very attractive—she carried herself with a confidence and cool self-assurance Stacie hadn't often seen in other women. She was perhaps a handful of years Stacie's senior. Her handshake was firm, and gave Stacie a sense of contained strength. And in spite of the smile, there was something about her guarded, calmly assessing gaze that told Stacie that very little would get past this enigmatic woman.

Earlier in the day, Alex had talked about her in relation to some sort of "special job"—looking at her, Stacie wondered exactly what that special job was, given what she'd overheard about this Guy, who was both the woman's boss and her uncle. There was something about the wariness in Ros' eyes that put Stacie on edge—it wasn't the woman herself, it was more the thought that the wariness was there because Ros Edwards had seen a side of life that people like Stacie couldn't even begin to imagine.

At that moment, Cam and Alex appeared. Both of them greeted Ros with a hug and a kiss that spoke of long-time familiarity, but Stacie only had a moment to feel left out before Cam turned to her, to take her hand in his and draw her into the conversation as well, as they walked back towards the ballroom to re-join the party.

The invitations had apparently said *carriages at midnight*—a rather quaint term to let the guests know when they should arrange their transport home—and a mere ten minutes after that time, Stacie found herself with just Cam and the Lombards for company. They were all together in the family room—the musicians had departed earlier, and the caterers would be returning in the morning to tidy up, along with a cleaning company to make good any remaining mess. For now, it was just the four of them in the house, sharing a final bottle of champagne before heading for bed.

"All in all, I think that went pretty well," Alex commented, once they'd all made themselves comfortable. "Did you have a good time, Stacie?"

She looked at the way Beth was held in his arms, seated on his lap, her head nestled close to his—it was such an intimate image that Stacie almost felt like a voyeur. "I had a wonderful time, Alex—thank you for inviting me. I've never been to a party quite like it before." Suddenly feeling gauche and provincial again, she focused on the glass of champagne in her right hand.

Warm, masculine hands gently removed the glass from her grasp. She looked at Cam, who was now seated next to her, and put up no resistance when his arm went around her and guided her closer to him.

Like Alex, he had removed his jacket. With his bow tie loosened and his waistcoat hanging open, he was a shining example of casual male chic at its lip-licking finest. If only she had the right to snuggle up to him the way her body clamoured to.

"Relax, honey," he whispered in her ear. "Time to unwind. Come here."

Stacie slipped off her shoes—beautiful though they were, the spindly heels were playing havoc with her ankles after being on her feet for most of the evening—and let herself be drawn in to rest at his side. She was barely aware of Alex's quiet departure, his sleepy wife cradled gently in his arms as he bade them goodnight and left.

"I really have had a wonderful time, Cam," she said with quiet pleasure, laying a hesitant hand on his flat stomach, half her mind wondering what it would feel like to unfasten a couple of shirt buttons and touch his bare skin instead.

"So have I, honey."

She felt a fleeting touch to her hair. A kiss maybe? It was certainly a fanciful thought… and one she had to admit she liked.

"I don't want it to end just yet, Stacie. Look at me."

"You want to have that talk."

"Yes, but that's just part of it."

Compelled just by his voice to obey, she lifted her head and as Cam's fingers flipped a flimsy strap off her shoulder, his mouth claimed hers in a deeply sensual kiss that coaxed her lips into parting and allowing his tongue to flirt dangerously with hers.

Oh, this felt way too good—she was responding far too hungrily, too needily, to this man. Wild images filled her mind, of him taking her up to the bedroom, of her limbs entwined with his, his magnificent body—and it would be magnificent, her fingers curling into his shirt told her that—covering hers, one hand pinning her wrists to the bed while his other stroked and caressed her, his mouth never leaving hers.

When she felt the warmth of his hand cradling her face, holding her in place so that he could continue to kiss her with that achingly sweet, controlled fierceness, Stacie knew she'd lost the battle—a battle that, truth be known, had been lost before it even started.

And if he was a Dom? Stacie felt her pussy ripple at an idea that appealed to something very basic that had been stretching and stirring into life ever since she'd first read Beth's book.

Too much, too soon! The voice was in her mind, that little spark of common sense that hadn't yet deserted her. If he was a Dom, if she let herself develop feelings for him—*and you aren't already on the way to doing just that?*—she could be letting herself in for a whole heap of trouble. Had she really fallen in lust in just a day?

"I know you've just come out of a pretty shitty relationship, but I would like to see you. Is it too soon?"

Stunned, Stacie slowly shook her head. Was he really asking her out? Yes, of course he was, she could understand English, she'd spoken it all her life. "No, not at all."

"Good. Now before you say anything else, we do need to have that talk, Stacie." His growling purr of a voice was thick with need of a different kind. "About the characters in Beth's book."

"The resemblance that isn't coincidental, right?"

"Right. As you pointed out, when it comes to physical appearances, Beth's characters are very loosely, but evidently recognisably, based on the three of us."

Ah. Then this would be where he told her that their characteristics—their sexual proclivities among them—bore no relation to their real-life counterparts. Or they did. At that precise moment, Stacie wasn't exactly sure what she wanted the answer to be.

"And?" she prompted carefully.

"And… there are certain other things about me that you need to know, and you'll need time—"

To hell with time. "I need you."

Did that treacherous, urgent whisper really belong to her? Whether it did or not, it spoke the truth—she needed Cam Fraser. She didn't need to know whatever it was he was going to tell her, whatever it was that she'd need time for. The attraction had been growing all evening… all day. He was awakening things inside her, wants and needs she'd never realised she had, and it was all mixed up with what she'd read in Beth's novel.

She needed to talk to Beth—the last scrap of sanity she had left demanded it, because even if the writer wasn't into the lifestyle she'd written about, she *knew* about it, and something about this man was now telling Stacie that she needed to know about it too. How she would start that conversation she had no idea, but instinct was telling her that Beth was the key to finding out more.

"Stacie, I've never been one to beat around the bush. I want you. If we were anywhere else, I'd be doing my damnedest to get you into bed tonight—"

"You think I'd argue?"

He cursed, loudly and colourfully. Stacie wondered if she'd said the wrong thing—maybe he liked his women to play a bit more hard-to-get. And why didn't she like the idea of Cam with other women?

"I wish you hadn't told me that, honey. It doesn't make this any easier."

"I don't make a habit of sleeping with a man on the first date, you know." Oh God, she didn't want him to think she was always this easy!

"I know. I know, Stacie," he reiterated. "I guess you feel it too. It's just as well our first night together can't be here. Not under Beth and Alex's roof."

Wow. Even as she dealt with the fact that at that this gorgeous hunk of masculinity had stated his interest in her and in so forthright a manner, another part of her admired him for the respect he was showing his friends.

And she wouldn't have it any other way. It never even occurred to her to question her agreement with what he wanted, that she wanted to sleep with a man she barely knew—that she was *going* to sleep with a man she barely knew, if not here and now, then soon and… somewhere.

"I understand—and I wouldn't feel comfortable either," she confessed. "Would it be all right if we stayed here, like this, just a little while longer? Please?"

She didn't need to ask him twice. In a heartbeat, she found herself lying alongside him on the sofa, daring to do what she'd dreamed of doing bare minutes earlier—first one shirt button, then the next, until she'd undone enough to reveal tanned skin over taut muscle, with a light feathering of dark-gold hair—just enough to tickle her fingers. When she ventured closer to a hard male nipple, her mouth began to water but that was as close as she got—Cam seized hold of her wrist, in a grip that was gentle but firm.

"Much further, honey, and I'll forget my good intentions and have you right here," he warned roughly, and with one swift movement pinned her errant hand behind her back.

Stacie's heart raced. He was doing what she'd imagined. In a blinding epiphany that stopped her breath, she realised that this was what she'd wanted since the day she was old enough to understand what sex and relationships were all about—a man who would give her the gift of taking control of her. She moaned softly under his mouth as he kissed her again.

"I know," he growled back, squeezing her hip. "I don't know how the hell I'm going to sleep tonight. I know I said we'd stay here a while longer, but I have to take you up to your bed and leave you there—right now. I only have so much self-control, beautiful. It's been spread thin all evening, and now I think it's about to run out. The rest of our talk'll have to wait a while."

Stacie buried her face against his chest, stifling a nervous chuckle even as she revelled in the power of being a woman who knew she was wanted by such a formidably masculine man. "If you say so, Cam."

Her reward was another kiss. "That's what I like," he said with clear approval. "A woman who does as she's told."

As much as the dress would allow her, Stacie ran her bare foot up his leg as she dropped a sequence of tantalising little kisses along his jaw.

"I don't always," she whispered against his cheek.

Hellfire and damnation!

When Cam arrived back in his room, he couldn't wait to strip off and get under a cold shower in an attempt to dowse the conflagration of wild lust that was consuming him from the inside out. He'd only just managed to deliver Stacie to her room without taking a diversion to his suite and had been on the verge of congratulating himself on not giving in to his baser impulses when the little witch asked him to unzip her dress.

That was bad enough—when she turned to thank him, somehow the straps were falling down and it was only her slender arms crossed over her luscious breasts that prevented the bodice from dropping down and revealing all. He'd made his excuses and left, flinging one last look over his shoulder, only to see her bidding him goodnight with a smile that told him she knew exactly what she was doing.

Christ, she'd make one bratty sub.

No woman had ever given him such a crazy case of need before. If they'd been anywhere else, if they'd already established limits and boundaries, he'd have turned around, slammed the door shut behind him and given her an intensive course in obedience and discipline.

The thought reminded him that they hadn't got round to the main subject he'd wanted to discuss with her. Was a real D/s relationship between them possible? He had to hope. There were no guarantees in life, but then again, she loved Beth's novel. He'd overheard her congratulating Alex's wife on her success and saying how much she was looking forward to reading the next volume. In the time between the release of the two books, Beth had become an accomplished sub under her Master's expert hand—it had been Cam's privilege to witness her development at close quarters—and it was reflected in the content of her second novel. What would Stacie make of that one?

As he dried off after nearly succumbing to frostbite under the shower, Cam reflected that his old friend was really going to rub it in when he told Alex that he was falling hard and fast for a woman he'd barely known a day.

CHAPTER FIVE

"Why don't you and I make the most of this sunshine, get away from the cleaners and go for a walk? The boys are talking business, so they'll be closeted away in the office for a good while yet."

Stacie looked up from her book to the woman who wrote it. If ever there was a woman who looked perpetually happy, it was Beth Lombard. She was dressed casually in jeans and a green sweater, with her hair gathered up in a loose ponytail. The gold chain was back around her neck. Knowing what she knew now, that Beth had written the novel she couldn't bear to put down, Stacie wondered if there was a deeper significance to the beautiful piece of jewellery.

Although the sun was shining, the unmistakable chill of autumn was in the air. The two women set off in a companionable silence. After they'd been walking through the woods that surrounded Winterleigh for a few minutes, Beth opened the conversation.

"Alex and I were talking last night, when we went to bed. You really like Cam, don't you?"

Stacie gave a slightly embarrassed smile. "Is it that obvious?"

Beth returned the smile easily. "Let's just say that I think I've seen something in the way you look at Cam that reminds me of how I feel when I look at Alex. Men like Alex and Cam have a certain way about them, for the right kind of woman." Her expression became slightly more serious. "I think that maybe you and I need to talk."

It was then that Stacie realised they'd arrived in a clearing. A gentle breeze rustled the few leaves left on the trees—the only other sound to be heard was birdsong. Used to the constant barrage of noise in the city, Stacie was only too happy to let the tranquillity of nature wash around her. Even though she'd lived in the city for as long as she had, she was still a small-town girl at heart.

Beth took a seat on a fallen tree trunk, and indicated that Stacie should join her.

"This is Alex's favourite place on the estate," she began. "Mine, too. It's where he proposed to me, just before last Christmas. Well," she laughed, "he didn't so much propose as tell me I was marrying him—but that's what men like Alex and Cam do."

Five words repeated in the space of moments, and they didn't escape Stacie. "Men like Alex and Cam—that's the second time you've used that phrase."

Beth nodded. "Those two are different from a lot of

men, if not most." Her face broke into a smile. "You've already seen what Cam can be like with what happened with your car."

Suddenly appearing a little on edge, Beth stood up and walked over to the other side of the clearing. "Last night you told me how much you enjoyed my first book. I know it's not to everyone's taste—people tend to love it or hate it."

"I'm definitely a love-it," Stacie confirmed enthusiastically. "And every time I've read it, I've found even more about it that I love."

"Thank you—I really appreciate the vote of confidence." Beth took a deep breath. "That being the case, Stacie, there's a conversation I think we need to have for a number of reasons, although you may want to tell me to butt out and mind my own business."

Stacie wasn't about to do that—it sounded like Beth was about to give her the opening that she wanted, to talk about Cam, the book, and exactly how much of the main characters was drawn from the real lives of the people who'd inspired them. "That's okay. Please… I'd like to talk."

"All right, then. It's difficult to know exactly where to start, but I guess the best place might be with the thought that you and Cam seemed to be getting on really well last night?"

Her lips curved into a hesitant smile. "Yes, we did—we are."

Beth nodded. "And, er, Alex and I were wondering

if… maybe you were going to see some more of each other?"

"It looks like we are." Stacie was quietly thrilled by the prospect. "We talked about it last night, and while we were talking, I realised that you might be the best person to ask about… certain things."

"Go on."

"I didn't know, until last night, that you wrote that first book. While I was out with Cam yesterday, he asked me who my favourite author was—with the benefit of hindsight, I think he was trying to steer the conversation round to telling me you wrote it, but I… I said some things that… I admitted to Cam that I'd fallen for the blond Dom in the book. I know—it's a silly thing to say."

Beth smiled—a kind smile that helped to put Stacie a little more at ease. "That's a great compliment, you know. And not at all silly. These books work better if the reader warms to the characters. You were saying?"

"Well, last night, when I came downstairs for the party and I nearly fell down the last step… it was because I saw that beautiful diamond collar you were wearing. It sort of rang a bell, and then taking into account the descriptions of the characters and the fact that the party was for your second book, I thought that the book I've enjoyed so much had to be the first one you wrote."

"And now you know you weren't wrong."

Stacie paused, trying to get her thoughts into some sort of order. "I couldn't forget what I'd said in the car—I felt I had to apologise to Cam for embarrassing both of us, but he said he owed me an apology for not explaining everything earlier. We talked again, after the party, He confirmed that the characters were based loosely on the three of you, but…"

Stacie's voice trailed off. How best to phrase the question she wanted most to ask? It was such a personal subject, so sensitive. If the D/s dimension to the book just came from Beth's imagination, Stacie could easily alienate her, and that was the last thing she wanted to do.

"It might be easier if you just come out with it and ask whatever's on your mind."

Beth was looking at her expectantly. *Oh well, in for a penny, in for a pound.* "How much do the characters have in common with you? Is it more than just their physical characteristics?" She paused, finding every scrap of courage to ask what was occupying her mind most. "Is Cam a Dom?"

The other woman looked at her for a moment, then reached to the back of her neck, and brought the catch of the gold chain to the front—except now that she could take a closer look, Stacie saw that it wasn't a catch but a small, beautifully engraved padlock. Beth held onto it as if it were some sort of talisman, the look on her face indicative of some sort of internal debate.

"I wouldn't normally discuss this with an outsider, Stacie, but I think there are a couple of reasons why it would be a good idea in your case. If you're going to be seeing Cam, there are things you need to know—and not being scared off by what I wrote in my book is a good start. I also think you're not going to be an outsider for very long."

Stacie felt warmed by the encouraging smile that lit Beth's eyes.

Beth continued. "Apart from a small circle of very close friends who share our interests, no one else has realised—which amazes me—that the three characters are loosely based on Cam, Alex and myself. I used some aspects of our physical appearances, as you're aware, but the most significant similarity between the characters I created and the three of us is the practice of D/s.

"This," Beth pointed to the gold chain and padlock and took a deep breath, "is my collar, as was the diamond necklace last night. I wear it through choice, but Alex holds the key. I can't remove it unless he unlocks it. To the outside world, we're a very ordinary married couple, but anyone in the D/s community will know from this, when I wear it with the lock here and not at the back, that I'm a sub." She paused. "Obviously, Alex is my Dom as well as my husband. And yes, you're right about Cam—he is a Dom, and a very good one."

So it was true. Confirmation of the fact from Beth drained all the air from Stacie's lungs as the implications of that statement rushed through her mind.

And he'd asked her out. Was this what he'd been going to tell her? That the character in the book was like him in more than just appearance, and that she'd need time to think about it before agreeing to see him? That seemed most likely.

"Stacie? Are you all right?"

"I think so." As she said it, Stacie realised that she was. "I feel as though I should be surprised, but somehow I'm not. Thank you for telling me all that."

"Has it changed your mind about seeing him?"

A blunt question, and Stacie sensed there was a certain protectiveness about it that was both odd and touching. A man like Cam didn't need a woman to protect him, yet clearly Beth didn't want to see her friend get hurt or be rejected because of something that was such a fundamental part of him.

"No. No, it hasn't. But I can't say I'm not concerned about it. I've never been in that kind of relationship."

"Have you ever thought about being in that kind of relationship?"

"Not until I read your book. It made me think about a lot of things, and it made me wish I could find a man like that," Stacie confessed. "But then again, I didn't think men like that existed. Just shows how much I know!" Stacie laughed. "I don't want to disappoint him. What's it like, dating a Dom?"

Beth sighed. "That's like asking what colour is a rainbow. The lifestyle, in all its forms, is something that many people outside the community can't or won't even try to understand. Alex is the only Dom I've been in a relationship with—we don't have a 24/7 power exchange, which to some people in the community isn't a true D/s relationship, but it's as true as we want it to be. He loves me, and he makes me feel safe in a way no other man ever had before I met him."

"You make it sound wonderful."

"It's as wonderful as any relationship—of any kind—that works. It doesn't mean it's perfect, though—we still work at our relationship, the same way any vanilla couple does."

"One thing that came across in your book was how much trust there was between the two central characters, once their relationship became established."

Beth's expression became thoughtful. "In D/s, trust is paramount. In fact, it's probably true to say that trust has to be in place *before* a relationship becomes established. No—trust is something that's earned. I think *trustworthiness* has to be a prerequisite. A Dom has to respect your safewords. And when you can have that level of trust in the person you love..." She gave a slightly embarrassed smile. "As a writer, I should have the words to describe what it's like."

"I think I can guess." It would have been easy to be jealous of what Beth had with her husband, but Stacie didn't begrudge her one bit.

"There are some things you'll need to remember, though, Stacie, if you're going to be involved with a Dom. If there's something they want, then they will go after it until they get it. That's another reason why they have to be one-hundred-percent trustworthy, especially if you get into the sort of activities that are generally classed as edgeplay."

Something about which Beth was clearly uncomfortable, as her next words confirmed.

"Alex has never done anything that could be considered edgeplay, nor has he ever wanted to. We are members of a club—on one visit, we were watching a public display that went too far. The Dom refused to respect the sub's limits and his safeword. Alex went to the DMs—that's the Dungeon Monitors—immediately. He didn't say anything to me, but I know he was as distressed by it as I was. It's a hard limit for both of us."

Stacie felt a cold shiver go down her spine. Although she made a mental note to look into exactly what edgeplay was, it sounded like something she wanted to avoid at all costs. And *Dungeon Monitors*? *They* hadn't been in Beth's book!

"Stacie, if you were involved with Cam, you wouldn't need to worry about anything like that—he and Alex are very much alike in a lot of respects. But if you do want to explore further, always remember where the real power in the relationship lies."

"With the sub." Stacie recalled how amazed she'd been when she'd first come across that fact.

"That's right, and if you find yourself with a Dom who doesn't respect that, then walk away—no, *run* away, just as fast as you can. If I wanted to, I could go back to the house right now, say the one word that will end it all, and I know that Alex would agree without hesitation.

"But… Alex isn't Cam," Beth continued. "As I said, they have many traits in common, the ones that come with having a dominant nature. If you belong to them, they take that sense of ownership very seriously. And their brand of ownership comes with certain rights and responsibilities that don't tend to enter into vanilla relationships."

"Rights?" Stacie found that more than a little alarming.

"Rights that you, as the sub, give them, and which you can withdraw at any time. What you will have in Cam is a protector for life, a man who will go to the ends of the earth for you, who will do whatever it takes to keep you safe, up to and including putting his life on the line. Alex is the same."

Stacie could see by her expression that the other woman was caught up in remembering. She could only guess that it was the memory of the events Cam had told her about.

"Cam told me a little about what happened last year—not that he went into any details. It's just… I was worried about you on Friday night, after dinner, when Alex came for you."

At that, Beth's face relaxed into a slightly self-conscious grin. "Knowing what you know now, you can probably work out what happened next. Alex is very good at getting me to focus on what's important—it's a Dom thing. And if you're going to see Cam, that's something else that you'll need to get used to."

Stacie swallowed the lump that had suddenly formed in her throat. Intimate images filled her mind, fantasies of the things that Cam might do to and with her. Beth's warm hands clasping her cold ones brought her back to reality.

"Don't worry, Stacie. Cam would never force you to do anything you didn't want to do. All you need to remember are three words: safe, sane and consensual. They are the cornerstone of this lifestyle. If you go out with Cam and you find you want to know more about Domination and submission, he'll guide you gently into it, at a pace you feel comfortable with, and you'll be able to stop it or slow it down at any time. What you need to think about is whether you can really hand over complete control to another person… to Cam."

"I never realised… Even though I've thought about it, it's still a lot to take in. As I said, I didn't think men like that could possibly exist."

"Nor me," Beth admitted. "At least, not back then, before Alex changed our relationship. I thought they were a figment of my imagination and that of every writer of erotic romance with elements of BDSM in it. I assumed that Alex was the inspiration for the dark-haired Dom because of certain aspects of his behaviour round the office—I didn't realise that what I was picking up on was the fundamental nature of his character, not just a shallow predilection for bossiness. He scared me to death when he turned our professional relationship into a personal one, but I've never regretted it."

Seated across the desk from Alex, Cam was waiting to hear his friend's answer to the proposal he'd just put to him. Alex seemed to be fixated on the view through the window.

"I don't know, Cam," he said at length. "I've been out of the game a long time. I'm not sure I have anything of value to contribute anymore."

Cam's muttered curse spoke volumes about irritation and disbelief. "That's a pile of crap and you know it. Cast your mind back twelve months—Underwood put a bullet in you but you still managed to put him out of action permanently with your bare hands. Besides," Cam went on, "it's not like you'll be doing fieldwork. I'm offering you a cushy office job, partner."

"I know." Alex turned back to his friend. "I'll think about it."

"Shit!" Cam rolled his eyes. "Not you as well! That's what I got from Ros when I asked her again last night."

The other man laughed, and after a moment's hesitation Cam joined in, laughing at what had turned into a long-running joke over the last couple of years.

"You could always go and badger her over at Guy's place—she's spending the weekend with him," Alex suggested.

"Any other time I might have done—I could really use her on the team," Cam admitted.

"Other priorities?"

Cam nodded. "Stacie. I might as well tell you now—I like her."

His friend gave him a shrewd look. "Tell me something I don't know. There were times last night when you were looking at her the way I looked at Beth when I first realised I wanted her."

"When did you reach that point?"

Alex looked uncomfortably embarrassed for a moment. "Five minutes into the fucking job interview. But we're not discussing me. We're discussing you. And Stacie. A couple of days ago you hadn't even met her. Friday night, you told me it wasn't going anywhere. Yesterday you told her you'd buy her a car, and you spent a thousand pounds on an outfit and accessories for her. Who are you, and what have you done with the real Cameron Fraser?"

"This from you?" The look on Cam's face was an eloquent expression of his opinion of the stance Alex had taken. "Do the words 'pot', 'kettle' and 'black' mean anything to you? Anyway, didn't you say yourself that she might be just what I need?"

"What I think is irrelevant—someone has to play devil's advocate here. Well? Don't you think you're going a little over the top for a woman you only just met?"

"*You* gave Beth a job, remember? You see, this is precisely my point. Fundamentally, there's no difference between your reaction to her and my reaction to Stacie, apart from the fact that it didn't take me three years and a sprained ankle to fucking well do something about it." Cam gave a dismissive shrug. "Besides, what the hell else am I going to spend my money on? She needed help—I'm in a position to give it."

"So you're going to be seeing more of her?"

"Looks that way."

"So it's not too soon, and you're not too old for her after all?"

Trust Alex to remind him about his objections. Cam shrugged. "What can I say? My timing's crap and my maths sucks."

"What if she's not submissive?"

The killer question.

"Thanks, Alex. That's really helpful."

"Hey, you were the one who said you needed a sub."

He had—Cam couldn't deny it. "She likes Beth's book. She's a huge fan."

Alex rested his chin on steepled fingers. "Cam, you know as well as I do—if every woman who likes Beth's book were a sub, every Dom in the country could have a different sub for every night of the week and two on Sundays. You also know that when it comes to our lifestyle, fantasy and reality rarely coincide. So what's your plan?"

Cam considered the question for a moment. "Get to know her. Gauge the level of her interest in submission, see if she has any inclination to take it further than just reading about it. See if things click between us."

"Suppose everything clicks except for the fact that she's *not* submissive? That she's not even interested beyond the fantasy version? Have you thought about that? How she might react when you raise the subject?"

"I don't think she'll freak out. Let me tell you something—she knows the main characters in Beth's book are loosely based on us. I didn't tell her—I just confirmed her suspicions. She worked it out for herself."

"Does she know to what extent?"

Talk about a dog with a bone. "Not yet."

"But she's probably wondering. If she's smart enough to make the connection in the first place, she'll want to know just how far it goes. You need to talk to her, and sooner rather than later."

He cursed under his breath—Alex was right. He wasn't telling Cam anything he didn't already know. "It still may end up going nowhere."

"The same place where most relationships end up, because it only takes one to be special. I know." Alex paused. "You do know that you're both welcome to stay here?"

"Thanks. Stacie was planning to take a few days off—if that's still the case, I thought we might stay here a couple more days and then head back to London."

Alex shook his head. "Cam, you need the break. Why don't you both stay here for the week, like you planned? Stacie's more than welcome. And hell, God knows we're no prudes—if the two of you end up ready to share a room while you're still here, go ahead."

Cam allowed himself a small chuckle. "Thanks, Alex. It's tempting, but having given this some thought, I want Stacie to be sure about this. What I don't want is for her to feel rushed into anything. I've given it some consideration, and I think we need to get to know each other in a regular environment. Not to mention the fact that I'd feel as uncomfortable as hell doing the horizontal mambo under your roof."

Alex roared with laughter. "Just so you know, the soundproofing in this house is excellent!"

"Yeah, well, I'm still not doing it. Besides, you and Beth need time together, now that you've decided to start a family."

It hadn't taken a genius to make the connection when the Lombards had asked him a while ago if he'd consider the possibility of being a godfather at some undefined point in the future. Looking back, the thought of his old friend having not just a wife but a complete family had probably consolidated his own change in attitude to such matters.

They finished their conversation and made their way to the family room, to find the two women enjoying mugs of hot chocolate. Judging by the laughter, they were getting on like a house on fire. In fact, looking at them, anyone could be forgiven for thinking they'd been friends for years. *A good omen, perhaps?* It certainly gave Cam an unfamiliar but very welcome buzz.

He watched Alex go to his wife, sit on the sofa beside her and wrap his arms around her. When Cam turned to look at Stacie, what he saw in her unguarded expression could have been an innocent longing for the same—from him?

Who dares wins?

"Hi," he greeted her easily. "Mind if I join you?"

Her answer was to slide along the sofa, just far enough so that he could make himself comfortable beside her—

not so far as to put too much space between them. Almost without thinking, he casually slipped an arm around her shoulders. When she didn't shrink away from him, a feeling of warm satisfaction, sweet like honey, flowed slowly through his veins.

"Stacie, I don't know exactly what you were planning to do for the next few days, but we need to take care of your old car. I was thinking that we might stay here for a day or two while we do that, then I'll take you back to London and we can look for a replacement."

Again, that look of disbelief in her eyes. "You really would do that?"

Cam raised a stern eyebrow—at that moment, he hoped that Stacie Matheson really did have an inner sub and would let her come out to play, because she had to learn that when he gave his word, it was final. He never said anything he didn't mean. For now, though…

"I told you I would, and I meant it. Now, when you came down here, what was your original plan? Did you intend to take the whole week off work?"

Stacie hadn't really thought about it. She'd asked her manager for a few days but hadn't specified a number. She knew, though, that taking the full week wouldn't be a problem—she'd had barely any time off during the year, and her manager had commented that it was about time, otherwise she might lose any vacation days that were still unused at the end of the year. When she told the three people around her, she was warmed by their reactions—

especially Cam's, when she felt his arm tighten around her.

"It's a pity you can't both stay here for the whole week," Beth said in response.

"I'm sorry, angel," Cam apologised. "When I promised Stacie I'd help her out with finding a new car, I figured we'd do that back in London. Stacie?"

Impossible though it was, it seemed like he was asking her opinion as if they were a real couple. Less than two days ago, she'd been wondering if he had a significant other, and now he was making her feel as if she *were* his significant other. Or at least on her way to it—that might be a slightly more accurate appraisal of her situation. Either way… *definitely* not in Kansas anymore. A boulder of burgeoning panic suddenly thudded into her chest. What was that she'd thought about this man being way out of her league again?

"Stacie? Are you all right?"

Cam's voice broke into her thoughts, and when she turned her head to look at him, she was surprised to see the genuine concern in his features.

"It's nothing, I'm fine… thanks." She gave him what she hoped was a reassuring smile. The look of concern, far from going, mutated into a slight but distinct frown of displeasure.

"Beth, Alex—would you excuse us, please? Stacie and I have something to discuss before we firm up our plans."

Open-mouthed, she wasn't quite sure how to react to the mug of hot chocolate being removed from her grasp, rapidly followed by a strong hand pulling her to her feet and out of the room. In the hall was where she found her voice.

"Cam! What are you doing?"

The question was futile—he wasn't saying anything, fixated as he was on hauling her upstairs. She expected to be taken to her room, but no, he went towards his room, dragged her inside and around to face him, at the same time as he kicked the door closed behind him. She decided to get the first word in.

"What? What did I say?"

"It's not what you said, Stacie—it's what you didn't say. Don't ever lie to me again."

That stopped her in her tracks and prompted her to mount a robust protest. "*What?* But… I didn't lie to you!"

"You didn't tell me the truth, Stacie. Something was bothering you, but you denied it. From now on, that never happens again, is that clear?"

"But it was nothing!"

Cam let her go. He was sorely tempted to drag her over to the bed and put her over his knee to administer the spanking she deserved. While he was pissed off by her refusal to tell all, his self-control was such that he was more than capable of employing such a punishment without letting emotion get the better of him. Had they been in an established relationship, he would have had no qualms about doing so. It was too early for that, and he didn't want them to get off on the wrong foot. The potential for disaster was huge, if a punishment were to be delivered without both parties being clear about justification and boundaries.

No, there was only one way to make her understand this time, and that was to have the talk he'd planned to have when they arrived back in London—once he'd had a chance to work out exactly what he was going to say to her. He had no choice but to wing it.

"Sit down, Stacie," he began, raking his hand through his hair—a habit he had when he was faced with a thorny problem. "I think that you and I had better have our little talk right now."

She was sitting on the bed—*his* bed, and it was a visual he really didn't need right then. He moved across the room, deliberately putting some distance between them.

"You've read Beth's book, and you know she modelled her central characters on the three of us—herself, Alex and me."

Stacie nodded, even though it was more a statement than a question. "Several times. While Beth and I were out for a walk a little while ago, we talked about it."

"Did she tell you to what extent she modelled those characters on us?"

"If you mean the D/s thing, yes, she told me about that." Stacie squirmed slightly. "I asked her if you were a Dom and she said yes."

Suddenly very still, Cam blinked. She knew? "Does that change anything?"

Wide-eyed, she looked up at him. Then her lips

pressed together—this wasn't looking good, he thought grimly. His thoughts became even grimmer when her shoulders lifted on a deep breath.

"For me it doesn't change anything, but I can't say I don't have any concerns," she admitted eventually. "I mean, I've never been in that kind of relationship, and apart from Beth's novel, I really know very little about the subject."

And no doubt what she did know, she'd learned from ill-informed, scaremongering sources. Cam silently cursed the lack of understanding of the lifestyle that seemed to prevail. "You've read her novel several times, though—you seem to be fascinated by it."

"I am," Stacie confirmed with a small, slightly hesitant smile. "There's so much love and trust between the two main characters. And communication. So different from the relationships I've experienced." She took a deep breath. "Beth said that trust and communication are important in the kind of relationship she has with Alex. I think I might know why you're angry with me."

"First of all, I'm not angry—not the way you mean. *Displeased* is more like it."

"Whatever. This is something to do with my not telling you what was bothering me, isn't it?"

Whatever? She'd actually dared to say *whatever* to her Dom?

And he did now consider himself just that, even if they hadn't ironed out the details yet. The fact that she knew what he was and hadn't backed out of seeing him was an implicit acceptance of his position in her life. Cam folded his arms and drummed the fingers of his right hand on his upper left arm. He continued to glare at her, one eyebrow raised. That way, he could see the exact moment when the error of her ways sank in.

"I'm in trouble, aren't I?"

"You could say that."

"What are you going to do about it?" She shifted slightly on the bed.

Now that was interesting. She was playing the game. "What do you think I should do about it?" Cam adopted the silkiest tone in his verbal arsenal, pleased to see that it scored a direct hit and made her squirm some more.

"I'm… not sure."

Understandable. Later on in their relationship, she would be sure. "Shall I tell you, Stacie? Assuming this was within the boundaries of our contract, you would present yourself to me for discipline. Do you know what that means?"

She shook her head.

"And that would add another ten to the count. You say, 'No, Sir'. You do not shake your head like that. Nor do you nod when in agreement. Shall we try again? Do you know what that means?"

"No, Sir."

Two words, barely more than breathed, and they went straight to his cock. Cam had to take a couple of steps away from her—not for the sake of putting distance between them, but for the sake of easing the stranglehold his jeans had on his unruly dick. He turned back to her.

"It means our current positions would be reversed. I'd be sitting there, and you would be standing in front of me. You'd strip off your jeans for me, without my having to tell you to do so, and you'd lie across my lap. I'd take your knickers down and you'd get the flat of my hand on your bare bottom. You would count out each and every stroke, and you would thank me for each one."

She stared at him, her mouth slightly open in shock. What was even more interesting was the way her nipples had become hard, proud points beneath the soft, clinging fabric of her top. The description of her punishment was clearly turning her on.

"What… would happen then, Sir?"

The best part. "The matter would be closed and I'd take care of you."

He hadn't thought she could open her eyes any wider, but wider they went and Cam felt a curious thrill at the thought of giving her the pleasure she was clearly anticipating.

"Now," he continued, "why did you look so worried when I mentioned the car and London?"

She took a deep, steadying breath. "I was worried about reading too much into this… the situation between us."

"Too much in what way?"

She squirmed again. "This is going to sound really stupid."

"Talk to me, Stacie."

"It's part of… it's the whole car thing. No, it's more than that. A couple of days ago we'd never even met, and now here we are—you've asked me to go out with you, you've offered to help me find a car and finance it for me. It's all more than a little overwhelming. I mean, people don't do that when they barely know one another. They hardly even do it when they've been seeing one another for years!"

"Okay. What else?"

From the way her expression changed, Cam guessed that the "else" was the crux of the matter.

"Socioeconomically, we're worlds apart. And there was the way you asked me about going back to London to look for a car. It struck me how quickly everything was happening. You were treating me like your girlfriend—"

"For want of a better way of describing it, you are my girlfriend."

"And it only seems like five minutes since I was wondering if you had someone special in your life!"

"Ah, I see. Too much, too soon."

"Yes. No. Sort of." She made an almost comic noise of strangled frustration. "I don't know!"

"Hmm. Well, that's cleared that up, then." He couldn't help it if he had a somewhat dry sense of humour.

She looked up at him. Her breath huffed out on a huge sigh and her shoulders slumped. "Not so much too much, too soon as an awful lot all at once. I just finished with Jonty—my ex—but I wasn't in love with him. I think that relationship had been more or less over for a while, or was getting that way, so it's not like I'm nursing a broken heart or having sleepless nights about it."

"Is there anything that *is* giving you sleepless nights—or likely to?" Cam enquired gently, serious again because he didn't like the thought of anything other than him keeping her awake at night. And he'd only be keeping her awake for the best of reasons.

"Well… you, mainly," she replied, staring at the fingers that were fidgeting on her lap. "Sort of, I mean, in the sense that I would probably be looking at sleepless nights… after talking to Beth about her book this morning. And they'd be sleepless for good reasons, not bad ones. Oh God, I'm making such a mess of this."

Not so sure that it was a good idea, Cam went to stand in front of her—close, but far enough away that he'd need to take another step to be in a position to touch her. As an extra precaution, he rammed his hands into his pockets. "No, you're not," he disagreed, not unkindly. "You're communicating and that's what we need you to do. Your clarity needs a little work, admittedly. So come on—tell me."

"I'm still embarrassed about what I said in the car yesterday."

"About?"

She looked at him with mutinous eyes. "Are you going to make me say it?"

"Yes."

She huffed again and looked away. Cam took the step he never intended to take, and with a single finger under her chin, he made her look at him again. He schooled his features into an expression of expectation.

"I'm still embarrassed about admitting to being attracted to a fictional character in the first place, compounded by the fact that I admitted it to the man who inspired that character. Happy now?"

Now she was glaring at him. Cam had a hard time keeping his amusement in check—instead he focused on the pleasure her reluctant obedience gave him.

"*Happy* may be an exaggeration, Stacie, but I am pleased by your open and honest communication. As for being embarrassed, forget about it—we dealt with that last night. Anything else worrying you and keeping you awake? Or likely to do so?"

He could see the question forming in her mind.

"Does it bother you that I'm a complete novice when it comes to this kind of relationship? I think that would worry me—if it bothered you."

That was an easy question for him to answer, difficult though it was for her to ask it. "It doesn't bother me in the slightest, honey. We'll take it slow and easy, starting with honesty, which is a good foundation for trust. For instance, when I ask you what's wrong, you answer me fully, honestly and immediately—no filters. If you censor anything you say to me, I'll just have to teach you the lesson the hard way."

She looked straight at him. "How would you teach me the lesson the hard way? A spanking?"

A question he wasn't expecting—not then, at any rate.

Was Stacie going to be a sub who would keep him on his toes? He bloody well hoped so. She was already showing clear signs of it. The one thing he didn't want was a slave incapable of thinking for herself.

Nor did he miss the way her pupils dilated when she asked the question. What was she anticipating? All of a sudden, Cam was burning to know how she wanted to be taught the lesson the hard way.

"Perhaps, but we have to discuss your hard and soft limits before we go down that road, Stacie. And that is a discussion we're not having here."

Was it his imagination, or did she look disappointed? Did she even know she looked disappointed? And what, in particular, was she disappointed about? Did she *want* to feel his hand on her bottom?

Cam was starting to get the idea that this relationship was going to be anything but predictable.

CHAPTER SIX

A couple of days later Cam found himself outside a large Victorian house in one of the less-fashionable areas of the capital, unloading Stacie's bags from the boot of his car. Her new car—at eighteen months old, it was as new as she'd let him buy for her and that had been under the kind of protest that would earn any sub a punishment—would be ready to collect in a couple of days. Picking it up from the dealer about ten miles from Winterleigh would give them another excuse to drop in on the Lombards. The original plan—to buy the car in London—had fallen by the wayside when Stacie's eye was caught by the fiery-red Mini on the dealer's forecourt, on the way from the scrapyard where her old vehicle had been laid to rest.

Until then, he was going to put the time to good use and spend as much of it as possible with Stacie, starting with dinner that evening and a night that—though she didn't know it yet—she was going to spend in his bed.

It was four days since they'd first met, and for most of that time they'd had the mutual pleasure of each other's company. What Cam had discovered about Stacie Matheson in that time pleased him immensely. Yes, she was physically attractive, but more importantly she had a mind too, one that he was growing more and more convinced was underutilised in her job as an administrative assistant in a large office. Not much got past her—over the last few days, they'd had some very lively discussions that had revealed more of her intelligence and character. The more he saw of her, the more he liked what he saw… the more attracted to her he became.

Something else that had given him great pleasure was dealing with the bastard she'd had the great good sense to ditch. He'd seen her thinly veiled annoyance at the latest text message to come from the loser, and having had enough of the pest, Cam had taken her phone from her and called her ex.

A few choice words had been enough to get the message across. When he finished the call, Cam had turned back to Stacie, intending to return her phone, only to find her standing there with her hands on her hips, absolutely furious with him. She had then told him in no uncertain terms that she was entirely capable of dealing with the arsehole and didn't need his help. Having put him in his place, she'd taken her phone back, switched it off, and then proceeded to kiss him sweetly. She was a feisty one all right.

It was time, though, to take things further. They'd discussed Beth's book, and as they'd done so it had become apparent that while Stacie had no firsthand experience, as she'd pointed out, she was definitely interested in not just reading about D/s but exploring it too, and exploring it with him. Cam hadn't realised how jaded he was in danger of becoming until Stacie's quiet enthusiasm began to infect him too.

"Thanks, Cam."

She went to take the bags from him, but he wasn't having that. "I'm carrying them up for you, Stacie. No arguments."

At that, her face fell—only a little, but more than enough for him to pick up on it. He looked at her, his expression one of expectation. He'd give her five seconds to answer him. *One… two… three…*

"Cam, you really don't have to, I can manage—"

"Stacie." He silenced her with no more than her name. "Enough. Whatever's going through your mind, it stops right now. I'm taking these up for you. Then you're going to make me a cup of coffee, we're going to have an hour or so together, and after that, while I run a couple of errands, you're going to get ready for me to pick you up at seven for dinner. Now show me the way."

The building housed half a dozen apartments over three levels. Stacie's was on the top floor and as he followed her through the front door, Cam's first impression of it was that it was clean and tidy, furnished for comfort rather than current fashion. Unlike his place, Stacie's home had never been subject to the whims of a professional interior designer. When he took the bags into the bedroom, he tried not to look at the bed. *Again.* Their first time together was going to be at his place, tonight, and if he had his way—not that there was any doubt on that score—she wouldn't be back here until after they'd picked up her new car.

"Now, how about that coffee?"

Again, she looked uncomfortable. "I only have instant, I'm afraid."

"Instant's fine, honey." He wanted her to be more relaxed around him, but it seemed like she was all nerves as she filled the kettle and put granules, sugar and milk in the mugs. He was quietly impressed, though, that she remembered how he took it.

Her back to him, she was watching the kettle boil. Her shoulders were stiff and he could almost feel the tension radiating from them. He pushed himself away from the cupboard he'd been leaning against and went to stand behind her. She offered no resistance when he wrapped one arm around her waist, anchoring her to him.

"Relax, beautiful," he urged her quietly, using his other hand to turn her head gently to one side. "We're going to be together tonight… all night. I'll look after you, I promise." He nuzzled her temple—she smelled of spring flowers. "You have nothing to worry about."

"Cam, I—"

"Nothing. To. Worry. About. Switch your mind off, just let yourself feel. Close your eyes, honey. Good girl."

He leaned down and kissed her mouth, his lips tenderly exploring hers. He'd kissed her many times over the weekend, and each time had left him wanting more of her sweetness.

Things were moving fast and going deep—Stacie knew it and she didn't care. Her head was trying to play the common-sense card, telling her to slow things down, but her female instincts had the upper hand. She was with Cam now, and the same instincts that made her want him so badly were also telling her that she could trust him.

He was a man like no other, she knew that already, and she wanted—so much—to experience everything that being with him had to offer. Having met Beth, seen at firsthand what a Dominant/submissive relationship could really be like, she wanted to find out for herself. It was a once-in-a-lifetime opportunity. The time she'd already spent with Cam had been an education. After he'd kissed her goodnight at the door of her bedroom while at the Lombards' house, she'd gone to bed and read more of Beth's book with new eyes.

And it wasn't just what Cam could offer in terms of a D/s relationship—it was the man himself, someone with whom she'd happily be in a relationship, D/s or not.

So she let herself relax into his strong embrace, wanting so much more than the touch of his mouth to hers, knowing that just a few hours from now, she would have it. No clothes between them… and no deceptions, no lies either.

"That's better, beautiful," he said, when their lips finally parted. "I want you to relax, ready for tonight. I have things to do when I leave here—when I go, I want you to take a nice long bath and then dress for dinner. Be ready for seven."

"Where are we going? For dinner, I mean."

"It's a surprise. Whatever you wear will be fine. You'll be staying with me until we go to Winterleigh and pick your car up on Thursday, so pack a bag for the rest of the week."

Just like that. What was it Beth had said? *If there's something they want, then they will go after it until they get it.*

And the thing about it was, Stacie was more than happy to agree. She wanted this. The thought of being with Cam in a full-on relationship made her want to do cartwheels; the thought of what was to come that evening filled her with nervous anticipation.

"I'll be ready," she promised.

Coffee was over too quickly—the apartment seemed awfully quiet and empty without him. Stacie checked the time. He'd be back in a little under three hours, so plenty of time to carry out her instructions. She smiled to herself, thinking how good it felt to have a man in her life who didn't have her on edge all the time. At least, not in a negative way.

With the laundry started, she packed one bag again with a variety of clothes, and then she filled the bath, giving herself plenty of time to relax and luxuriate in the bubbles. She washed her hair too, dried it carefully, and was still ready for Cam's arrival a good half-hour ahead of time. Her heart leapt when she heard his voice through the intercom. She buzzed him into the building and was waiting for him at the open door to her apartment.

And oh, he looked good. The crisp black dress shirt, open at the neck and teamed with an immaculate black suit and perfectly polished black shoes, showed off his tanned skin, blue eyes and dark-blond hair in a way that would reduce any woman breathing and over the age of consent to a boneless mass of panting need. She could *so* vouch for that.

Those eyes held hers for a second, and then he stepped through the door, closed it behind him and laid one hand against her cheek, holding her to receive a kiss that pulsed through every cell, every atom in her body. In a response she couldn't control even if she'd wanted to, she put her arms around him and pressed closer, moaning into his mouth as he took what he wanted from her—took what she gave freely and without reservation.

When the kiss ended, he laid his forehead against hers. His voice was hoarse when he spoke her name in greeting.

"You look incredible," he continued, his eyes sweeping over her. "Just right for this evening."

Stacie had chosen to wear a dress—it wasn't new, but it was one that she felt good in and judging by the appreciation in Cam's expression, the effect was pleasing to him. "Thank you." She stood on tiptoe to touch a brief kiss to the corner of his mouth. "You look pretty tasty yourself."

He gave her a lopsided grin. "Do that again, honey, and we won't be going anywhere. Where's your bag?"

While Cam collected it from the bedroom, Stacie checked around the apartment one more time, and then she was leading the way down the stairs, out to where Cam's car was parked. He opened the door for her, saw her safely into the vehicle, and stowed her bag in the boot. Moments later, they were on their way.

Their destination was a riverfront development—a stunning example of modern architecture, and Stacie didn't want to think about how much it cost to live there. To do that would just emphasise the yawning financial chasm between them.

"So, what's the plan for tonight?"

"Drinks, dinner… getting to know one another a little better," Cam replied easily, switching off the engine. "Thanks for having dinner with me tonight."

What a strange thing to say. And what woman *wouldn't* want to have dinner with him? Stacie felt a surge of that nervous excitement again. "It's my pleasure—thank you for asking me."

"And you're okay with staying the night?"

She took a deep breath. "I'm okay," she said simply. "I want to be with you tonight. We've waited long enough."

Cam's penthouse apartment was everything that hers was not—modern, minimalist, expensively sophisticated. A small bathroom and three bedrooms off the entrance corridor—he showed her two of them, but not the master—and then the corridor opened up into a huge living space, with a kitchen area, a dining area and a seating area. Floor-to-ceiling glass stood between them and a private terrace with views of the river and some well-known landmarks.

"Which you could see properly if it wasn't dark," Cam added, joining her to look out across the lights of the city and their twinkling reflections in the river. She felt his hands on her shoulders as he took up position behind her. "I've put your bag in the bedroom. Now, what would you like to drink?"

Stacie couldn't help herself. She brushed her cheek against his hand, and was rewarded with a fingertip that caressed her skin in return. "Dry white wine, please, if you have it."

"Good choice," he approved, "I have a particularly good Chenin Blanc in at the moment—I think you'll like it."

She did. She also liked sitting beside Cam, sipping her drink and talking about a thousand different subjects. When she complimented him on his beautiful home, the smile he gave her held a hint of something that in anyone else might have been construed as sadness, an emotion she found difficult to connect with the image Cam projected so easily.

"It's a place to stay when I'm in town, honey, that's all. Hardly a home."

She could be wrong, but it sounded to her like a real home was the one thing he wanted above all else… as if it were something he'd never had. It made her wonder about his past, all the things that had made him the man he was today.

Their conversation continued around other subjects, some personal, some not. She found out that Cam's business was security—he didn't go into too much detail, but Stacie had a feeling that it had nothing to do with men in dodgy uniforms looking out for shoplifters at the local supermarket. It was a business he and Alex had originally started together, but after a couple of years he'd bought Alex out, for reasons Cam didn't go into. Now, though, he was now looking to bring the other man back into the organisation as a full partner again.

She also discovered that they weren't going out for dinner, because Cam was cooking for them.

"Nothing complicated," he said, with a somewhat more relaxed smile this time, "but I can guarantee it will taste good."

Completely stunned, all Stacie could do was stare at him. Including this time, she could count on the fingers of one hand the number of occasions a man had cooked for her and still be able to enumerate the Four Horsemen of the Apocalypse on the remainder. A restaurant couldn't be more exclusive than that. "What are we having?"

"Pâté to start, then chicken with dauphinoise potatoes and wilted spinach, and for you, mojito cheesecake for dessert."

Cam refused all offers of help in the high-tech kitchen, so all Stacie could do was sit at the breakfast bar and drink her fill of the way he moved around the space as he prepared their meal. There was a masculine, animal grace about him that spoke to her primal female core and conjured up deliciously decadent images of how he would move in the bedroom. The delicious aroma of the food wasn't the only thing that had her salivating.

The meal tasted as good as it had sounded, but when it came to the final course, Cam escorted Stacie from the dining table to the seating area that gave them a fantastic view of the river and the city beyond. He also carried a small spoon and the glass that held the delicious-looking dessert, both of which he put down on the low table.

"Before you sit down, beautiful," he said, "I want you to do one thing for me."

"Of course."

She looked at him—and saw his expression change, a shift so subtle that it could easily have been missed. The easy-going, charming dinner companion was gone, and in his place there was a man who looked as if he were in control of the world. Stacie's mouth went dry, and she knew… this was Cam as a Dom, a man who would not be disobeyed. Her body went on vibrating high alert.

"Take your panties off and give them to me."

She hesitated only a moment—barefoot since she'd sat down with that first glass of wine, it was easy to do as he commanded. He slipped the scrap of silk into his trouser pocket, after removing something else that he kept hidden in his hand, and then he sat down.

"I want you here, on my lap, honey."

Why on earth did he have to ask that of her? Stacie

wasn't skinny—the bathroom scales told her that every week, with monotonous regularity.

"Stacie, when I give you an instruction, I expect you to obey me without question or hesitation."

"But—"

"Now, Stacie."

She tried to perch so that she took most of her own weight, but Cam had other ideas. He moved her into the exact position he wanted her, so that her feet weren't even touching the floor, and then he revealed the item he'd had stashed in his pocket—a black silk scarf. It made an excellent blindfold.

"We'll discuss limits soon—this evening maybe, tomorrow at the latest. What we're about to do now requires only one thing, but without it we can't even start. Trust is important in all relationships, beautiful, but in a relationship between a Dominant and a submissive, trust overrides everything."

She felt his fingers checking the fabric; she could only presume to ensure that she could see nothing.

"This will be your first easy step towards trusting me. I'm going to feed you your dessert. You will trust me to pay attention to your needs. You will trust me not to give you too much at once. You will trust me not to embarrass you by getting it all over your face, or spilling it all over your dress. You will trust me to keep you safe, not let you fall, and to give you an entirely pleasurable experience. And since we haven't discussed safewords yet, you will trust me to stop if you say the word *stop*. Do you understand, Stacie?"

"I understand, Cam."

She felt him move—she presumed to reach for the dessert glass, which he then placed in her hands—and then he was telling her to open her mouth. Stacie knew the spoon was small—the first taste was half the size of the spoon, and he was telling her to eat it slowly, to savour every nuance of its minty, zesty deliciousness, to focus on what her senses other than sight were telling her. Between spoonfuls he kissed her, making love to her with random delicate touches of his mouth, while the movement of his other hand over her body was slowly stripping her bare mentally, until all she wanted to do was curl up in his arms and give to him whatever he desired from her.

Inside and out, Stacie was the most beautiful woman he'd ever met and Cam knew, as he fed her the last morsel of cheesecake, that she was going to play a seriously important role in his life. No, he realised, not *going to*—she already *was* playing a seriously important role in his life. He wanted to know everything about her—her likes, her hopes, her fears… her loves.

He set the glass and spoon to one side. Even though he'd not yet removed the blindfold, she nestled in his arms, quiet and restful, waiting for him to make the next move. Her serenity calmed him in a way he'd not experienced with any other sub. No fidgeting, no impatience—she seemed to be content just to be what he needed at that moment.

He stroked her thigh, his hand over the material of her dress intended to accustom her to his touch. He was a leg man, no mistake, and she had legs that went on forever, firm and toned, but not overly so. He'd explored the lush curves of her bottom several times over the last few days, always over her clothes, never in any way that might embarrass her. It was time to take her to the next level. One more stroke down to her knee, and then…

He heard Stacie's sharp intake of breath when the upward sweep of his hand remained in contact with her skin, up her thigh to her hip, where his fingers pressed gently but firmly into the soft, silky curve. She shivered against him, but she didn't move away, didn't even try to.

"That's my girl," he whispered. "Will you open your legs for me, honey?"

She wriggled—her leg brushed against his cock, which was already straining against the fabric of his trousers, reminding him unnecessarily how much he wanted her, but her thighs parted for him.

"How do you feel, Stacie? Comfortable?" Her mouth was curved in a tranquil smile and she nodded, her head resting close to his. Her response was good, as far as it went.

"Talk to me, beautiful. I need to hear you say it, remember." As he would need to hear her communicate verbally in a scene. He reined in his imagination before it could go charging off to a place of silk ropes and other restraints, and toys that would bring her to the brink of orgasm time and time again, before finally he allowed her to come apart for him.

"Yes, Cam." Her voice was low but clear. "I'm comfortable."

And delightfully wet, as he discovered when he caressed her clit with his fingertip. Her mound was completely smooth, and as a result she was sweetly responsive to his touch—the pitch of her breathing changed as he continued to stroke the sensitised flesh. Her hands clenched into his shirt held him captive, as did the soft, almost anguished moans that whispered from her lips. He half-expected her to try to close her legs against his touch, but she didn't—she was staying with him.

He dipped his fingers into the slick heat of her pussy. She whimpered again, buried her face against him, and the hand that had been curled into his shirt transferred to the other side of his neck. He began to move his fingers, each one alternately tapping her G-spot, the rhythm unrelenting, and he felt a satisfying flow of wetness in response, the automatic contraction of her body trying to milk his fingers as if his cock were inside her.

"Let me know when you're ready to come, honey."

There was desperation about the way she clung to him now, and not unexpectedly he soon heard her give the warning he'd asked her for. It was his cue to make the decision—to delay her orgasm or intensify it.

She'd earned her reward. He chose the latter, slipped a finger back inside her, and when he found the precise spot on the wall of her vagina again she unravelled in his arms, crying out over and over again.

"Shh, it's okay, honey," he soothed her, rocking her gently in his arms as she drifted back down from her shattering orgasm. An experienced submissive could scarcely have done better.

There would be plenty of time to take what appeared to be Stacie's natural inclination towards submission and train it, hone it to perfection... help her to become the sub he'd always needed, the sub he sensed she was born to be. Very gently, he loosened the blindfold and tucked it back in his pocket.

"Stacie." He spoke her name softly, with a tenderness that was new to him. "Eyes on me, beautiful."

She obeyed instantly. He saw lightly flushed cheeks, and eyes that shone with satisfaction and a little apprehension. *So sweet... so submissive.* "That's my girl," he said, glad to see that hint of anxiety leave her. It was time to take her to bed. "Come with me."

The dress she wore was perfect, he decided—it buttoned down the front, so he was able to unfasten it slowly, relishing each area of delicate creamy skin as it was revealed. When she was naked, it was all he could do not to worship her—Stacie Matheson was all woman, all soft, voluptuous curves that made a man ache to take control. And again she simply accepted what he wanted to do—she stood there while he cupped her breasts in his hands and pinched her nipples between his thumb and forefinger. At her sharp gasp he released them, only to take each one in his mouth in turn and suckle gently, soothing the sting of the pain he'd purposely inflicted.

"Into bed, honey—I'll be right with you."

Her eyes were on him as he undressed, and when he joined her under the sheets, she nestled close. She seemed fascinated by his tattoo. Her finger was following the bold lines that adorned his upper arm and shoulder in a way that set his entire body on fire with need—especially when she reached the ink that strayed over his chest. Perhaps it had something to do with the way the tip of her tongue peeped out between her lips as she concentrated on the ink—his kitten had come out to play again.

"When did you have this done?" she asked at length, her voice low and slightly husky.

"When I was too young to know better," he admitted with a wry grin. "Do you like it?"

She considered the question as she traced more of the pattern. "I do. It's like you," she concluded, a faint satisfied smile curving her delicious mouth.

He was intrigued. "How so?"

"Straightforward, but at the same time… complex."

And with that, she leaned forward and pressed her lips to his shoulder.

Cam felt as if his balls were about to explode. However, instead of allowing his concentration to focus on all points south, he framed her cheek with his hand, coaxed her into looking up at him. Before this went any further, he wanted to see if she remembered what he'd said about communication—straight questions, honest answers, no filters and giving verbal responses.

"Stacie, honey, how do you feel? Is there anything

we've done so far that you don't like, or don't feel comfortable with?"

She looked up at him, took a deep breath... and her eyes lit up, almost glowed with a happiness that came from a place she hadn't known existed, until he'd shown it to her. He could almost see her thinking, choosing her next words with the kind of care that meant it mattered to her. *It mattered.*

"Nothing, but it's more than just tonight, Cam—it's the last few days, ever since we met," she began quietly. "I need you to know, though, that I don't... I've never... rushed into getting to this point, but being with you just seems right, as if I were always meant to meet you."

She was telling the truth. He could see it in her eyes, even if he hadn't already known it. Right from the start, he'd known she wasn't the kind of woman who slept around. "I know, Stacie."

"That doesn't make sense, I know, because we've only just met, but I've realised that trying to make sense of it is a pointless exercise. It is what it is. And this evening's been just as wonderful as the rest of it. I've never known a man like you, Cam. No one's ever affected me like this before."

Warmed by her words though he was, he had to be absolutely sure. "And none of it has made you feel awkward? In any way?"

"None of it," she confirmed, her voice a silken whisper that wove its magic around him. "I'm nervous, but excited too. I want to know more, to experience more. And I want to give you pleasure too, Cam."

"You do," he said simply. "And now I want you to sleep for a little while. Tonight isn't over yet—I have plans for you, so you need to rest."

Skin to skin, they lay wrapped in each other's arms—something Cam had never really done with a sub beyond the requirements of aftercare until this moment. He'd scened with them at the club, or if he had a relationship with a sub that included sex, then the act had always taken place at the club, a hotel or her place—never his. It was easier to leave that way, before involvement could run too deep and expectations were raised.

While Stacie slept, he thought—about her and the things she'd said. With this woman he wanted none of those boundaries. He wanted her submission, yes, but he also found himself wanting the simpler, less formal pleasures of vanilla too. And the question—for later—would be how far did he want those pleasures to go? As far as marriage, like Beth and Alex? Just meeting this woman had been enough to trigger that thought.

A while ago, before he'd opened up to the possibility of a meaningful, lasting relationship being a part of his life, that alone would have had him backing away at the speed of light. Knowing where his friends were taking their relationship, he found himself imagining Stacie pregnant with his child—and far from scaring the shit out of him, it simply heightened the protective feelings he already had for her.

He stretched out a hand and grabbed a condom from

the nightstand drawer, tossing the foil packet next to the alarm clock. He'd never gone bareback with a woman in his life and he wasn't about to start now. At this stage, protecting Stacie included protecting her from an unplanned pregnancy. But one day? Was it wrong of him to hope so soon that she might eventually want that too?

Her hand was resting over his heart—he took hold of it and turned it palm up, so that he could place a kiss in the centre. She smiled, even though her eyes were still closed. *Bratty little sub.* She'd woken up without owning up. Stifling a grin, he added it to the list of reasons for disciplining her at a later date, once her training started in earnest. Tonight was about tenderness and pleasure, and gentle introductions.

And knowing that she was awake, Cam decided that it was time to move on to the next stage of their first night together. In one movement, he rolled onto his side and put Stacie on her back, pinning the hand he still held to the mattress. Startled eyes opened and looked at him questioningly as he threw his leg across both of hers—his mouth descended and he kissed her as if it were the end of this world and the beginning of the next.

CHAPTER SEVEN

No longer startled, Stacie looked up at him with a heady combination of blossoming trust and blatant desire that made Cam want to make their first night together even more special for her. He wanted to do something for her that he'd never done for any other sub, and he knew exactly what the perfect something would be.

"Wait here. I won't be long." He headed for the bathroom.

When he returned a few moments later, it was to find her watching him with eyes heavy with wanting—the same wanting he felt for her. He dropped the towels at the end of the bed, left the bottle of lotion handy on the nightstand and in one movement, knelt on the bed and kissed her again.

When he transferred his attention to her breast, she arched into his mouth. He fed hungrily, catching the hard, puckered nipple between his teeth, cupping the soft flesh, squeezing it, revelling in the sweetness of her responses as he drew her deeply into his mouth. He moved again, to kiss the column of her throat, trying to calm himself and his need so that he could indulge her the way he intended to. Or was he indulging himself?

"Turn over, Stacie, and then I want you to relax. Leave everything to me."

Her hair was a golden, glinting mass around her shoulders. Cam combed it with his fingers, loving the feel of the cool silken strands against his skin, before gathering it together and lifting it to one side. On impulse, he leaned forward and buried his nose in it, inhaling the fresh scent of her shampoo mingled with the fragrance of an infinitely desirable woman, a drug-like combination that wove a hypnotic spell around his senses. He wanted to cover her body with his and melt into her until the world ended.

But this was for her, not him. With a stubbornly lingering degree of reluctance he moved to kneel between her legs, his eyes drawn to her glistening pussy and the tight pucker of her anus. His cock was already primed to take her, but for now his desires would have to wait.

He poured lotion into one of his palms, warming it between his hands before he laid them on Stacie's body and began to knead her shoulders. Almost instantly she relaxed—he could have sworn he heard her sigh with pleasure.

Her sweet curves belonged to a voluptuous, toned body that was a perfect fit for his hands… and then there were those legs that went on forever. In his mind's eye, he could see her at the club. In a stylish, appropriately minimal outfit that hinted at the treasure beneath and emphasised the glorious length of those legs, she would turn the head of every Dom there… and probably one or two Dommes as well. With heels—at least four inches—she would be truly stunning. It was just a pity that as a submissive, she wouldn't be wearing them in the club. No matter—with or without them, she had the potential to be a sub any Dom would be proud to own. He knew he would.

"That's it, honey," he approved, working her back and letting his fingers curve around her ribs to stroke the sides of her breasts, moving down to her waist and then her hips, where he applied a little more pressure and enjoyed the intimate glimpse of her, already denuded of hair. The Dom in him rejoiced silently as she eased her legs a little further apart, giving him an almost perfect view and a silent invitation for him to advance.

His gently questing fingers found her clit again, hard and swollen with arousal. He teased it between his thumb and two fingers, and when her body responded with a fierce quiver he slipped his fingers into her deliciously hot and wet pussy, thrusting into her in anticipation of what his cock would be doing soon enough.

Stacie was a pure delight. She began to writhe beneath his touch, making delicious little sounds of pleasure, but stilled instantly when he placed his hand on her back and quietly ordered her to be calm. Spirit and submission in one oh-so- sweet package.

He leaned forward, taking his weight on his right hand while he stroked the narrow indentation of her spine with his fingertip, then followed the same path with his lips, lacing a network of open-mouthed kisses down her back, tasting her skin as if it were the finest wine. Leaning over her like this, his dominant nature roared to the fore—he wanted to cover her with his body and stake a claim to her that no man would challenge. Images flashed through his mind of the things he'd like to do to her—the things he was *going* to do to her, once she was completely comfortable with the dynamic of the relationship he wanted for them.

Her breathing was becoming more laboured now, as one of her hands twisted into the cotton sheet bunched at the side of her. He recognised the signs—sensation and pure pleasure combined to overwhelm her. She could no longer fight the onslaught. For Cam, it was an exquisite victory. He picked up the bottle of lotion again and resumed the massage, this time concentrating on her buttocks, thighs and calves. By the time he was done with her, she'd be relaxed, receptive… and ready to be claimed.

"Time to turn over again, honey," he instructed when he was ready, wondering if his self-control would get him through to the end of the massage once she was on her back beneath him. Missionary wasn't his favourite position for making love—not when there were so many other exciting possibilities—but he sure as hell wanted those legs wrapped around him when he buried his cock in her body for the first time.

Oh shit. She was way too much temptation. Those lush breasts were a siren call to his mouth, inviting him to lick and nibble so that he could hear her moan with arousal and need. His hand framed her rib cage, cradled the soft globe in the crook of his thumb and forefinger, and then she filled his mouth again. Only when she made a fumbling attempt to push his head away did he release her nipple. When he thrust his now free hand between her thighs to rub her pussy, she arched again and cried out.

"Talk to me, Stacie." His voice was ragged as he welded his self-control together once more. "Show me what you want."

He already knew what she wanted, what she needed—it was there in her face, in her panting cries, in all the ways her body moved beneath his touch, but he wanted to find out if she would tell him. If she *could* tell him.

He didn't have long to wait, and what she did rocked him to the core. She offered him her hands, crossed at the wrists, in a gesture of pure submission, the like of which he'd seldom experienced. If ever. How could a complete novice have him reeling with such grace and beauty?

"Please, Cam. I'd like to know what it's like…" Her gaze dipped to her wrists. "I need control, Sir."

With that one word—*Sir*—she delivered the final blow and took his breath away.

"You've never experienced it before, honey?" A person didn't necessarily need to be in a D/s relationship to enjoy a little playful bondage now and again.

She shook her head. "No, Sir—I never wanted to, before you."

And he wasn't about to question that. No, Cam acknowledged—he'd simply rejoice in it, accept it for the honour it was and treat it with the respect it deserved.

As it was her first time, he used silk scarves to bind her, tethering her wrists to the bars at the head of the bed but leaving her legs free—there were things he wanted to do with those legs that required more flexibility than any bindings would allow.

"Comfortable, beautiful?" he asked between the kisses he littered across her deliciously curvy, delightfully real body—such a perfect match for him in so many ways. He pushed aside thoughts of how it would feel when she came around his cock, when her pussy milked every drop of seed from his balls. They had all night—no need to rush into burying himself in her body even though every cell in *his* body cried out for it. Instead he turned his attention to all the things he could do to bring her to the edge of orgasm—the first of many he planned for her in his bed… and other places.

"Yes, Sir," she whispered. "What are you going to do?"

As soon as she uttered the question, Stacie pressed her lips together. She'd questioned a Dom, something no sub should ever do when scening, according to one of the private little chats she'd had with Beth Lombard. She'd have to do better than that.

Or maybe all she needed was a little more time… and a lot more training. And oh, how her girly bits tingled at the thought of what that training might entail.

She loved the dominance she'd seen in Cam. It promised to fulfil a yearning she'd never realised she had until a few days ago, for a man who would be in charge and take control—a man she could rely on. Cam was all that and more, and Stacie was convinced she could give him what he needed.

She was under no illusions, though—just as Beth had cautioned, she'd been guided gently so far, nothing too outrageous, nothing that made her feel nervous or uneasy, but what would come after this? Not necessarily tonight, but later—days, weeks from now.

"Stop thinking, Stacie." The command was in his tone as well as the words he used—it snapped her attention instantly back to the man who was looking at her with breathtaking intensity. "I'll let the question slide this time because you need to learn that you can trust me without question, no matter what. What I won't let slide, though, is this habit you have of zoning out on me."

What are you going to do about it? She swallowed the words before they could get her into more trouble. Instead, she held his gaze, trying to prove to him that she could focus.

"That's better."

For a moment she hoped for a reprieve, but then he spoke again. "So that you learn from this, you are not allowed to come until I give you permission. Do you understand, sub?"

That last word, the sensual growl that accompanied it, answered the question she'd silently asked herself, created a tempest of aching need that instantly drenched her pussy. He'd effectively put her in her place—and it was a place that kept her centred entirely on the man beside her. "Yes, Sir. I understand."

In the muted light, his handsome face acquired shadows that spoke of power and authority. His mouth was fixed in a straight line above that stubborn chin, and although he said nothing more, she felt the energy of his will as if it were a living thing, independent of the man himself, coiling around and through her body and claiming it for him.

And it was that force of will that kept her from moving when he replaced the blindfold, prefacing the action with a tender kiss to her mouth. Then he shifted position and began to make love to her.

What she didn't expect was for him to start at her feet.

"Be still, Stacie," he warned when she jumped at the first contact. "Remain quiet and calm, and remember—you come only when I give you permission."

She felt his lips on her right ankle first, then more light and insidiously seductive kisses as he worked his way up the inside of her lower leg to her knee. There, where the sensitive skin of her inner thigh began, the sensations changed—it was no longer his mouth but something light, feathery maybe, swirling loops and scrolls up and down her thigh. She started again, this time when he lifted her leg and draped it over his shoulder. She'd never felt so open, so vulnerable… so helpless. His hands were warm, stroking over her flesh, venturing closer to her hot, wanting pussy but then retreating, teasing her, tormenting her with a scorching, sinful pleasure, advancing again, more teasing, another retreat.

And then he was working on her other leg, repeating the sensual seduction of her body, inch by tantalising inch, but this time he carried on and…

As Cam caressed her body from her shoulders to her toes, she discovered that she'd known nothing of just how arousing a man's hands and mouth could be, how he could feast on her body. He stroked and kissed and nipped, zeroing in on erogenous zones that she never even suspected she had.

Oh God, her legs were resting on his shoulders and his mouth was on her pussy. His arms were a band across her hips, effectively pinning her in place so that his thumbs could hold her labia apart and expose her clit… he was suckling on it the same way he'd done her nipples. She was completely open to him—the tiny puritanical part of her mind, that last stubborn vestige that maintained sex wasn't supposed to be this good, was trying to work out how to put things on a more modest footing when all of a sudden something snapped and bitch-slapped the mental prude out of existence. With something that was neither scream nor howl but somewhere between the two, Stacie gave up everything to the mouth that wouldn't let her go.

When Cam's tongue flicked teasingly over the hard little button of sensitised flesh she cried his name, her back arching away from the bed. Teeth nipped again, sending erotic bolts of lightning zinging along her nerves. Her hips bucked and writhed, still trying in vain to lessen the sensual onslaught, but Cam wouldn't let her get away. He held her firmly in place, hands roaming over her belly, fingers splayed, pressing so hard into her flesh that she could feel each one of them—leaving her with no illusions as to who was in charge.

She loved it.

She was a prisoner for his mouth to torture with pleasure… a prisoner with no desire to escape. His fingers slipped inside her again, pinpointed her G-spot with unerring accuracy, and pushed her closer to the climax she was forbidden to experience. Her soft moans turned to harsh little cries as the last shred of her sanity struggled to hold on.

And then in the same instant, his mouth and his fingers left her and she was plummeting from the heights of pleasure, like a diver plunging from the cliffs at La Quebrada—the world had gone from beneath her and she had no way of finding it again… until strong hands framed her face and firm lips claimed her mouth. She responded hungrily, tasting her own flesh on his lips, straining towards him, silently begging him for more.

"Easy, honey," he murmured against her skin.

He moved again, and Stacie's world exploded into flames.

For Cam, it was like playing a fine musical instrument—he stroked, he plucked, and she came alive under his hands, a living orchestra of vibrant responses. Silk, feathers, ice—he loved the way she reacted to all of them. Her skin had begun to glow with a dewy sheen that became more pronounced each time he drove her close to orgasm. His focus was entirely on her pleasure.

And now it was time to finish for both of them—she'd earned it. He'd seen every moment of her struggle to obey his command. He eased up her body, feeling every quiver she gave, to release her wrists—when he took her, he wanted to feel her hands on his body.

"No, beautiful," he warned, when she would have removed the blindfold. "That stays on."

"Yes, Sir," she whispered, as he kissed her again, one hand stroking her thigh as he wrapped her leg around his waist. Christ, she was perfection—so bloody perfect that he nearly forgot the damn condom. He sheathed himself in the latex and then, unable to wait any longer, he powered inside her, his thrusts deep and rhythmic.

Shit, this was heaven—he'd died and gone to fucking heaven. His wonderful sub was holding him to her as hard as she could, and the gasp she gave every time he went deep turned him on even more. Wrapped in the cradle of her thighs, he felt as if he could fuck her for hours, give her orgasm after orgasm, and still conquer the world.

"Come for me, honey," he growled. "Let me feel you come for me."

Her body pulsated around his cock. He could feel each

and every ripple, counting down to the explosion building in his balls. It was then that something broke inside him. He rode her harder, faster, deeper, driven by the same instincts that had compelled primitive man to claim a mate and perpetuate his genes. Stacie was his mate, the missing part of him, the better part of him—he knew it without any doubt. It didn't matter that they'd known each other less than a week. She belonged to him as he belonged to her, and he'd do whatever it took to guide her and teach her to be his.

She came as hard as he did—her orgasm lit up the heavens and the aftershocks cascaded over him like splinters of starlight as his cock pulsed inside her. He rolled onto his side and as he held Stacie in his arms, his body still joined with hers, Cam felt an intimate connection to her that he'd never experienced before—with anyone.

"Shh, baby, it's all right," he soothed her. She was crying quietly, her whole body shaking—their coupling had affected her as deeply as it had him. He untied the scarf and looked into eyes that were shining with fulfilment and a sense of wonder.

"Tell me how you feel, beautiful." Cam held her close. Then he felt her hand gently stroking his chest, followed by her lips pressed to his sternum.

"It's never been like that before, Cam," she whispered. "Never."

He loved the sound of her post-orgasmic voice—it was the voice of a woman who had been well and truly loved. It was a voice that wrapped itself around his cock and made him hard all over again.

"In a good way or a bad way?" He held his breath, not daring to guess her answer. It was too important for that.

"How could it be anything other than good?" She pressed closer to him—he could feel her need for him to hold her. "Good doesn't even come close."

His finger under her chin, he lifted her head so that he could kiss her—a gentle kiss this time, but one that held the promise of passion yet to come. "Sleep now, Stacie." His tone was unmistakable in its command. "The night isn't over yet, so you need to rest."

"Can we stay like this, Sir?"

"I wouldn't have it any other way."

Sometime later Cam was woken by a line of sensual, erotic kisses being placed with precision down the centre of his chest. He half-opened his eyes and saw Stacie making her way toward his groin. He felt her soft chuckle as much as he heard it, and knew exactly why she was chuckling. His morning wood was a few hours ahead of schedule and the honey-haired enchantress was entirely responsible for its appearance. When her lips encircled said wood, he couldn't hold in the grunt of pleasure.

"Stace?"

Those sweet lips left his cock and then she was smiling at him. "I normally hate it when people call me that," she said, "but from you, it sounds good."

Dom's privilege—no one else was going to call her

that anytime soon. "Come here, baby. On top of me."

She came towards him on all fours until he could put his arms around her and kiss her. Her beautiful legs—God, how he loved those legs—trapped his hips and his cock was twitching to thrust into in her pussy again. One hand held her head in place while he ravished her mouth with a series of rough kisses—the other stroked her soft, silken body, over the curve of her hip and down her thigh, where he tugged her closer, succeeding in pulling her off balance so that he could put her on her back beside him.

Where she belonged.

Stacie was lying in the crook of his arm, looking up at him. For long moments he simply devoured her with his eyes, taking in the miracle of her. Her hand was resting on her thigh—on impulse, he picked it up and turned it over, so that he could start a chain of kisses at her wrist. When he reached the crook of her elbow, he felt her hand curve gently around the back of his head—she was smiling, and he couldn't resist. He tasted her mouth, pulled gently on her lower lip and then teased her tongue with the tip of his.

"I want you."

Cam breathed the words into her mouth, as if by doing so he could infect her with a similar desire for him.

She closed her eyes and leaned her forehead against his shoulder. He liked that—it indulged his Dom's instinct to protect.

"You have me, Sir."

The admission set his blood on fire. Instinct guided his

hand between her legs. He slipped two fingers inside her wet heat and stroked deeply, resisting her attempts to push his arm away from her—her face was telling him a different story. Arousal was in the faint flush in her cheeks… need glittered fiercely in her beautiful eyes.

Stacie moaned softly, but she felt like screaming. Or crying. Or both. Or maybe even howling—howling felt like a good option. She'd given up trying to stop the exquisite pleasure with which Cam was tormenting her—all she could do was accept it. Weak-limbed now, all her energy was gone… waves of sexual pleasure washed relentlessly over her. Her ability to think and reason was all but gone, and when the orgasm hit, that last scrap of control was swept away on a torrent of overwhelming carnal bliss. She had become a mindless creature of pure sensuality.

He made her come again and again, with his hands and his lips, and the words he growled in her ear, the things he told her he was going to do to her—things she'd never heard of, but they sounded so good and she wanted him to have the power to do them. He tapped into a wantonness in her soul that she'd never imagined existed, but it was a wantonness she wanted to explore… only with him. *Only Cam.* The man who made her feel cared for and protected, but more than that—he gave her the confidence to want him and show that she wanted him.

"Cam… Sir." She reached towards his face, only to have her hand caught by his, held so that he could press his mouth to her palm.

"What do you need, honey?" he asked. "Tell me what you need."

She needed him inside her again. "You. I need you, Sir," she whispered. "I'm empty without you."

His hand framed her cheek. "What do you want me to do, baby?" he said. "You need to tell me what you want me to do."

Fuck me. The words formed in her mind—words she'd never actually spoken to any man. Sex had never been like this, so raw and powerful. With one or two of her previous lovers, it had even been something to be endured, not enjoyed—and *enjoyed* barely did justice to her reaction to what she'd experienced with Cam Fraser.

Did she dare say those words now? She closed her eyes to mask her embarrassment. "Please fuck me, Sir."

"Then open your eyes and ask me."

The intensity in his gaze took her breath away. His eyes burned with blue fire, and as she hesitated to obey, his hand moved. She gasped when he pinched her nipple, the shock of it bringing her mind sharply back to its source.

"Tell me, Stace. Tell me what you need."

"I need you to fuck me, Sir. Please."

Cam wrapped his arms around her and then she was lying on her side, with his heat and strength at her back. She felt sheltered, protected… desired. She felt as if she was owned by him, and she didn't care if anyone thought it was wrong for her to feel that way. He was showing her a world she'd thought couldn't possibly exist for real…

and it was electrifying. Whatever this man wanted from her—things she probably couldn't even begin to imagine—she'd give it to him. She'd give him anything, because she knew that this man would keep her safe, no matter what. *He promised.*

"I will, honey. Tonight you're mine—and before morning, every part of your body will know it."

Lying on his side behind her, Cam hooked her leg over his thigh, opening her wide so that he could slide his thick, hard cock inside her. Holding her thigh in place with one hand, he curved his other arm around her neck, guiding her head so that she was looking up at him as he slammed hard and fast into her. So young, so precious—in his mind, the thoughts jostled for prominence with his primitive desire to take her over and over again, and the feral satisfaction he found in her wild cries and the way she was looking at him, as if she were about to fly straight to heaven from the highest peak in creation.

Sensing how close she was, through the exploding tendrils of his own impending release, Cam fastened his mouth over hers, and when she came he took her scream of shattering release into his own body—a scream that triggered a climax that drove him so deeply into her that he thought he'd never be apart from her again.

Before his brain went into complete meltdown, Cam withdrew and removed the condom so that he could get back to the serious business of taking care of his sub. He eased her leg from over his thigh and guided her into a more comfortable position—still close to his body, still cradled in his embrace. With a tenderness he'd seldom felt before, he brushed threads of sweat-damp gold from her flushed face.

"Stace?"

The smile she gave him held a bewitching sensuality that spoke of complete satisfaction—she looked like a woman who'd been pleasured from head to toe and back again, and then some. And she was looking at him with a blatant adoration that made him want to beat his chest in a way that would sweep aside thousands of years of civilisation.

He settled back and brought her closer to the protection of his body, unable to resist kissing her again—gentle, loving kisses that he knew would help her to relax and have confidence in him to take care of her. She responded with a tender touch of her own, her palm against his cheek, her eyes soft with caring. No sub had ever looked at him quite that way before.

He found himself wanting her to go to sleep in his arms—if she did that, he could start to process his own feelings and responses to what they'd experienced together. Waves of emotion were rocking him towards an inevitable conclusion.

She nestled against him. He watched her eyelids slowly close, aware of the way her breathing gradually settled into the even tempo of sleep. Her hand was back on his chest—he pictured a cuff around the wrist, to match the collar he would put around her elegant neck while they played. But that was for the future—right now, she needed to take baby steps along the path to submission, and so far… she hadn't faltered.

He was glad that she was asleep now, because God knew he had enough to think about. Stacie consumed his mind and his body was already aching for her again—aching for her scent, her taste, her heat around his cock.

The feelings he was developing for her were more powerful than he'd imagined possible. Under his care, he was determined that she would discover everything that submission had to offer. He'd always done his utmost to ensure that the subs he played with had the most pleasurable experience possible, but with Stacie, it was going to be different, because for him, it was going to involve far more than his head and his need to be in control.

It was going to involve his heart. His fall—hard and fast—was complete.

He was in love.

CHAPTER EIGHT

"So what's all this about a new car?"

Stacie glanced up from stirring her coffee to see her colleague, best friend and surrogate sister, Jenifer Peterson, standing a couple of feet away. She grinned. "And good morning to you too. Coffee?"

She poured a second cup, saying nothing in response to Jen's question until someone else from their office had left the kitchen and they were alone again.

"What makes you think I have a new car?"

Jen rolled her eyes. "I saw the fob on your desk earlier on. Is that what you were doing last week while you were off?"

"I might just have a new key fob." Stacie passed the drink to her friend, trying her best to turn the grin into a convincing poker face.

"Oh sure. And that might have worked if you'd got an ordinary key ring, not one that opens the doors and starts the damn thing. Stop trying to wind me up and start spilling the beans!"

"Okay, okay. I'll put you out of your misery." Stacie sipped her coffee. "It was one of the things. You know Jonty and I have split up?"

"Oh, shit. I'm sorry."

There was no doubt about her friend's sincerity—the language proved it. Jen didn't prevaricate. Stacie took a deep breath. "Don't be. You always said he was a bastard and you were right. I took last week off because the previous week, I found him in bed with some bimbo. I just needed some time to myself."

Jen swore again. "I can understand the Stacie-time thing, but buying a new car? That's one hell of an expensive way to get over a broken heart!"

Stacie took another sip of coffee to mask her reaction. *If Jen knew that the car was a gift…*

"He bruised my pride more than anything else, Jen," she elaborated once she'd composed herself. "Besides, you know as well as I do—probably better than I *did*—that that relationship was on its way out anyway. You've been telling me for weeks what he's really like and you were right."

Both women lapsed into silence when another one of their co-workers came in to make a cup of tea. Since they'd already been there too long anyway, they went back to the office, Stacie giving her friend a quick *sotto voce* promise to explain more over lunch on the way.

A week off work meant that the morning went quite

quickly while Stacie was playing catch-up. The work was routine enough, so it gave her a chance to mull over recent events at the back of her mind and decide exactly what she was going to tell her friend. It would be the truth… to a degree. She'd tell Jen that she'd met someone special, but she wasn't sure that her friend was ready to hear in what way he was special.

Stacie was learning not to blush at the thoughts and the memories. Cam Fraser was proving to be a gentle, demanding, dominant lover, and she loved every moment she'd been with him. The morning after their first night together he'd woken her with a kiss and breakfast in bed, allowed her to shower in privacy, but had proceeded to spend every minute thereafter with her until they'd driven out to the Lombards' house a day later.

The return visit had given Stacie the opportunity to talk to Beth again, with the aim of finding out more about the D/s lifestyle—or at least, the version of it that suited the woman with whom she was becoming fast friends and her husband. What had fired Stacie's imagination in particular was what Beth told her about Club Aegis.

Before reading her novel, Stacie might have been shocked by what she learned from Beth—no, not shocked, maybe rendered speechless was a more accurate description, but now that she was discovering a little more about the scene, she was starting to understand what lay beneath. It wasn't just egotistical exhibitionism, Beth had said—in some cases maybe, she'd then qualified with a laugh, but they tended to be the exception, not the rule.

For most, it was an opportunity to make a statement in the presence of their peers about the depth and true nature of their relationships as Dominants and submissives—relationships that weren't always between romantically linked partners and didn't always include sexual intimacy

And then there were the displays and demonstrations—classed as public, but within the private environs of the club. Beth herself had never taken part in one with her husband. She'd gone on to say that she doubted she ever would, but she'd watched quite a few and said she'd been in awe of the participants and their willingness to expose the intimacy of their relationship.

The concept of a public display had given Stacie plenty of food for thought. She'd wondered what it would be like to do something like that with Cam, to be so focused on him that she wasn't aware of anyone else in the room—to have him so focused on her that no one else mattered. It sounded almost frighteningly intense.

Then Beth had become serious and told Stacie that there was something she needed to know. She'd explained that play sessions in the community could often include more than two people, and all three of them—herself, Alex and Cam—were of the opinion that Stacie should know that such sessions had sometimes taken place between the three of them in the privacy of Winterleigh. They had also agreed that there would be no more, now that Cam and Stacie were in a relationship, and Beth had volunteered to be the one to talk to Stacie about it.

It hadn't been easy to hear all that—she'd admitted as

much to Beth. What made it easier was listening to Beth explain the basis for the closeness of their friendship. Filling in the gaps that Cam had left when he told the story, she related in detail the incident a year earlier, when Cam had been instrumental in saving both her life and Alex's. It was an event that had created that almost indestructible bond between the trio, but they'd always acknowledged that things would change when Cam became involved with someone else.

I love Cam, but only as a very dear friend, Beth had assured her. *I'm very much in love with my husband. Cam has touched me and held me, and helped Alex to care for me after a scene, but no more than that.*

Stacie had known it for the truth, and though she'd not known Beth for very long at all, she trusted what the other woman told her. There was something about her genuine, warm friendship that was infinitely reassuring.

Cam had come to her after that conversation. She'd sensed his unease when he'd asked her if she was all right with what Beth had told her. The answer she gave him had been a truthful one, and one that had put a flicker of something like fear in his eyes—and then she'd seen that flicker vanish when she told him that even though she didn't fully understand right now, she knew she could trust him and that one day she would understand.

Jen's quietly forceful voice broke in on her musing.

"It's lunch time. You can take that dreamy look off your face now and tell me what the hell you've been up to."

Ten minutes later, in the upmarket café around the corner from the office, Stacie was sitting opposite her friend, having just given her lunch order to the waiter. She took a sip of water and waited for the barrage of questions to start.

"Okay. You dumped the bastard, bought a new car and took a week off. What *don't* I know?"

Plenty. Stacie looked at the petite, raven-haired woman, who was currently wearing an expression that could only be described as one of impatient anticipation. Jen had been her friend ever since she'd arrived in London, and had graduated to best-friend status very quickly thereafter. They watched out for each other at work and they'd seen each other through some pretty crappy relationships.

Stacie tried winning her over with a smile. "Did you have a good weekend?"

"Sta-cie." The two-tone warning was unmistakable.

"You're not going to let me off the hook, are you?"

"Nope—not a chance, so come on, tell all. You found lover-boy in bed with the trollop and headed out of town for some Stacie-time—can't say I blame you," Jen allowed generously. "How does that translate into a new car? And an almost brand-new Mini at that—did you win the lottery and not tell me?"

Stacie had to smile—in one way, she'd done just that.

"Not in the way you mean, Jen. I met someone."

"What?!"

Stacie winced. She should have known her friend

would implode, and counted herself fortunate that the volume of the verbal expression of that reaction was turned right down. "Now don't go blowing a gasket—"

"I'm going to if you don't tell me how all the pieces fit together. You dumped Jonty, left town, and came back with a new car and a new man. You're worrying me!"

So Stacie explained how her old car broke down and she was rescued by a tall, blond, handsome stranger who took her to stay with his friends.

"And something clicked between us—that's all."

Jen's eyes narrowed. "Wait a minute. Are you trying to tell me that you met a man, and five minutes later, he's spending thousands on a new car for you? What have you *done*? And don't you know better than to get into a car with a strange man? You were in the middle of nowhere—he could have dragged you off somewhere, raped you, killed you and hidden your body where no one would find you! And why the *hell* didn't you call me to let me know what was going on?"

"Jen, please. Credit me with *some* sense! It's not what you think. Not that I'm entirely sure *what* you think, but I'm pretty sure it's not *that*. And I didn't call you because… because they were—are—good people and I felt safe!"

"Stacie, leaving that aside for the moment, he must be after *something*! Men just don't do things like that, not without wanting something major in return."

But Cam had, and to Stacie that was one of the many things that meant he was unlike any man she'd ever known. If there'd been no attraction between them, she was absolutely cast-iron certain that he would have stood by his offer to finance her car purchase and allowed her to pay him back at a rate she could afford. He was gorgeous, and sexy… and entirely honourable.

Stacie could see that her friend was genuinely worried, though.

"Look… his name's Cam Fraser. I've never met anyone like him before, Jen. I mean it. He's just…" She shook her head slowly, trying to find the right words to describe the powerhouse of a man she'd met.

At least her friend held back until the waiter had finished serving their food before carrying on with her questions.

"He's just *what*?"

What could she say? That he was more of a man than anyone she'd met before? That he threw political correctness out of the window and made her feel more feminine than she'd thought possible? Jen—fiercely independent and notoriously unwilling to compromise her standards when it came to the men she deigned to date—would go ballistic if she even hinted at anything like that.

"Jen, I know this is something you're not going to like hearing, but he makes me feel things about myself that no one else ever has. Jonty… He almost treated me like—" Stacie broke off as a phrase came to mind, one that she despised but it described her previous relationship to a tee. "Regardless of what he said, Jonty treated me like a friend with benefits. With Cam, it's so different—he makes me feel like a desirable woman."

"Have you slept with him yet?"

That was Jen through and through—as forthright as it was possible to be. And Stacie's lack of an immediate response told her friend all she needed to know.

"Please be careful, Stacie. I don't want to see you get hurt again. Does he know about—"

"He knows about Jonty, yes." Stacie stabbed a prawn with her fork. "I never loved him, you know. I should have finished with him ages ago—it was long overdue, you know that. And Cam… like I said, he's different."

Jen wound spaghetti around her fork—far more elegantly than Stacie could ever manage in public. "So when do I get to meet Mr. Sex-on-a-Stick?"

Stacie had known that that question would come sooner or later. And as soon as she finished spluttering, she answered it. "Soon, I promise. I just want to get to know him a bit better."

Her friend nodded. "Okay. So these friends of his—what are *they* like, then… besides being *good people*?"

By the time they were heading back to the office, Stacie had been able to assuage her best friend's worst fears. Most of them, at any rate. She had a feeling that Jen still harboured the grim thought that she might end up being shipped off to a life of sexual slavery.

Stacie almost giggled. Now *there* was an interesting thought… sex slave to Cam Fraser. Not just interesting, but seriously… hot. She told herself sternly to park that thought, otherwise she'd get nothing done that afternoon.

The backlog of work gradually dwindled as the day progressed. She also succeeded in fending off Cam-related mental distractions, until her mobile phone gave a discreet beep just after 4 p.m. It was a text message from *him.* Stacie's heart was racing as she opened it up to read it.

Picking you up at your place at 1800. Have a change of clothes for the office tomorrow. You won't need anything for tonight, just your toothbrush. C.

Wide-eyed, Stacie glanced around the office. Surely someone must be able to hear the tribal drumbeat of her heart? It felt like it was about to knock its way through her ribs. And he didn't even ask if she already had plans. A small smile teased the corners of her mouth—political correctness be damned, she was seriously turned on by the thought of Cam's assumption that she'd obey his edict.

She grinned even more at the thought of what he might do, should she refuse. And all she was going to need was her toothbrush… that required some serious mental fanning.

"Is that from him?"

A mug of coffee landed on Stacie's desk, courtesy of Jen.

"Uh-huh."

"So? What's he said?"

"Nosey!" Stacie laughed. "He's picking me up at six o'clock."

"And?"

"And what?"

Jen made a rather strange, half-strangled noise of frustration. "Where's he taking you? What's the hot date?"

"I have no idea, Jen," she confessed. "All I know is, he's picking me up at six, and I need to take my toothbrush."

Jen nearly choked on her coffee. "Shit! If I weren't busy tonight, I'd be around at your place for six to check him out. Just be careful!"

Stacie rolled her eyes. "Yes, Mum. It's not like he's a stranger!"

"I beg to differ!" The indignant words were a strained, forceful whisper. "You've known him how long, exactly?"

In one way, Stacie had to admit that her friend had a point. Looking at the number of days since she and Cam had first met, it wasn't many. On the other hand, though, there was the matter of how much time they'd actually spent together on those days. That had to equate to a few weeks' worth of average dates by now.

"Long enough! I'm meeting Cam tonight, so stop fussing!"

"I'll stop fussing if you promise to call me and let me know where he's taking you!"

"If that's what it takes… I promise!" In spite of her protestations, Stacie was glad she had a friend who would look out for her the way Jen did.

For once, Stacie was able to leave the office on time,

which meant she could get home, shower, and throw some clothes into a bag for work the next day, just in time for Cam's arrival on the dot of six o'clock. When she opened the door to him, her heart pogoed from her stomach to her throat and back again.

Oh God. It just wasn't right for a man to look so… damn… edible…

He'd been thinking about her all day but even so, when Cam saw her again he still wasn't prepared for the kick-in-the-gut reaction he experienced. He leaned forwards, inhaled the now familiar scent of her hair and claimed her mouth with a gentle kiss. "Hey, you," he said with a smile. "Good first day back?"

"Better now," she replied, stepping back to let him in. "How about you?"

"Better now." He deliberately repeated her words, momentarily surprised to find that they were true. All of a sudden, even though it was nearly over, the day *was* starting to look up. Because of her. He caught sight of the overnight bag, sitting to one side. "Ready to go?"

Cam couldn't help himself. As he escorted his woman down to the car, he had to hold her hand. It felt so small, tucked into his. It also felt right, just like everything else about her. He settled her into the Jaguar, stowed her bag in the boot—just as he had the night they first met—and then they were on their way across London.

It wasn't long before they were sipping soft drinks on

the terrace and enjoying the nighttime view across the river. For the time of year the weather was surprisingly pleasant, but Cam still made a point of drawing the gorgeous young woman who had captivated him so completely closer to his side.

She was already changing his life for the better. Being with her like this made his pain-in-the-arse day fade into insignificance.

"This is lovely," she murmured quietly, burrowing into him. "It's one of those moments you want to last forever. I wish I didn't have to go to work tomorrow."

"Don't think about that—we have the whole evening ahead of us."

"We do, don't we? Did you—"

She broke off suddenly. For a moment or two Cam waited to see if she would continue. "Honey?"

"It was nothing."

"Stacie." He used her name as a warning, his intention all in the tone of his voice.

"I'm sorry," she said quietly. "I was going to ask if you had anything special in mind for tonight. I'm in trouble again, aren't I?"

Cam suppressed a smile. "Do you think you should be?"

"Probably. I'll probably get into trouble a lot."

At least she was honest, he had to give her that. And honesty went hand-in-hand with trust in a relationship such as theirs. "For that, I'll let you off—just this once."

"Thank you, Sir. May I ask you something?"

"Go on."

"The last time I saw Beth, there was something we were discussing, and I wanted to know some more about it." She paused. "She told me a little about Aegis, and suggested that I talk to you about it."

Of all the things he might have guessed that she wanted to ask him about, Aegis wouldn't have even made it to the list. *Interesting*. "What do you want to know?"

"Will you take me there sometime?"

And that turned the surprise into a double whammy. He'd think about it, of course he would, but one thing was certain—she was nowhere near prepared to go there yet. "Not this week, beautiful. You're not ready yet. How much did Beth tell you?"

He listened while she spoke with enthusiasm of the demonstrations and public scenes his friend's sub had told her about. In his time, Cam had taken part in one or two such activities with the more adventurous subs with whom he'd scened, and although he'd enjoyed the experiences he could take them or leave them.

"Stacie, going to a place like Aegis would be a huge step for someone as new to the lifestyle as you are," he told her patiently, not wanting to put the brakes on her eagerness but at the same time needing to keep her safe and protect her—including from her own overenthusiasm, if necessary. "As my sub, you'd be required to dress and behave a certain way."

"I… know that." She sounded a little less certain. "The dress thing…"

"Minimal," Cam replied bluntly, watching for her reaction. "For some subs, you could even say optional, especially for something like a public display of whip work involving a St. Andrew's Cross, or a demonstration of hot-wax play."

Stacie paled visibly, as he'd feared she might. At the moment the kind of activities he'd mentioned were way beyond her—she'd need time, gentle encouragement and total, unshakeable trust in him to cope with anything even remotely like that. There was pushing a sub's limits… and then there was outright aversion therapy, which was the last thing he wanted for her.

"Honey, there are two things to consider here—going to Aegis, and what we do when we get there. For the former, you need to feel comfortable being on display, because make no mistake—when we go to Aegis, you *will* be on display. As for the activities I mentioned…" He kissed her temple in a manner intended to reassure. "I have no desire to see your skin marked by a single tail or hot wax."

A finger under her chin and she was looking straight at him. Such beautiful eyes. So expressive. "Now, a flogger, on the other hand…"

Her mouth opened in a startled O, matched by innocent wideness of her eyes. Then the innocence was gone, banished by an eagerness that took him by surprise. He was going to have to watch her, Cam realised. His Stacie was going to try to run before she could walk. He couldn't allow that.

"Not yet, baby. And don't argue."

He half-expected a spirited discussion—to put it mildly—but instead he was pleased to see an acquiescent smile appear just before he kissed her.

Damn, but he enjoyed kissing her.

They sat in silence a while longer. Cam was mulling over the conversation, wondering how he might facilitate his sub's introduction to the feast for the senses that was Aegis. As he'd warned her, she'd need to be comfortable with the idea of wearing very little around other people, some of whom would be dressed in as little as she was, or even less. Over the years he'd known several novice subs, and they'd all said the same thing—even though it appeared to be not that different from wearing a bikini on a beach, or even going topless, the first time was always more daunting than they'd anticipated.

Of course. A visit to the spa would be ideal. A special session, preferably with Mari, at Alessandra's place, in the extensive suite known simply as the Annexe. He would be there with her, and if she really hated being naked in front of a stranger, then he would ensure that she was dressed in a similar way to Beth when Alex took his wife to the club.

He was smiling at the thought already. And the sooner he could arrange the spa appointment, the better.

"Stacie? Are you busy on Saturday?"

Whatever Cam's reasons were for asking her about Saturday, Stacie's curiosity about the matter was forgotten some time later, in the face of a level of sexual arousal that almost had her writhing in frustration—except she didn't dare move without permission.

She was naked and on her knees in front of Cam—a spectacularly sexy-looking Cam. He was wearing tight leather trousers and a matching leather waistcoat that was hanging open. Oh, the temptation of that broad chest and accompanying oh-so-lickable six-pack. She was almost drooling. The supple black outfit made him look sexy and dangerous—a living, breathing Adonis, dressed by Hades himself.

With her hands behind her head, shoulders and elbows both pulled backwards so that her breasts were thrust proudly forward, she was keenly aware that her backside was still smarting from the sound spanking she'd received a short while ago.

It was a delicious sensation—a sentiment with which her pussy was entirely in agreement. After the spanking, he'd kept her sprawled across his lap so that his fingers could explore her intimately and play with her clit. All the time he'd been talking to her about the news reports they'd watched on television a short time ago—and expected her to take an active part in the conversation, when all she could deal with was his hand between her thighs. He was a complete and utter fiend. Then, just as she was about to come, he'd set her on her feet and told her to kneel down with her legs apart.

What she'd called him then was best left in her head.

Stacie was acutely aware of the way her arousal was

evident on the hardwood floor. None of her previous boyfriends had been capable of turning her on like that. Masturbation had never done it either, but for Cam she was so wet it was almost shameful. Especially with him looking blatantly at her pussy and the floor between her thighs.

When she'd first knelt before him, he'd changed her posture to his liking, making small precise adjustments to the placing of her knees, the position of her chin, the angle of her arms, and then he'd settled comfortably into the armchair from where he'd been watching her ever since without saying a single word. The one time she'd attempted to speak, he'd merely raised his eyebrow to silence her.

Cam was a study in relaxed, confident comfort, one long leg draped casually over the arm of the chair. He continued to observe her in silence. She'd been in this position for what felt like hours, but was really only a matter of minutes… and she was starting to feel more than a little uncomfortable. That was secondary, however, to her desire to please Cam—to show him that she could be as patient and focused as he needed her to be.

"You look beautiful like that, baby," he told her at last as he stood up and came towards her. He went down on one knee in front of her and cupped her cheek, so that he could run his thumb lightly over her lower lip. "You see? Patience isn't such a bad thing, is it?"

Stacie asked her question by the look in her eyes and the tilt of her head. His response was a warm smile and a nod. She heaved a sigh of relief. "I never realised that it could be so difficult not to speak. Sir," she added after a slight pause.

"You did well. We're done with the scene now, Stacie. Give me your hands and let me help you up."

She did as he said, and luxuriated in the feeling of him rubbing life back into her arms and shoulders. His touch was firm but gentle, in a way that she was coming to know so well.

"I'm going to carry you to the bedroom now, Stacie," he told her. "When I pick you up, I want you to wrap your arms and legs around me."

She had only a moment to be puzzled by his instructions; when he held her tightly against his body in that position, she knew exactly why. Her mound was slammed hard against the wall of his formidable abs. She was mortified by the sudden desire to rub herself against him, but he wouldn't allow her to ease away from him at all.

And with his hands cupping her bottom she was only going to embarrass herself even further.

"Look at me, honey," he commanded softly. "Do you know how it makes a man feel to know his woman's so wet for him and only him?"

"Good?" she whispered.

"That's one way of putting it."

In the bedroom, he slowly lowered her till her feet touched the floor again. For Stacie the process was an excruciating torment as her pussy slid over the rock-hard erection beneath his leathers. She almost came from that alone.

Without words, Cam ordered her to lie down on the bed. With that heavenly, familiar touch, he eased away the niggling aches that were just starting up in her legs. She was almost ready to melt when he lifted the duvet over her. She watched him pull the vest off, full of admiration for the way the muscles moved across his powerful shoulders. He really did have a beautiful back—the definition of his muscles was a living work of art—to go with the beautiful everything else about him. Her body was inwardly squirming in anticipation of having him close to her, his skin like hot, rough silk next to hers.

The bed moved and then he was pulling her into his arms. With a deep, contented sigh, she nuzzled his chest. At that moment there wasn't a better place on earth to be. "Cam?"

"Yeah?"

"I've been thinking." She paused, collecting her thoughts—Jen would be totally scandalised by what she was about to say. "I know we haven't been seeing each other long, but… the thing is, I've never had unprotected sex. *Never.* I'm on birth control, and if there's no other reason for using a condom—"

"Stacie, you don't have to do that—"

"I don't want anything between us," she blurted out. "I've never wanted that with anyone else, Cam—just you. I want to feel you inside me."

Cam needed all his self-control not to pull Stacie on top of him and give her the cock she wanted. With a feral growl, he rolled over and grabbed a condom out of the drawer.

Protect her. The words ran through his mind on an infinite loop and served two purposes—firstly as a reminder of one aspect of his role in her life, and secondly, it helped to block out the siren call of her voluptuous beauty tempting him to throw caution, condoms and his principles to the winds. He should never have mentioned the regular health check-ups and blood tests that always came back clean. If he hadn't, this goddamned stupid idea would never have entered her head.

He was about to rip the pack open when a feminine hand closed over it. His eyes locked onto hers.

"Please, Cam." Her whispered words suggested an intensity of feeling that matched his own. "I can't explain why—I just know I want to feel you inside me. I know it's right… for both of us."

The declaration was repeated with a sincerity that spoke to the core of the man that he was—one soul bared to another.

"Stacie, stop. You haven't known me long enough for this."

"I trust you… Sir. That's all I need to know."

The context was different, but subs at the club trusted him because of his reputation there, because they understood the dynamics of Dominant/submissive relationships and respected the protocol of that world. Stacie trusted him… why?

Lying beside her, leaning over her, he stroked her hair

and feasted his eyes on her flushed cheeks and sparkling gaze. She was so special—so vital to him already. Questions about the future were starting to form at the back of his mind again… he already knew how he felt about her, what he wanted with her, and now he was starting to want it more, but what of her feelings?

He moved fully over her, taking his weight on his hands. "Spread your legs for me, honey," he commanded roughly. "Wrap them around me."

With her gorgeous legs cradling him, he took her with a single deep stroke, held still while he relished the hitherto unexplored sensations of having a woman on his naked cock.

Not just any woman… my *woman.*

CHAPTER NINE

Alessandra di Montecatini was a strikingly attractive woman, from her immaculately styled, cocoa-brown hair—currently in an elegant knot high on the back of her head, loose tendrils drawing the eye to the delicate sweep of her neck—to the soles of her Manolo Blahnik-shod feet.

Italian-born, she was the widow of a senior MI6 officer, and every inch the Domme, even when she was in attendance at the spa, one of the many business enterprises in which she had an interest in and around London. Reputed to be in her early fifties, she was a stunning woman who looked a good decade younger.

Cam smiled as she entered the office where he'd been waiting for her. Regal in bearing and all business, clad in a skirt suit that was designer chic at its best, she offered her hand, and in a courtly gesture Cam raised it to his lips to kiss the back of it—greeting her as one Dominant to another.

"Why, Cam, what a pleasure it is to see you again," she purred as she glided towards the less-formal area of her domain. With perfect grace she took a seat in one of the two high-backed Queen Anne armchairs, and with an elegantly understated gesture invited Cam to join her in the other. "Please, make yourself comfortable. Tell me—what can we do for you today? I must admit, I was quite intrigued when I was informed that you'd requested an appointment in the Annexe."

"Alessandra, my dear, it's lovely to see you again—it's been too long." Cam unfastened his suit jacket and sat down, one leg crossed over the other. "I brought a very special guest with me today. And I apologise for the short notice."

She gave a slight nod of acknowledgement. "I'm just glad we were able to accommodate you. Yes, I saw your lovely guest. Is she yours?"

He nodded. "She's new to the lifestyle, still very much finding her feet, but she has courage. I'd like her to experience one of Mari's special treatments."

Alessandra raised a questioning eyebrow. "A session with sweet Mari can be quite intense, *caro*. You think she's ready for this?"

"I do." There was no doubt in Cam's mind on that score. "Especially if I'm in there with her. She's already asked me about Aegis, and while she's way too much of a novice to go there as an active participant, I thought a session here might help her to acclimatise to being exposed to strangers in a safe environment."

At that, Alessandra's expression became thoughtful. "This is the first time you've brought one of your subs here—and for a session with Mari too. I think, perhaps, your Stacie is a little more to you than you're telling me, Master Cameron. How far do you want Mari to take her?"

A good question—he'd been giving the matter a lot of thought since he'd made his initial decision. "With your permission, Mistress Alessandra, I want to challenge her limits. She has a set of safewords—red, yellow and green with the usual meanings—and I'd like Mari to use her skill to take her all the way to a climax."

Alessandra was the Dominant in a ménage relationship with two beautiful submissives, both bisexual, as she was herself. Mariposa and Gregory were both qualified to give all the usual spa treatments, but in addition they were trained to give a special intimate variation on some of those treatments in the most private area of the spa. It was known simply as the Annexe, and it was reserved for members of Club Aegis or anyone endorsed by a member of the club.

"Of course," she agreed graciously. "I'll inform Mari of your requirements, and at the end of the session I'll ensure that you have time alone with Stacie."

"That won't be necessary, Alessandra." Cam had every intention of taking his sub straight home after the session, where he could take care of her properly.

The woman laughed delicately… knowingly. "You think so, Cam? Your sub is really quite delightful, and once you've seen her dissolve beneath Mari's touch, I can *guarantee* that you'll want time alone with her there and then... especially since I've replaced the chaise longue with something that's large enough for two." She gave a casual shrug that belied the mischievous lift of her mouth. "Maybe even three, depending on how well they know each other."

The Domme rose with her customary grace. "Let me have a few minutes to give Mari her instructions, then go to Room Six. You know the way."

Stacie cast an anxious glance over her shoulder, watching Cam as he went in the opposite direction, his destination the office of the elegant Italian woman whose portrait behind the spa's reception desk proclaimed her to be the establishment's owner. The impression she'd got from his demeanour suggested clearly that he knew her very well. She told herself not to be jealous, but a frisson of insecurity ensured that she wasn't in any mood to listen. How could a man as devastatingly attractive as Cam be interested in a dull little nobody like her, when he knew women as stunning as the spa's owner and could have any female he wanted?

She sighed. What on earth had possessed her to agree to this crazy idea? And why in the name of heaven would she need a safeword for a *massage*, of all things? For a massage from Cam, then maybe—who knew where *that* would lead!—but in a place like this?

"Miss Matheson? If you would like to change behind the screen, you'll find a robe ready for you. I'll be back in a few minutes."

Stacie turned her attention back to the beautiful young woman who had escorted her to the treatment room and who—as far as Stacie knew—would be the one to administer whatever extravagance Cam had ordered for her. The staff badge pinned to her white vest-style top declared her name to be *Mariposa*—Spanish for "butterfly"—and Stacie had to admit that it suited the dark-eyed Latin beauty down to the ground.

Didn't Cam know *any* ugly women?

The door clicked shut. Stacie found the robe and quickly changed into it, grateful that she'd delayed her shower until shortly before Cam was due to pick her up. While she was waiting, she took the opportunity to look around the treatment room. With its subtle décor, dimmable lighting and pleasant ambience, it was the ideal place to relax and be pampered. The air held the gentle fragrance of the scented oils and lotions used in the treatments and a CD was already playing on the compact player, the music gentle and relaxing.

The treatment table occupied a central position, of course, all shiny chrome and thickly padded white leather, draped in pristine white towels. Stacie had to admit that it did look pretty comfortable. In the corner, there stood a gleaming high-tech shower cubicle.

By far the most curious feature in the room was the daybed, though to call it that barely did it justice. The large raised platform with its thick mattress looked like a jumbo-sized chaise longue crossed with some sort of Turkish divan, but it had a seating area that had the width of a bed. Two, perhaps three, people could occupy it with ease. It was littered with an assortment of jewel-coloured cushions. Logically, it was out of place in a room like this, yet somehow it seemed to belong. What its purpose was, Stacie had no idea.

The one thing she wasn't too enamoured of, though, was the huge mirror on one wall—combined with the smaller one on the opposite wall, it was showing her far too much of herself that was… well, what was generally well out of sight.

"Miss Matheson? If you'd like to remove the robe and make yourself comfortable on the table, face down, we can start."

Having dimmed the lights, Mariposa laid a solid wedge-shaped cushion on the massage table, with the taper towards the small pillow for her head. Stacie almost groaned aloud when she worked out what she'd look like.

You can always safeword out of this.

With no sign of Cam, was that still an option?

And that wasn't all—Stacie had been to places like this once or twice in the past and had always availed herself of the use of disposable underwear. On this occasion, however, that luxury didn't appear to be on offer. Still, they were all girls together… the masseuse was a professional, she must have seen naked bodies of both sexes, in all shapes and sizes. Stacie would be just one more face—

er, body—in the crowd.

Having just about talked herself around to what she needed to do to go through with this, she was just about in position on the table when she heard the door open and close again, followed by familiar, clipped footsteps going around the foot of the table and the sound of someone making themselves comfortable on the daybed. Startled by this unexpected development, she turned to look—and saw Cam stretching out as if he were a sultan from the Arabian Nights, looking like a movie star in the aubergine-coloured silk shirt and mid-grey suit. The jacket had been carelessly discarded to one side. Her eyebrows rose on an unspoken question, while her treacherous pussy twitched hungrily at the sight of him. *Down, girl.*

"Just relax, honey." He soothed her suddenly jangling nerves with soft words and a smile. "You look beautiful. Mari's going to get you nice and comfortable. Whatever she does, just go with the flow. Understand?"

Beautiful? Like this*?* In spite of that disbelief, whatever happened next, Cam wouldn't let her be harmed—Stacie knew that. So, while she remained more than a little apprehensive, she moved her head to a more comfortable position, let the haunting New Age music flow through her… and tried to calm down as much as she could, with her backside stuck in the air. Oh yes, this was definitely *undignified*… in neon letters six feet high. And this was supposed to be relaxing? Nobody had warned her that she'd have to leave her dignity on the other side of the door…

Oh lord. Just when she thought it couldn't get any worse, gentle hands were moving her thighs apart, exposing her intimate parts to the world. Every part of Stacie's body tensed—although she'd had a massage at a spa before, this was the first time she'd ever been touched so intimately by a woman, by hands as light and slender as her own… so different from Cam's firm, possessive caresses. She swallowed hard, as if by doing so, she could force down the swelling wave of panic that could easily engulf her.

And then it started… the trickle of warmed oil over her lower back and bottom, followed by the soft touch of careful feminine hands spreading the liquid over her skin. *That's okay.* The hands moved down her thighs and along her calves, even massaged the soles of her feet and her toes, before sweeping upward again, all the way to her back and shoulders.

Mari's expert touch was so soothing, from her shoulders down Stacie's arms to her wrists where the young woman carried out a gentle manipulation of her fingers and other joints. Stacie was barely aware of the gentle kneading of her shoulders and the strokes down either side of her spine. It was all so divinely comforting, and little by little, she began to relax. This wasn't so bad after all—a touch more personal than she'd anticipated, but it wasn't challenging her boundaries too much.

The masseuse continued to move around her, graceful and silent as she administered the treatment. Her mind up among the clouds, Stacie was finally calm, even beginning to entertain the vague thought that she could get used to this. The rude awakening came when the hands that had been touching her with impersonal care parted the cheeks of her bottom, and she felt fingers that had no business being there apply an intimate caress to her pussy.

Stacie's fight-or-flight reflex sprang into action. In a second, she was sitting on the edge of the massage table, ready to make a grab for her clothes and run. It was only the strong hands taking a firm grip of her upper arms that stopped her in her tracks.

"Easy, honey."

Watching for the moment when Mari would change the nature of the massage, Cam anticipated that his sub would react in exactly the way she did. He was up and there in front of her before her feet could hit the floor. When he saw the fear in her eyes, he contemplated calling a halt to the session—but only for a moment.

"Cam?"

"Here, you call me Sir," he said gravely. After all, this session was part of her training, in preparation for the visit to Aegis that she'd requested. "You remember what I told you?"

"Go with the flow… Sir." After a moment's indecision, she resumed her position, her movements stiff and jerky with self-consciousness. By the way her hands clenched into the towel covering the massage table, she still wasn't entirely at ease—in spite of that, she wasn't safewording out of the situation either. Not yet, anyway.

Cam went to the head of the table, where he dropped to one knee so that he could look her in the eye. He caught her attention by stroking her hair, and it was then that he saw the apprehension still shadowing her gaze.

"Stacie, eyes on me," he instructed her with quiet, absolute authority. "You know I'll protect you. I swear it. Do you really think I'd allow anyone or anything to harm you? Nothing will ever hurt you while you're with me. But if you want to go to Aegis, you need to know that you will be on display to a lot of people, maybe wearing not very much, and you need to be comfortable with that—with your body. This is a very private, low-key introduction—Aegis is an exclusive club, but if I'm to take you there, you'll have to be prepared to cope with the close scrutiny of a not-inconsiderable number of people." He put his hand close enough to hers for her to take it, if she wished.

She squeezed his fingers. "It's all right, Sir," she whispered for his ears alone. "I can do this."

At that moment, Cam knew what it was like to be truly proud of his sub. He resumed his position on the daybed, reassured now that Stacie would be able to handle what he had planned for her, provided that he was with her. He caught Mari's eye and gave her the pre-arranged signal to take things easy. He wanted to challenge Stacie's limits without pushing her too far. And from a purely selfish point of view, he had to admit he was enjoying the scene immensely.

Mari was highly skilled in a number of ways… as a

masseuse and beauty therapist, and as a submissive to her Mistress, Alessandra. The loose white trousers and white top gave her an almost-ghostly appearance as she moved serenely around the room. Cam's focus, however, remained on his sub. Once or twice she opened her eyes, her suddenly nervous gaze seeking him out for reassurance—at those times, he gave her a small encouraging smile or a slight nod of approval, and then she'd close her eyes again.

Mari's strokes gradually became more intimate again, and this time Cam was pleased to see that the light touches to the sides of her breasts and the gentle skimming of her pussy no longer alarmed Stacie. Having spent so much time with her, exploring the delights of her body and its wonderful responses to physical intimacy and stimulation, he could recognise her tells more easily now… and she was starting to become aroused, just as he was.

It looked as if Alessandra might have been right after all…

In her mind, Stacie slammed the door on reality and allowed her body to define its own reactions to what was being done to her. Cam—Sir—was just a few feet away, and he was there to take care of her.

No woman had ever touched her so intimately before, yet it was gradually dawning on her that the contact held an impersonal quality that made it easier to bear, even as it was turning her on—almost as if she were being prepared for Cam. One hand was stroking her back, while the other was…

Oh God. Mari's fingers weren't just stroking over her clit now—they were venturing more intimately. Not deeply but rhythmically, and that rhythm was so close to Cam's when he was inside her that she couldn't stop herself from moving restlessly and whimpering. She needed Cam.

She turned her head to look in his direction—what she saw sent a sensual pulse of desire through her body, centring low in her abdomen. He was lounging on the daybed, yet every bit of his attention was on her and what was being done to her. He was calm and unmoving, and as she continued to watch him, that calmness transferred itself to Stacie. He wouldn't let any harm come to her, he'd promised, so this must be all right.

As the panic subsided, Stacie began to adjust, to accept what was going on. She wanted Cam so much—he wanted her too, the evidence was plain to see, yet he seemed to be able to ignore what was happening to his body while he focused on her. Stacie clutched at the edge of the massage table, but it didn't help. She was going to come and Cam hadn't given her permission. Her orgasms belonged to him, and he hadn't given her permission for this one.

"Let it go, Stacie."

She had Sir's approval. The realisation zinged through the multi-coloured lights exploding in her mind. He wanted this… to see her come apart under Mari's touch, so it had to be all right. This was happening because Cam wanted it to happen, and that made all the difference.

All the difference in the world.

The orgasm shuddered through her instantly at Cam's low words—she couldn't help herself. Mari's hand stroking her back eased Stacie through her climax. As she finally calmed, she felt more oil being drizzled between the cheeks of her bottom, followed by Mari's expert fingers, as light as the wings of the creature that shared her name.

The masseuse continued with the intimate treatment, stroking Stacie's mound and dipping her fingers into her pussy, penetrating her with more fingers this time, and before Stacie knew it another orgasm was building inside her, combining with memories of other orgasms, when Sir had bound her to his bed in a similar position and made her come until she could barely move.

When she climaxed this time she cried out, so deep in the pleasure of it that she was only vaguely aware of Cam's approving murmur.

And still it wasn't over. Mari removed the cushion so that Stacie could turn over and lie on her back. The change in position allowed Stacie to look at her Dom more easily.

No man had ever looked at her with such intense desire or made her feel so wanted, so protected. He looked as if he'd eat her alive, and oh God, she wanted to give herself to him completely, submit to him in any way he wished. She wanted him, she adored him… she loved him.

But it couldn't be love, not so soon, not so quickly. Lust, yes. She'd entertained lascivious thoughts about Cam Fraser almost from the moment she met him, but love didn't happen like that. It took time to get to know a person—more time than they'd had together. She'd had six months with Jonty, slept with him for most of that time, but still hadn't developed the depth of feeling that she had even now for Cam.

Yet, as she continued to look at him, her eyes connecting with his in a way that made Mari's intimate exploration of her body fade into the background, Stacie felt something happening inside her—not a physical reaction to what Mari was doing to her, but an emotional reaction to Cam so strong that it was verging on the physical. Cam was the man she wanted… no, *needed* to be with, until the sun no longer lit the day, nor the moon the night.

Overwhelmed by the turmoil inside her, Stacie broke eye contact with the man who was the cause of that turmoil. Consumed by the implications of what she'd just discovered about herself, Stacie offered no resistance to what the masseuse was doing. After all, it was done with Cam's blessing… for both his pleasure and hers.

"Stop thinking, Stacie. Just give in to it and let yourself feel everything."

He thought she was fretting about what was happening to her body. Understandable—after all, how could he know what was going on with her heart? He was the man she loved… and so much more. He was her Dom and his wish was her command. All she had to do was please him. And she knew what was pleasing him right now.

Those delightfully capable hands caressed her neck and shoulders, weaving their magic and banishing tensions and worries. When they strayed towards her breasts, moved slickly over the soft flesh, she let herself feel the sensations as Cam wished her to. Her pleasure-clouded mind surrendered to the knowledge that he wanted this for both of them. Control was his, responsibility was his—and if it was what he wanted, she was free to give in to what was being done to her.

What was to be her final orgasm under Mari's care came on a crescendo of decadence and sheer hedonism. One of the young woman's hands lay still over her heart, while the other was massaging her clit the way only someone completely in tune with the responses of the female body could. Arousal built like a wildfire, too much, far too much, but she couldn't escape it. Her limbs were like lead and wouldn't move, so all she could do was give in to the boiling waves of sensuality.

Stacie moaned softly and looked back at her Dom. She wanted him on top of her, taking her for his own over and over again, filling her with his heat and strength. She wanted him to make her body ache from having his thick, hard cock inside her.

The climax erupted from the depths of her soul. Her back arched off the table as she cried Cam's name, repeating it again and again with each pulse of pure sexual euphoria that made her pussy throb with need. She was flying through the stars with Cam beside her, flying into eternity… with him.

Stacie let herself drift back down to earth as Mari finished off the massage with soothing strokes across her shoulders and down her arms. That last orgasm was receding like an ebbing tide now, leaving behind it limbs that were as flimsy as seaweed, and with her senses gradually returning to normal, Stacie realised that she felt like a completely different woman…

"Mistress A gave me a message for you, Master C—this room is yours for as long as you wish," Mari informed him quietly as she washed her hands. "There are towels and robes behind the screen, and soft drinks in the refrigerator over there."

"Thank you, Mari," Cam acknowledged as he rose from the divan. "I'm very pleased with what you've done, and I'll be sure to let your Mistress know."

"Thank you, Sir." She inclined her head in a gesture of respect and quietly left.

The door closed behind her. Cam let out his breath on a long sigh—alone with his sub at last, something for which his body had been clamouring for the last twenty minutes.

She was still lying supine on the massage table, covered by a thin cotton sheet and wearing what he could only describe as a drunkenly beatific smile. He went to sit beside her, his hip resting next to hers, one leg braced for support. Unable to be apart from her a moment longer, he entwined his fingers with hers.

"How do you feel now, baby? Was this—" he gestured around the room "– anything to be scared of?"

She shook her head. "No, Sir. I was nervous, especially when she began to touch me…" her eyes glanced down her body, "but as soon as I reminded myself that you were right here and I trust you to keep me safe, it was all right. Be careful—don't get too close. The oil will stain your suit."

Cam shrugged. "It's only clothes, but since you're so concerned…" He stood up and unfastened the platinum and diamond cufflinks at his wrists. A few moments later, he was as naked as she was.

"Come on, let's get you cleaned up."

He lifted her into his arms, unwilling to risk letting her slip on the marble-tiled floor, and carried her to the luxuriously large shower enclosure. Now he could understand why Alex enjoyed having Beth in his arms so much—there was something infinitely satisfying for a Dom to hold his cherished sub in a way that meant she was totally dependent on him.

Cam adjusted the water to a comfortable temperature then set about washing Stacie's hair and sponging her skin clean. He was grateful that Alessandra insisted on using only subtly fragranced products in her spa. It was one thing for Stacie to be surrounded by the fragrance of a summer garden—he liked that—but when it came to himself, he had no desire to smell like a walking florist's shop.

After drying off, he fastened a robe around her delectable body and a towel around his hips, and led her by the hand to the divan. The lighting was still low and now lent the room a kind of romance that had been missing while the masseuse was present. Cam lay down first, and in one fluid movement pulled Stacie down beside him.

She looked drowsy and sated, a long way from his worst-case scenario of hysteria at being touched by another woman. When he kissed her softly, she snuggled against him, one arm draped over his waist.

"Honey, that was beautiful," he told her. "I don't think I've ever seen anything so truly erotic. You know I want you now?" His cock surged under the towel, pressed against her thigh.

"I know, I need you too, Sir—but what if someone comes?"

He unfastened the robe, pushed the sides apart and let his eyes feast on her curves—the fullness of her breasts, the indent of her waist, the flare of her hips, and most of all, the length of her incredible legs. Unable to resist, he hooked one over his thigh, so her pussy was intimately acquainted with his towel-shrouded erection.

"Do you still not trust me to protect you?" he queried gently. He bent his head and suckled at her breast, catching the nipple between his teeth with an intensity that had her arching beneath his touch.

"I do, but—"

"No buts, beautiful. Do you trust me?"

She lifted her hand and touched her fingertips to his

jawline. "I trust you, Sir."

CHAPTER TEN

"I love him, Jen."

Stacie looked at her best friend and gave a slightly sheepish smile, knowing that it was going to feel like a long lunch hour while she explained why she hadn't yet introduced said friend to the man with whom she was now ready to admit that she was in love.

Not that she'd even told *him* that yet.

"Stacie Matheson, you—are—*crazy*!"

"Shhh!"

She glanced around the restaurant, then back at Jen. "Can you keep it between us, please? I don't want the world to know. Not before I've had a chance to tell Cam, at any rate. I feel bad enough telling you first, but I had to say something to someone."

"Well, before you *do* tell him, has he said anything about how he feels about you?" Jen prodded salad ingredients with her fork and wrinkled her nose. "You know my views on that subject."

Stacie did—beyond a shadow of a doubt. One spectacularly bad experience had soured Jen for life when it came to declarations of love. After that, she'd enclosed her heart in an impenetrable ring of steel and sworn that never again would she be the first to say those three little words. She dated infrequently, to the best of Stacie's knowledge, thanks to her impossibly high standards and expectations.

"Yes, I know your views," Stacie conceded, her voice quiet with understanding. "And no, he hasn't said anything yet, but he must feel *something* for me."

"Why must he? Because he's a fantastic lover? He makes you feel like you're the only woman on the planet? Stacie, they all do that… until they decide they want a change of scenery, and then you're yesterday's newspaper wrapped around the fish and chips."

"They don't actually use newspaper anymore," Stacie pointed out, aware that perhaps she wasn't being particularly helpful, but at the same time not wanting to let Jen's viewpoint affect her own attitude towards Cam. She hoped a little levity might lighten the mood.

Jen huffed. "You know what I mean. How long have you been seeing him now?"

"Over a month—and I've seen him virtually every day."

"Until now," Jen reminded her.

Stacie had another mouthful of risotto. Friday lunch at the little Italian restaurant was becoming a regular habit for the pair of them—they were both grateful to spend some time away from the office at the end of the week. She had a feeling that her friend would only be a little happier and a little less prickly once she got to meet Cam. Stacie checked her watch.

"He has a conference and meetings in Edinburgh for the next few days—that's the only reason I'm not seeing him again until next week. His flight leaves in a couple of hours, so he'll be on his way to Heathrow, if he's not there already. He's due back on Wednesday evening's flight, so how about if we arrange to meet for a drink after work next Friday? You'll be back from your break by then, won't you?"

With a little more sweet-talking, Jen eventually agreed to Stacie's plan for her to meet Cam. She'd just have to remember to forewarn him about her friend's somewhat prickly nature, and that he should be prepared to win her over.

After lunch the two women returned to the office. For Stacie the afternoon dragged by even more than usual, and she knew exactly why. For someone she'd known a relatively short period of time, Cam had quickly become an essential part of her life. What lay ahead of her was not just a weekend but close to a week of going cold turkey from the irresistibly addictive drug that was Cameron Fraser.

After a weekend that had, as she had anticipated, dragged by—apart from the relief of a handful of brief phone calls from Cam when he was between meetings—Stacie started off the new week with the challenge of entering expense claims on the computer system. The task itself was simple—the challenge came from coping with the mind-numbing boredom combined with the frustrating slowness of the system.

At first she put it down to that Monday-morning feeling, but as the day continued the uncomfortable feeling in her chest became more and more painful and simply breathing required a greater effort. By early afternoon, Stacie was ready to head for home but she struggled on, determined to get through the stacks of receipts so she wouldn't have to face more of the same the next day.

When she left the office at the usual time, having mentioned to her manager in passing that she didn't feel one hundred percent, Stacie headed straight for home and bed, convinced that all she needed was a good night's sleep and she'd be fine the next day. When she arrived at her apartment and all but collapsed on the sofa, she finally had to concede, however, that what she had wasn't some silly little virus. She'd only had flu once in her life before, and as ill as she was, she had no choice but to accept that she'd caught it for a second time.

Frozen to the core, Stacie huddled under the duvet. After making it to the bedroom, every joint in her body ached. Her head hurt, her throat was sore and although she was exhausted after the journey home from the office, she couldn't get to sleep because she could barely breathe.

Feeling sick wasn't helping either. She'd only just

made it to the bathroom in time, and even though she was sure there was nothing left to throw up, she was still queasy.

If she'd had the energy, Stacie would have been calling herself all the names under the sun. Jen still wouldn't be back for a few days yet, but even if she hadn't been away, Stacie couldn't have called her friend to ask her to go to the pharmacy for something to alleviate the symptoms—the pitfalls of not having a landline phone and relying on a mobile. All it took was leaving the damn thing in her desk drawer, and she was cut off from the outside world. She'd just have to tough it out.

Please let me sleep. If only she could sleep through it—or at least the worst of it. Her stomach was in no mood to let her, though. Her tortured body barely made it to the bathroom for yet another session of dry heaving, her hands shaking uncontrollably as she filled a glass with water afterwards. A few sips soothed her parched mouth and throat, but almost immediately her stomach rebelled again.

Stacie crawled back to bed. She didn't need a thermometer to know that she had a fever. In her single-minded determination to get home, she'd omitted to pick up anything that might have helped with the symptoms and now she was paying for it. Already wearing pyjamas, a sweater and two pairs of socks, she pulled on her dressing gown and burrowed under the duvet again.

"Cam."

She whispered his name as if it were a talisman, something she could use to keep the worst of what she was feeling at bay. Logic told her that the illness would pass, but there was a part of her that was convinced she'd never feel warm again.

Stuck in Edinburgh for five days of meetings with both domestic and foreign clients, all arranged around a security conference where he'd agreed to address the attendees on one of the latest hot topics in the field, Cam had missed Stacie more than he'd thought possible. Next time he was away on a trip like this, she was going with him.

On the final day, when he came out of his last meeting, the first thing he did was try her number again, and again it went straight to voicemail. There'd been no problem over the weekend, not unless he counted the number and duration of the meetings he'd attended, half of which had been unscheduled. It wasn't so much the meetings themselves as the knock-on effect of limiting his opportunities to talk to his sub. Consequently, to compensate, he'd called her whenever he had the opportunity, but since the last call on Sunday evening, it had been an entirely different story.

On Monday the phone had rung and rung with no reply, eventually going to voicemail, a situation that had continued through the following morning, but ever since the previous afternoon his calls had gone straight through to voicemail without ringing out first. Initially he hadn't been too concerned that Stacie hadn't answered her mobile—he'd rung during office hours so she was probably working, but when he'd called from the hotel in the evening, after the business dinner, there was still no reply. From there it had gone steadily downhill.

He didn't know whether to be angry, worried or both.

Thank God he was flying back tonight. The first thing he was going to do, once he got back to London, was to go straight to her apartment and find out what the hell was going on. The second thing was to find out her work phone number and put it in his contacts list.

Why he hadn't done that before now, he didn't know—he didn't even know where she worked, one of many oversights for which he was now cursing himself. What the fuck had come over him? Being in love had completely addled his brain—he should have had a complete mental dossier on her long before now, known where she worked, who her friends were, how to contact them. Overdosing on sex probably hadn't helped either.

At least he was on the shuttle flight and not driving back. With luck, he could be at Stacie's by seven that evening.

Thankfully, the plane departed on time and kept to its schedule. Having collected his hold luggage, Cam headed straight for the business car park and then he was on his way back to the city, making more attempts to get through to Stacie via the hands-free kit in the car.

No joy.

Within an hour the Jaguar was parked outside her building. The light on in the window indicated that she was probably home. Cam gave her mobile number one more fruitless try and then went in, slipping unannounced through the main door as another resident was leaving.

On a surge of adrenaline, he went up the stairs two at a time and knocked forcefully on Stacie's door, calling her name—no reply, and no suggestion that there was anyone there to make a reply.

His mouth set in a grim line, Cam looked at the lock, one eyebrow raised in a combination of gratitude for its flimsiness and uneasiness for exactly the same reason. *She'd better have a couple of deadbolts backing up this piece of crap.* He picked it in under ten seconds and prepared to break the door down.

When it opened effortlessly under his hand, he made a mental note to do two things—the first was to give her security measures a thorough overhaul and the second, which would give him infinitely more satisfaction, was to turn her over his knee and deliver a suitable punishment for having such a cavalier attitude towards her personal safety.

"Cam, how did you get in?" Stacie was clinging to the door frame for support, having just about made it to the bedroom door in time to see him appear in front of her.

"You need better security on your front door—a ninety-eight-year-old great-grandmother could get in here without breaking a sweat. Stacie? Whoa, come here!"

Cam swept her up in his arms just before her knees buckled under her. "Stace, you look like crap—what's wrong?"

She shivered in spite of the heat radiating from Cam's body. "Flu. That's why I couldn't get to the door before you broke in. Can't get warm. You need to go or you'll get it too."

"Fuck that. You need someone to look after you. Let's get you back into bed and take it from there."

He tucked her in, under a heap of sheets and blankets piled on top of her usual duvet. Through tired, bleary eyes, she watched him as he moved around to the empty side of the bed and began to shed his clothes. "What are you doing now, Cam?"

"Getting you warm, honey." Naked, he slipped into bed beside her and then pulled her against the delicious heat of his body.

"Cam, go home. You're going to get it, too."

"So you said," he observed dryly. "There's not a cat in hell's chance I'll get it. Now stay close and get some sleep."

She'd been like this for over two days now—two days of feeling like death. It felt like a lot longer, though, and as yet there was no end in sight. She'd tried to sleep through most of it and had been only partially successful. Until now.

Warmth was finally seeping through her frozen body—the source of that heat shifted slightly, bringing more of his body into contact with hers, and it was that contact, as much as the change in temperature, that was finally causing her to drift towards a more restful sleep.

Soft words came from behind her. The cotton wool inside her head prevented her from making sense of them, but there was no mistaking the comfort and care in the tone and in the arms wrapped tightly around her.

Cam Fraser wasn't a miracle cure for the flu, but he was certainly one hell of a way of alleviating the symptoms. Her lips curved into a slight smile as his presence lulled her into peaceful sleep.

He could tell by her breathing the exact moment when Stacie finally fell asleep. Judging by the shadows under her eyes when he'd first seen her, it looked like this was the first time she'd been able to rest properly for however long she'd been laid low—potentially a good couple of days, if this was the reason he hadn't been able to get through to her on the phone.

Cam's worry and frustration had evaporated the moment he'd seen that she was all right—relatively speaking. He'd never imagined that it was something as simple as the flu that had got in the way.

She needed someone to take care of her. She needed *him*. Until this moment, Cam hadn't realised just how much he disliked the fact that she was living alone. Solitude was all well and good—he lived a largely solitary life himself—but when something went wrong, like this, it brought home just how vulnerable it made someone like Stacie.

He was going to take better care of his sub. Perhaps it was time to start guiding this relationship to the next level. Three days of not being able to contact this incredible woman had taught him one thing above all else, and that was how necessary to him she was. And when she was well again… perhaps it was time to pay their first visit to Aegis as a couple, so that she could absorb the atmosphere and get an idea of what it was truly like there.

But that was for later—for now what Stacie needed more than anything else was something to help with the flu symptoms. With the utmost care, he left her asleep in bed and quickly dressed. There was a late-night chemist a couple of miles away—he could be there and back before she knew he'd gone.

It was a good theory and might have worked out, had it not taken forever to buy what he needed at the pharmacy, which seemed to be full of people suffering from the same thing as Stacie.

Having had the foresight to take her keys with him, he let himself back into the apartment, and the moment he closed the door behind him his keen hearing picked up on the sound of hushed sobbing. *What the…?* He deposited his purchases on the coffee table and hurried to the bedroom.

Stacie was still in bed, but curled into a ball, quietly weeping. The sound tore his heart out.

"Stace? Are you all right? What's wrong? Tell me."

He went to the bed and gathered her in his arms, rocking back and forth while she calmed down.

"I woke up and you weren't here. I thought you'd gone," she croaked. "Or I'd dreamed you and you hadn't really been here at all. God, I'm sorry—this is so pathetic."

Not pathetic—she was tired, she was sick, her resistance was low, and it just made things seem a hell of a lot worse than they really were.

"Honey, I know this is stating the bloody obvious, but you're not well. Just let me take care of you, all right?"

Cam liked the way she was resting her head against his shoulder—she was just where she belonged. "I'd have been back sooner, but it seems like half the city has the flu at the moment and most of them were in the queue ahead of me. Let's get you back into bed, honey."

Her pale face suddenly flushed with colour. "Umm, I need the bathroom first."

Without further ceremony, he lifted her into his arms and took her to her requested destination. "Take your time, baby. Where do you keep the bed linen? I'll change the bed while you're in here."

He was done by the time he heard the bathroom door open again. He turned and saw her leaning against the doorway, looking totally drained of energy. She made no demur when he carried her back to the bed and settled her under the covers, sitting up with the bank of pillows at her back.

"How do you feel?"

"Like death warmed over." She looked up at him. "Thank you for looking after me. You don't have to stay, you know. You must be so tired."

Cam sat on the edge of the bed. He was tired, yes, but

not so tired he couldn't take care of what was important to him. "You might as well stop trying to get rid of me, honey, because it's not going to happen. I'm going to make you one of those foul-tasting drinks, so we'll see if we can get you feeling a little less crappy, and then I'm going to make you something to eat. Is there anything special I can get for you?"

She shook her head. "I'm not hungry. I haven't been able to keep anything down anyway. But you must be starving—if there's anything you fancy, please help yourself."

Cam laid his hand against her cheek, looking straight into her weary eyes. "What I fancy isn't in the kitchen." He leaned forward and kissed her forehead. "You just rest and get better. I'm here to take care of you now, and I'll be here for as long as it takes. Would you like some music, or maybe we can find a film to watch?"

She thought for a moment. "A film. That would be really nice."

A short while later, Cam was back in bed beside Stacie. She'd finished her drink and until a few minutes ago, had been watching the film with him. Now, though, she was asleep again, nestled against him with his arm around her. The rightness of the situation could tempt a man into weaving all sorts of fantasies for the future.

Instead, though, he focused his attention on the here and now, and the practicalities of the fact that Stacie needed him. She was breathing a little more easily, he thought, and didn't seem to be quite so feverish. And by far the most important thing, she was sleeping. Not such a bad idea.

Cam yawned. Between one thing and another it had been a long day and he was ready for some sleep himself. He switched off the reading light and the television, and then very carefully, so as not to disturb Stacie, made himself comfortable beside her.

A couple of days later Stacie was feeling considerably better, although Cam—who had remained at her apartment for the duration of her illness—refused to let her return to work too soon. He was still there at the weekend, when an unexpected visitor seemed hell-bent on testing the door buzzer to destruction. His best guess was that it was the mysterious Jen, and if looks could kill, the one she gave Cam when he opened the door to her might easily have planted him six feet under.

"Jen!"

Stacie's happy greeting confirmed his suspicions. He watched the two women hug, which gave him the opportunity, albeit a brief one, to form a first impression of his sub's best friend.

What she lacked in height, she made up for with the explosive force of her personality. Objectively she was very attractive, although not his type. A curtain of shining jet-black hair, poker-straight, fell to beyond her waist, creating a truly stunning image. It was so perfect that for a moment he wondered if it was a wig, before dismissing the thought as a product of his professional imagination. Her ivory complexion provided the perfect setting for her green eyes and rose-tinted lips, and with a figure comprised of a slender waist and hips and remarkably generous breasts, he could see her appealing to either Dylan Baxter or Conor Devlin—two members of his team who seemed to share an extraordinarily similar taste in women, going by what he knew of their romantic exploits.

"Stacie, are you all right? I rang the office when I got back yesterday afternoon, and they said you'd been on sick leave all week. Then, when I tried your mobile, I couldn't get an answer. I didn't know what to think, I've been out of my mind with worry. I'd have been around here yesterday, but—"

"Jen, I'm fine, honestly—well, almost. I accidentally left my mobile at work, and then I've been off with the flu all week. Cam's been looking after me." She glanced over at the man in question and gave him a small smile. "I think I'd better introduce you to each other. Jen, I'd like you to meet Cameron Fraser. Cam, this is Jenifer Peterson, my best friend and colleague from work."

Judging by her expression, Cam concluded that he might well have his work cut out to get Jen Peterson on his side. Part of him was glad that his woman had such a fiercely protective friend to rely on, while another part was busy figuring out how he could get her to stop looking daggers at him. He took the hand she offered and raised it to his lips, stifling the urge to grin at her ascending eyebrows.

"I'm very pleased to meet you, Jen—if I may call you Jen, Miss Peterson?"

She acknowledged him cautiously. Her voice was pleasant enough, but he sensed a certain holding back, as if she were reserving judgment on him.

"Can I get you some coffee? I was just about to make some for Stacie."

Stacie watched her friend stare at Cam's back as he headed for the kitchen, wondering what Jen would say when she had the opportunity. She didn't have to wait long.

"He's older than I thought he'd be," Jen whispered. "Forty-something?"

"Forty-four," Stacie confirmed. "He doesn't look it, though, does he?"

"I'll grant him that. He certainly knows how to turn on the charm."

Jen didn't sound charmed. Stacie felt her energy flagging again. "Do you mind if we sit down? I still haven't fully shaken off the bugs—don't worry, I'm not infectious anymore."

"Has he really been looking after you?"

Stacie nodded. "I was going to see about returning to work yesterday, but he wouldn't let me. Please don't worry, Jen—he's taking really good care of me. I've not had to lift a finger since he got back from Edinburgh on Wednesday night. He came straight here, and he's only been back to his place once or twice, to pick up his mail and a change of clothing."

Sitting beside her, Jen glanced towards the kitchen door. "There's something about him, Stacie… I don't know what it is, I can't just put my finger on it, but he's not like other men. And I don't mean the kissing the back of my hand business, either."

Jen really was too perceptive. She was a good judge of character too, when her judgment wasn't affected by her prejudice against men in the context of intimate relationships.

"Give him a chance, Jen. Get to know him better—you'll see."

She could see the doubt in her friend's face… what she could also see, though, was the first hint of a willingness to give him that chance.

"He really means a lot to you, doesn't he? You really do love him."

Stacie checked the kitchen—no sign of Cam returning just yet. "Yes, but I haven't told him yet. Jen, he's one in a million."

"I hope so, Stacie—I hope he's everything you want him to be."

If only she knew. The phrase *Too good to be true* played at the back of Stacie's mind on a continuous loop. Cam was everything she wanted and more besides, and that was what worried her.

Especially when he made coffee as good as this, she thought a few minutes later. After bringing the drinks from the kitchen, Cam had made himself comfortable in one of the armchairs and immediately engaged in a major charm offensive to win over her best friend.

Stacie tried not to let the spectacle amuse her too much, because it really wasn't funny, but seeing Jen and Cam weighing one another up was rather like watching two jungle cats circling each other, working out their opponent's strengths and weaknesses, and gradually coming to the conclusion that a messy fight might not be the best option after all. By the time Cam was inviting Jen to join him and Stacie for lunch, and Jen was declining the invitation with clear regret and a gentle, slightly sad smile, Stacie was hopeful that two of the most important people in her life might actually be able to be more than barely civil to one another.

And that brought to mind the prospect of introducing Cam to her parents, which was a battle to be saved for when Stacie had acquired the powers of the average superhero… or when she was more certain of how Cam felt about her.

When Jen was ready to leave, Stacie insisted on seeing her to the door, grateful that Cam had been astute enough to pick up on the fact that she wanted a few moments to talk to her friend alone and had consequently taken himself off to the kitchen again.

"Now that you've had a chance to talk to him properly, what do you think?"

Jen looked thoughtful for a moment. "He's a man—therefore, by definition he's not perfect. But he does seem decent, and I saw the way he was looking at you. I'm not sure if I could be comfortable with a man looking at me that way."

That puzzled Stacie. "In what way?"

"You'll probably think I'm being really weird here, but I couldn't make my mind up whether he was looking at you as if he owned you, or if he wanted to eat you up alive."

At that, Stacie had to smile. "Don't stress about it too much, Jen—I sometimes look at him in exactly the same way."

Cam let her go back to work on Monday, but had said nothing about remaining at her apartment. That being the case, she was surprised to see him there when she arrived home at the end of the day. She was even more surprised to see him wielding power tools and testing what had to be a new lock on her front door… to go with the new bolts and security chain that he'd fitted to the inside.

"Hi, beautiful," he greeted her, catching hold of her waist and drawing her to him for a bold kiss of welcome.

"Hi yourself," she smiled back when he released her mouth. "What are you doing?"

He raised an eyebrow, and Stacie got a rapidly sinking feeling in her stomach. That quirk meant only one thing—her backside was about to have a close encounter with Cam's hand. She was in trouble for something, but she had no idea what it might be.

"Just finishing up, and then you and I are going to come to an agreement regarding your responsibilities as my sub."

She wasn't fooled for a moment. There would be no coming to an agreement—he was going to tell her what her responsibilities were, because sure as the sun would rise in the morning, in his eyes she'd failed to fulfil at least one of them. His words, his tone, his demeanour… all three combined almost gave her an instant orgasm as she stood there with his arm holding her close to his hard body. Her eyes automatically fell, focusing her gaze on the v-shaped area of tanned skin between his Adam's apple and the first fastened button of his open-necked, dark blue shirt.

He continued. "Go inside. Put a cushion on the floor, three feet in front of the centre of the sofa. Strip, kneel on the cushion and wait."

Her breathing fast and shallow, Stacie knew that this was not a time for playful disobedience. "Yes, Sir."

She didn't hang around wondering further what had specifically rattled his cage—instead she focused solely on his instructions, wasting more time as she fumbled slightly with the buttons of her blouse. She assumed the required position, and seconds later, long legs clad in dark-grey trousers came to stand in front of her. The knees bent, and then she was looking directly at Cam's crotch as he sat in front of her.

Oh shit. She was in so much trouble and *still* the man could turn her on with zero effort on his part.

"Stacie, there are some things you need to learn, and in this case, you're going to learn some of them the hard way. These things are important, because they concern your health and safety.

"Firstly, you left your mobile phone at work and I couldn't contact you—"

"But I wasn't well! If I hadn't caught the flu, I'd have had it with me!" How could he possibly be mad at her for being ill, something over which she had no control?

"I know that, but I had no other means of contacting you, which is something we are going to remedy. In addition to getting a landline installed—which I will take care of—you are going to give me your contact numbers for friends and family.

"For the avoidance of doubt, Stacie, I am not going to spank you for not telling me that you were sick, but only because you didn't have the means to tell me. If you'd had your mobile phone and not told me, I'd have been disciplining you for that. From now on, you tell me *everything*—is that understood?"

His voice was stern, but what Stacie felt was the care beneath the strict tone. "Yes, Sir, I understand."

"But that's not all, Stacie. What disturbed me even more is the blatantly careless disregard you have for your personal security. A few days ago it took me seconds to get in here—I can only thank God that your ex is an even bigger dickhead than I gave him credit for, given that he didn't manage to get in here when you dumped him. I've fixed that now, but the point is, I shouldn't have had to, because you should have put more value on your own security a long time ago."

She couldn't argue that point—it was one of those things she'd been meaning to do, but just hadn't got around to it. "I'm sorry, Sir."

"I know you are."

The softness of the tone startled her. She looked up into Cam's face as he leaned forward, hands clasped, forearms resting on his strong thighs. He remained still for a few moments, then his hands parted and his fingers caressed the line of her jaw. "Over my knee. The sooner we do this, the sooner we can put the whole episode behind us."

Her insides squirmed as Stacie assumed the position he'd ordered. It was downright humiliating, being treated like a recalcitrant child, but at the same time she couldn't deny that she was turned on by being placed in such a vulnerable position. A large hand flat on her back held her in place.

"Stacie, I'm disciplining you for one infraction. That on its own would earn you a minimum of twenty swats. However, due to the severity of that infraction and the fact that it concerns your personal safety—the safety of *my* property—you'll be getting an extra twenty."

Forty swats wasn't so bad—she was sure she'd had more when they were playing. His next words, though, made her quiver… and not in a good way.

"And don't make the mistake of thinking that you'll enjoy this, Stacie—you won't. This is for punishment, not pleasure, and it certainly does not please me to be put in a position to have to do it."

When the first spank landed, Stacie yowled—she couldn't help it. He was right—there was no way this was an erotic spanking… and she was facing thirty-nine more of those? "Cam… Sir… I'm sorry… please stop!"

It wasn't her safeword—she had no intention of giving her safeword, because as the hand of the man she now thought of as her Master continued to spank her rapidly burning backside, Stacie found a new place of refuge, in the certain knowledge that Cam cared deeply about her, even if he wasn't in love with her.

CHAPTER ELEVEN

"Why didn't you tell me about your birthday?"

Stacie glanced over her shoulder on her way to the kitchen to make coffee. Cam was standing at the mantelpiece, looking at the birthday card from her parents that had arrived that morning—one of the dozen or so she'd received in total. Not a vast number, but she'd always preferred quality over quantity.

She shrugged. "It's not exactly come up in conversation, and I wasn't going to make a point of mentioning it. It's okay, it's no big deal."

He replaced the card and picked up another—the one from Jen. "It's today?"

"Yep—another year older," she admitted with a self-conscious grin.

The second card went back. "Don't think of it like that, Stace. Clocking up another year is not the be-all and end-all of a birthday."

"So how should I think of it then?"

"A celebration," he replied easily. "Of the day your parents graced us all with your presence."

Stacie chuckled—*grace* had not featured heavily in her life when she was a child. Her ballet teacher had despaired, and Stacie had the dubious distinction of being the first—and to the best of her knowledge, only—pupil to be expelled from the school. "So when's yours?"

"March, but you're not getting out of it that way." He moved to sit on the arm of the sofa. "Come here."

His long legs were braced a foot and a half apart for support, and when she took the hand he offered, he drew her inexorably into the space between his strong, muscular thighs. His arms wrapped around her hips, and when his head was laid against her breasts, she couldn't help but kiss his hair.

The freedom to give such gestures of affection afforded her a warm glow inside. Her own arms went over his shoulders and rested on his back, fingers splayed to feel as much of the taut muscle as she could. She could stand there for hours, just as close to him as she could get. He had the kind of body a woman just couldn't get enough of—especially when there was no clothing in the way, when they were skin to skin and he was driving her towards another of the mind-blowing orgasms he delivered so effectively.

When he drew away from her a little, she let her hands slide to his broad shoulders. He looked up at her, the movement slow and deliberate—the electric-blue desire in his eyes stopped her breath. She dipped her head slightly, hinting for a kiss, and in one fluid movement he stood up, taking her completely off-balance but holding her upright with an arm that was a band of steel around her waist. His other hand was at back of her head, holding her in place to receive the hard pressure of his mouth on hers. She was instantly wet for him.

"We should celebrate," he murmured roughly. "It's too late to get a table at a decent restaurant, but I can still get what I need to make it an evening to remember. Give me an hour or two. While I'm gone, you stay here, make yourself even more irresistible—although I doubt that's possible—and when I get back, I'll make dinner and we can have a party for two."

Whatever Cam had gone to do, it took him almost all the time he'd estimated. When she opened the door to let him in again—it really was time she gave him a set of keys—Stacie found herself staring at a huge bouquet of classy, quality blooms that had apparently sprouted a pair of denim-clad legs. The flowers also appeared to be carrying a bag of groceries, along with a metallic cerise gift bag that had a sizeable envelope sticking out of the top.

"Cam, what on earth…?"

"I hope you have something big enough for these," he declared cheerfully as he went past her.

In the end, it took all three of her mismatched vases to do the job properly. When it was done, with the arrangements placed strategically around the room to give it splashes of vibrant colour, Stacie felt Cam's arms around her again, and his attention exclusively on her. All of a sudden, she was glad she'd changed into the short, light-coloured dress that made the most of her curves.

"Honey, you look incredible," he breathed against her cheek. "Happy birthday, birthday girl."

The first kiss was sweet and tender... the second warm and caring... the third explosive and earth-shatteringly sexy. When Cam finally released her mouth, it was all she could do to rest her forehead on his shoulder while she regained her equilibrium. Boy, could that man kiss a girl clear into the next century. "Thank you."

Somehow she sensed his smile.

"We haven't even started with your birthday celebration, honey. I'm just glad tomorrow is Sunday, because I have plans for you tonight."

The sultry, sensual tone of his voice sent delicious, anticipatory shivers of ecstasy up and down her spine. Stacie had no way of knowing what those plans were, but she felt the overwhelming urge to kneel before him and offer herself for anything he desired.

She was permitted to open her birthday card, but not her present. The design on the card was just the kind of silly picture she would have chosen herself, but the only message inside the card was the one that Cam had written. The handwriting was as bold and masculine as the man himself—strong, slanting script in black ink. It dominated the blank card the way his personality dominated his environment.

For my stacie... my special girl, my birthday girl... my

girl. Master C. There was a flourish after the *C* that may or may not have been a kiss—it was difficult to tell.

Neither did she miss the way he'd written her name, all in lower case. That, and the look in his eyes, hinted at the nature of his plans. Something told her this was going to be a birthday she'd remember for a long, long time to come.

"You get your gift later, beautiful." His finger slipped beneath the neckline of her dress, moving sensually up and down against her skin. "What are you wearing under this?"

She'd quickly developed a sixth sense when it came to this man. While changing into the dress, a little voice had suggested that it might be a good idea to leave off the lingerie.

"Something that I hope will please you, Sir," she replied, the tone of her voice reflecting the mischievous light in her eyes. "As it's my birthday, I thought it might be appropriate to wear my birthday suit."

The sudden flare of his nostrils told her that she'd said—and done—exactly the right thing.

"Good girl. I'm going to freshen up—I won't be long."

He was only in the bathroom for a few minutes, but when he emerged, Stacie's mouth watered in anticipation of feeling that magnificent naked torso next to her skin. Now *that* was a birthday present and a half! He'd stripped down to just his jeans, teasing her with a glimpse of that sculpted line that ran from the top of his hip to the treasure that filled the denim so perfectly, and as he padded barefoot towards her, Stacie doubted that there had ever been a finer example of *Homo sapiens masculinus*. Or whatever the Latin for the male of the human species was. The long-dead language hadn't been one of her stronger subjects at school.

She felt the heat radiating from him as he stood inches from her, teasing her with that chest… the one she wanted to lick all over, to explore in the most intimate ways possible. One finger lifted her chin, so that she was looking directly into his intense, heavy-lidded eyes—all powerful alpha male, staking his claim to her.

"Strip."

Holy crap. One little word and she was ready to come. How the hell did he manage to do that so easily?

"I want you naked while I'm getting dinner ready. I'm feeling generous—you've got twenty seconds, and I want to see your clothes neatly folded on that chair. No dumping them in a heap to beat the deadline."

The fact that he turned his back on her to go to the kitchen ramped up her desire to something close to fever pitch—it was a highly visible affirmation of his expectation of her obedience. She achieved her objective with about three seconds to spare, and when Cam returned from the kitchen, she was on her knees, her hands clasped behind her head.

"Excellent, honey, but there's one thing I want you always to remember." He grabbed a cushion and crouched down in front of her, one knee resting on the floor. "Always use one of these when you assume a position like this. Dinner won't be long. Nothing fancy, but for your starter, you're going over my knee, and this time, beauty, it's purely for our mutual gratification."

He palmed her breast, and Stacie had to close her eyes against the carnal waves of pleasure that washed over her when he drew her nipple into his mouth, grazed it with his teeth. She trembled when he swiped his finger through the wetness anointing her pussy, and again when he licked his finger and gave his approval in one word.

"Delicious."

Once he was seated on the sofa, she tried to arrange herself over Cam's lap with as much grace as she could muster. Since the last time she'd been in this position was when he'd taken her to task over her personal safety, she was more than a little nervous about how this was going to go.

She shouldn't have worried. Last time, Cam had merely held her in the position he wanted while he did the deed. This time… the first thing she felt was a gentle touch stroking down her spine, fingertips exploring her erogenous zones, a palm cupping her bottom with incredible gentleness.

"There's nothing more beautiful than a sub waiting for her Dom's touch," Cam began, his voice, low, seductive… as sensual as the caresses he was lavishing on her body… stroking her as if he owned her. "She's wondering exactly what he's going to do to her, because even if she thinks she knows… he may change his mind."

But he hadn't. The first smack landed firmly. The hand

lingered in place for a few moments, and then it was slowly caressing the sting away—so different from the last time. The second was applied to the other cheek in exactly the same way, and very soon thereafter Stacie began to feel very warm, very comfortable and very turned-on. In desperate need of some rather more intimate attention, she wriggled slightly, hoping that Cam would get the hint.

"Stacie, I'm only going to say this once—lie still. And don't pout." A sharper but somehow still playful slap drove the point home.

Stacie squeaked. She wasn't pouting. "I'm not pouting!"

She heard a low chuckle. It was the kind of chuckle that implied that the chuckler knew differently.

The spanking continued, with a rhythm and a pattern that lulled her into that idyllic state, taking away the world and leaving behind the bliss of pure sexual arousal and lust. Her Dom was keeping her safe, cradling her in his care, wrapping her in the warmth of words that were the missing jigsaw pieces of her soul. And when the hands moved to stroke her thighs, to explore her moist slit, she shuddered deeply, with a need that only this man could satisfy.

"Honey, now that you're nicely warmed up, I want you to do something for me." He helped her to sit up by the side of him.

"Anything, Sir."

His grin broadened. "Oh beautiful, that's music to a

Dom's ears." He touched her cheek with his fingertips. "I'm going to make dinner now. While I'm doing that, I want you to lie down here and make yourself comfortable—because once you're comfortable, I don't want you to move. At all."

It was only when she was in place that Stacie realised that her Dom had a prime view of her naked body from the kitchen, but apart from the ceiling, she couldn't see a damn thing…

As he moved around the kitchen, preparing dinner from the supplies he'd brought back and what he found in the well-stocked cupboards, Cam couldn't help but keep glancing towards his sub, stretched out on the sofa. He was particularly enamoured of the completely wanton position she'd taken up—legs splayed so that he could see her pussy and arms flung up over her head. Shit, he wanted to take her fast and hard.

The main course wouldn't take long, but it was the dessert he was looking forward to. Not so much the ice cream itself, but the dish he was going to eat it from. It was going to be cold and messy, and he could guarantee he was going to have a screaming, squealing sub on his hands. This was going to be *fun*.

"Up you get, beautiful—your birthday dinner awaits."

"Does that mean I can get dressed now?"

"Not a chance, honey. Come and sit down."

He watched her eat. As she chewed the first mouthful of steak—medium-rare, as she'd requested—a look of such bliss crossed her features that his body hummed with the primal satisfaction of a male providing for his mate. He shook his head, trying to rid his mind of the primitive nonsense that was in danger of filling it.

"Cam, I know you've cooked dinner for us before, but this is incredible! I have to ask—where on earth did you learn to cook?"

He laughed. "Once I left the Regiment, it was a case of learn to cook or starve."

"And being the perfectionist you are… here I am, slapping the results straight on my thighs." She sighed and looked at him, her gaze pointedly falling on his chest. "It's all right for you—I mean, the calories you burn off with all the stuff you do for your job. You can eat like this and not put any weight on, whereas I…" Her voice tailed off and she looked down at her gloriously naked breasts and beyond, to her thighs.

All of a sudden, the food didn't taste quite so good. "Stacie, eyes on me. Question—do you trust your Dom?"

She put down her knife and fork and met his steady gaze with her own. "Yes, Sir, I do."

"Then I only need to say this once, and you *will* get the message loud and clear. Stacie, you are beautiful. There is not one inch of your body that I do not adore. You are a woman most Doms can only dream about, and you know why? Not only are you gorgeous to look at, but far more importantly, you have real intelligence, a generous heart and a personality that makes you beautiful inside as well. You have spirit and determination. Since we met, there hasn't been a day when I haven't wanted to be near you, to have you in my bed, to have you kneel in front of me—to hear all the sexy sounds you make when I give my sub what she needs from me.

"And that is just the way you are *right now.* I do not want some scrawny-arsed supermodel, I want a real woman, and the real woman I want is *you.* Is. That. Clear?

She smiled… a hesitant smile that told him she wanted to believe, she was willing to believe… but she needed to get used to the idea. "Yes, Sir."

"Good." Her response would do for now, but her attitude towards herself was something he was going to keep an eye on. "Now, finish your steak—you're going to need the energy for your dessert."

"Ice cream? We're having *ice cream* for dessert?"

From the way that her Dom had been talking, Stacie was expecting some sort of confection worthy of the world's greatest pastry chefs. What she was getting was… ice cream. Quality ice cream, she had to admit, but ice cream was still only ice cream. She huffed. Oh well—maple and pecan had to be better than plain old vanilla.

Cam grinned lasciviously. "Don't knock it till you try it, honey. Come with me."

When he led her to the bedroom, she became more confused than ever—and seeing the bed covered in towels wasn't clarifying matters either. Although it did explain what he'd been up to when he'd disappeared into the bedroom after he'd polished off his steak. "What—"

"Lie down. Head on the pillow, and get comfortable."

Stacie sat down and swung her legs up on the bed. "What are you going to do? Cam?"

"Just relax. You said you trust me, right?"

She couldn't exactly deny it—hadn't she said so, just a short time ago? "I did—and I do. I'm just a little… curious, that's all." She shot a pointed look at the half-litre tub of ice cream.

"Then allow me to satisfy your… curiosity."

Cam quickly stripped off his jeans, and as naked as she was, straddled her thighs. His beautiful thick cock was already hard and erect, straining upwards and weeping at the tip that almost touched his annoyingly flat belly. He was as turned on as she was. She watched as he opened the new tub, stuck the spoon in and tasted it. He beamed his approval. "Excellent—but I know what would make it taste even better."

"Don't I get some?"

He raised an eyebrow. "Beautiful, you're going to get more than you can handle. Open your mouth."

Maple and pecan ice cream caressed her taste buds, and as soon as she swallowed it she screamed, as something ice-cold landed between her breasts. "You—"

A second freezing dollop landed a couple of inches lower, then a third and a fourth, and while Stacie was squealing, gasping for breath and trying to think of something suitable to hurl at her Dom, he was gleefully dropping more blobs all over her.

And they were starting to melt. Stacie felt the trickle of creamy rivulets following the curve of her ribs, until finally she found her voice again. "What are you *doing*?" she shrieked, followed by three stunned words. "Oh… my… God."

They say that actions speak louder than words, and what Cam was doing didn't just speak, it yelled—loud, proud and crystal clear. He was licking her, scooping up the softening dessert with his tongue, and as the ice cream was melting, so was she, trapped beneath Cam while his lips played havoc with her senses. Wet, open-mouthed kisses sucked at her skin, reinforcing all the submissive feelings that were tumbling through her.

He was on all fours now, caging her body beneath his, his eyes dark with passion. When he kissed her mouth, she tasted her own body mingled with maple and pecan, and felt the loss of him when he rose to his knees. His cock bobbed against his rock-hard lower abs. Stacie opened her legs at his touch, and when he positioned himself between her thighs, she couldn't help herself—she reached for his cock and wrapped both hands around it, using her palm to smear his precum around the shaft.

He gave a low, guttural growl of warning as she began to milk him. "Stacie."

"Please, Sir—let me."

He gave her permission with a jerky nod. Stacie laced her fingers together over the top of his dick, with her thumbs underneath, and resumed the up and down motion. His balls were heavy globes at the base and he groaned again when she moved one hand to cradle the sac, gently rolled the testicles between her fingers. His thighs, hard with straining muscle, were almost trembling under the onslaught.

"Enough!"

He grasped her wrists and moved her hands away from his genitals… and then he was lying on top of her, all delicious, hot, heavy man. Her hips lifted for him, granting him easy entrance to her body, the thickness of his hard cock stretching her and filling her with each supple movement of his hips against her, each slap of his body colliding with hers in a passionate frenzy.

Baring everything to him, she threw her head back, offering her neck for his kisses, a gasp escaping her lips as he bit down on the curve of her shoulder. He moved again, and his teeth fastened on to her nipple, sending brilliant shards of crystal pain through her entire body. Pure sexual pleasure washed over her and around her, the man she held so tightly the source of the eddies and swirls of her sensory overload.

"Please... Cam... Sir... please—"

"Come for me, Stacie. Let it go. Fly for me."

She needed no further urging—a scream signalled her climax, an orgasmic wave crashed over her again and again with each relentless plunge of her Master's cock into her body, taking her, claiming her, branding her as his and only his… until the last decadent ripple jolted through her and he came, rigid in her arms, spilling his seed deep inside her.

Instinct wrapped her arms and legs around his shuddering body, holding him, soothing him, calming him, until his breathing resumed its normal rhythm. And when he looked into her eyes again, she almost stopped breathing at the sight of so much rage to possess. His mouth ground down upon hers as he withdrew from her body.

"Never… *never*… doubt how much you mean to me, Stacie," he breathed against her neck, nuzzling and licking the sensitive skin behind her ear.

"Never."

He was going to give Stacie her birthday present after they'd showered. The intensity with which they'd made love had dissolved into helpless laughter as they'd unstuck their ice cream-coated bodies—Cam's light covering of chest hair had turned into darker spiky curls that clung to Stacie's inquisitive fingertips. After they'd tidied up the mess in the bedroom, they'd cleaned up in the snugly intimate shower enclosure, in a glorious session of playful intimacy. Once that was done, Cam told his sub to get into bed while he retrieved the gift bag from the living room.

Returning to the bedroom, bag in hand, he allowed himself the indulgence of committing to memory just how gorgeous she looked, all freshly scrubbed and sitting up in bed, waiting just for him. Her arms were wrapped around her raised knees, and she looked as relaxed and happy as he was. Wearing his collar, she would be… perfection.

"Happy birthday, beautiful."

Beside her in the bed, he couldn't resist kissing her while she opened the gift. The cerise gift bag was camouflage, hiding another bag in classy dove grey. Engrossed though he was, he didn't miss the way her hands trembled slightly when she saw the jeweller's name.

"Cam, what is this?"

"The first part of your birthday gift," he said easily, determined to remove the concern from her voice. "I hope you like it—you didn't give me much time to look, so I thought I'd get you a little something for the day. We can go shopping tomorrow for something special."

"Wait, please." She held up her hand. "Please… just slow down. This… I've looked at their window displays, I know what their price range is like… I can't accept this." She started to push it back at him—a reaction unlike any he'd ever seen before, when he'd given a gift of any kind to a woman he was dating.

"Stacie! Christ, woman, don't you know I want to spoil you? And if I can't do it on your birthday, when *can* I do it? Look at me, honey."

Tears were not what he expected or wanted to see. When he'd chosen the piece of jewellery—a simple bracelet in yellow gold, with bezel-set grey sapphires—he'd only wanted to please her. The sapphires had reminded him of the colour of her eyes—eyes that were now looking at him in something close to distress. *Shit.* This was not supposed to happen.

"Cam, you've already bought the car for me—"

"We're not going to rehash that, are we?"

A couple of days after they'd picked up her new car, she'd broached the subject of a payment plan, so that she could repay him for the cost of the car—something which, by that time, he'd had no intention of allowing to happen. That was when he'd found out just how stubborn and pig-headed she could be. The argument had continued for far longer than he'd anticipated, but eventually she'd capitulated, albeit reluctantly.

"No, we're not," she agreed quietly, "but this—"

"Stacie, I want you to open the box. It's nothing to be afraid of. *Open it*," he repeated softly.

With the greatest of care, she unfastened the shiny grey ribbon that held the gift bag closed. The box she found inside was enclosed in equally tasteful wrapping paper, secured by another bow. She hesitated a moment, and then unfastened the second bow and removed the paper. And then she simply stared at the grey box with the gold lettering.

"You've come this far," Cam urged. "Don't you want to see what's inside?"

She was still more than a little nervous. With his arm around her, he felt the deep breath she took… and heard the gasp when she opened the box.

"Oh, Cam." She closed the box. "It's lovely, it really is, but I still can't accept it."

"Yes, you can." He took the bracelet out of the box and fastened it around her wrist. Then he lifted her hand to his mouth, kissed it, and then kissed her cheek.

"It looks beautiful—just like you, birthday girl."

CHAPTER TWELVE

"What do you think, Sir?"

What Cam thought was that he was the luckiest bastard alive. A week after her birthday, Stacie stood in front of him, modelling the outfit that she was going to wear for their first visit to Aegis as a couple.

And she looked amazing.

At the moment, what she was wearing wouldn't look too unusual in any mainstream nightclub. The royal-blue patent leather heels were perhaps a little too high for dancing the night away, but they looked perfect against the sheer black thigh-highs that adorned her incredible legs. As she walked around, the lacy tops occasionally put in an appearance beneath the black satin miniskirt that cinched her waist and flared from her hips. Between the waistband of the skirt and the bottom of the black bolero jacket that just fastened over the fullness of her breasts there was a tempting flash of the satin corset, also blue to match the shoes.

Once they arrived at the club, the heels and sheer black thigh-highs would have to go, of course, as would the miniskirt and the short bolero jacket. In the corset, which barely covered her nipples, and black lace thong, wearing the collar he would put around her graceful neck before they entered the public lounge at the club, she would be the most stunning sub there. *Guaranteed.*

Over the last couple of weeks or so, since Stacie had recovered from her bout of flu, they'd spent as much time together as possible—unfortunately not as much as Cam would have preferred. His team in the Middle East was proving to be so successful at their job that he was now having to turn down additional work due to lack of available manpower, with the result that Cam was facing the prospect of another spell out there, just when it was the last thing he wanted or needed.

He dragged himself away from those pessimistic thoughts. His woman had asked him a question and he still owed her an answer.

"I think every Dom in the place will be convinced I sold my soul to the devil to have a sub like you. Now lose the skirt and the jacket."

First, she laid the jacket over the back of the chair behind her, and then she turned her attention to the skirt. The sexy little wiggle she gave to shimmy it over her hips lit another fire under his already blazing libido.

With his cock already eager to find its place in her pussy, when she stood before him the level of discomfort at the top of his thighs increased a hundredfold. He made a circular motion with his finger and she turned slowly in response, a full circle until she was facing him again.

"You look incredible, honey."

Cam moved to the centre of the long sofa. They were at his place—the lighting was low, and behind Stacie was the panoramic nighttime view of the city. And Christ, how he wanted her.

"Now take off the panties and come here."

She wobbled slightly on the impossible heels as she obeyed his command. A little uncertainly, she stood just in front of him.

"On my lap, knees here—" he patted the sofa to either side of his thighs "– and put your hands on the back. I want your pussy here." He put a hand over the bulge in his jeans.

She moved into position—it was the sweetest agony he'd ever known and judging by the gasp she gave, she wasn't expecting to feel the hard length of him against her moist folds.

"Now, listen carefully. You are not to move your hands—no matter what I do, they stay there. You can move your hips, but you are not permitted to break contact with me. Is that clear?"

"Yes, Sir."

He began by running his hands over the boned satin that encased her torso. She was, quite simply, a living example of the corsetiere's art. The corset fastened down the front as well as lacing at the back, so very slowly—

tormenting himself as much as he was tormenting her—he unhooked the front, just enough to enable him to lift her breasts out. As her nipples were on a level with his face, all he needed to do to draw the hard, puckering tips into his mouth was lean forward.

He could never get enough of the way she tasted—sweeter than honey, smoother than cream. Her body was made for his pleasure, and he knew just how to use that body to send her spiralling out of control. His teeth grazed her nipple—she threw her head back in response, and in doing so gave herself up to the mastery he had over her willing flesh. He drew harder on her nipple, knowing she'd feel the sharp sting of pain zero in on her clit… knowing she loved it.

His arms wrapped around her waist and hips held her in position. As he continued to tease her breasts with his mouth, the sounds she was making became more and more urgent. Her hips began to move, undulating back and forth, grinding her pussy against his denim-covered dick, just the way he intended.

Cam stopped suckling her breast long enough to take in her enraptured expression. Her eyes were tightly shut, almost as if she were in agony.

"Look at me, honey."

His voice, although a whisper, still held the power of command. With a visible effort, she opened eyes glazed with pleasure and met his gaze.

"Do it, Stacie. Ride me," he urged. "Take what you need. And keep your eyes open."

She was gasping now, perilously close to her climax. Would she ask for permission, the way he'd trained her to?

"Please, Sir. I need… may I come?"

"Not yet, honey. Ride me some more. That's it."

She was pushing down hard now, fucking his cock through his jeans. Her movements were getting jerky, less controlled, and his need to get inside her was growing more and more imperative. He unfastened the corset completely and flung it to one side, then lifted Stacie away from him and laid her down on the sofa.

The fly of his jeans was wet with her juices, but he didn't let that distract him from freeing his aching shaft. Then he was on top of her, wrapping one leg around his hip as he went fast and deep inside her, his instincts as primitive and savage around her as they always seemed to be now. That primal drive to claim her as his mate meant that every time he made love to her, he wanted to mark her somehow as his. So everyone would know.

"Come for me, beautiful. Now."

She needed no further encouragement. Close to his own climax, he felt her convulse around his dick as she cried out, almost as if in pain. With a harsh, rasping cry of his own, he came too, relishing each exquisitely violent jerk as he filled her with his seed.

Stacie didn't want to let him go.

Naked beneath Cam, his cotton shirt as soft against her skin as his jeans were rough, she'd never felt more possessed by the man who'd claimed her heart, her body and her soul. She wanted to tell him how she felt, wanted it so much, but she was too afraid that it would spoil the moment.

More than that, she was terrified that it might destroy everything that they had.

His cock still inside her, his body a welcome weight on hers, she stroked the back of his head. He'd let his hair grow longer over the last few weeks—it had softened the military look considerably, but at the same time it made him seem more dangerous. *Bad-boy* dangerous.

The contradiction teased her lips into a small smile. How could he seem more dangerous when she'd never felt more protected? The sense of belonging that he gave her was precious beyond belief.

On her way back down to earth, Stacie suddenly realised that Cam was chuckling… that low, sexy laugh that she always found very difficult to resist. "What are you laughing at? Sir?"

He lifted his head to look at her and planted a brief smacker of a kiss on her lips. "I haven't done anything like this since I was sixteen!"

What had he been like as a teenager? The question popped into her mind and she pictured a lanky youth with tousled blond hair… or had he been forced to grow into a man too quickly, living in a series of homes that had been anything but that? Allusions to his past had hinted at time spent in the care system, and for him to have joined up at the earliest opportunity, as he'd also told her at one point… it all suggested a childhood no child should ever have to endure and a desire to leave it all behind as soon as possible.

"So who was she?"

"Who was who?"

"The woman to whom you lost your virginity." Stacie wasn't jealous, just curious. "And how old were you at the time?"

His mouth quirked up in a half-smile. "You really want to know?"

Keeping her expression light and jokey, she nodded. "Of course I do. So?"

"So…" He drew out the word, considering his response. "I was fifteen—she was thirty-eight and my then-best friend's mother. Close your mouth, Stace, or you'll be in trouble if the wind changes direction."

He was completely unabashed, while Stacie was struggling to find the words. "But… wasn't that… you were… wouldn't it be…?"

"It was the night before my sixteenth birthday. What can I say?" He shrugged, trying to look innocent. "At least she waited till after midnight, so I was legal. Just. Veronica was divorced, and when she needed some furniture moving that weekend, Phil was two hundred miles away, visiting his father."

"And it absolutely *had* to be that weekend?"

"Apparently."

"So she asked a fifteen-year-old schoolboy?"

He gave her a little-boy grin guaranteed to vaporise

any woman's panties with laser-like precision. "Technically, I was sixteen when she did the deed. And I was big for my age!"

Stacie looked pointedly in the direction of his groin. "I bet you were!"

It earned her a reprimanding look.

"As I said, I was supposed to be helping her move furniture in the bedroom, and she seduced me. The third time I was with her was when she asked me to handcuff her to the bed and spank her until she came."

And at that, Stacie started coughing… choking actually, until Cam sat up and pulled her upright with him. "Relax, try to remember how to breathe, and I'll get you some water."

She gratefully sipped the cool liquid while Cam explained that it had been Veronica's parting gift, bestowed over a small but memorable number of occasions before he joined the Army—an introduction to bondage and discipline and later, to Domination and submission.

"And then I joined up and didn't give it another thought, not until Alex and I were on a training exercise in the US. That changed everything. Better now?" He took the glass from her.

"Yes, thanks." Stacie looked down at her lap and suddenly realised that she was still naked and in need of a shower. "Hadn't we better—"

"In a minute. There's something I need to ask you, Stace. Are you all right with this? Us?"

She frowned. "I'm not sure what you mean."

"I mean the age difference."

She couldn't help the frown. The conversation about the older woman must have been the trigger for the question. Although he'd never mentioned it before, it was clearly something that really bothered him. For the life of her, Stacie couldn't figure out why. "Cam? I've never given the age difference a thought—it doesn't matter one bit to me. It's just a number, and not a big one at that. All that matters to me is being with you." It was the simple, unvarnished truth.

For a few seconds he just looked at her, then acknowledged her statement with a nod, as if he didn't trust himself to comment further on it. "Okay. Shower now, then we'll talk some more about the club."

"Ready, beautiful?"

Seated beside Cam in the Jaguar, Stacie smoothed her palms down the suddenly frighteningly short skirt, taking care not to risk snagging the sheer black thigh-highs—not that it would have mattered that much, as they would be coming off soon… once she was inside Club Aegis, in the changing room to which one of the house subs would take her on Cam's instructions. Shoes, thigh-highs, thong and jacket—all would come off, and then she'd emerge to meet her Dom and enter the club proper. She took a deep breath, using it to help her get into the right place in her mind.

"Yes, Sir—I am."

"Good girl. You know what to do when we go in?"

She repeated what he'd told her, right down to the moment when she would join him in the lobby… and he would put the narrow collar around her neck, which would signify that she was with him. She'd also be provided with a color-coded wristband that would indicate that she was a sub who wasn't looking for a Dom—it shouldn't be needed, but it would provide an additional layer of protection.

Nerves roiled in her stomach as she followed Cam into the club. The confidence she'd gained from the kiss he'd given her before they got out of the car evaporated as she stood behind him at the reception desk while he signed her in. Her eyes were fixed on the centre of his back at waist level—she didn't dare look to one side or the other, and it wasn't just because she was a sub and that was what a sub was supposed to do.

"Stacie, it's time. Go with Emma and be back here in ten minutes."

The voice was Cam's… but not Cam's. Nerves fluttered again in Stacie's stomach. This wasn't a game anymore, it was very real, and Cam had certain expectations of her behaviour… behaviour that would reflect on him as her Dom. Moisture pooled in her pussy at the thought. *Snap out of it.*

"Yes, Sir."

Emma was a sub—that much was blatantly obvious. Barefoot, she wore a skirt not unlike Stacie's in length, and with it a sort of halter-neck soft leather harness, an arrangement of straps that framed her pert breasts while leaving them uncovered, rather like a very kinky bra.

Stacie had expected the changing room to be like a locker room in a gym, so she wasn't prepared for the luxury that greeted her when she followed the petite brunette inside… nor was she prepared for the sudden change in Emma's demeanour. From being calm, controlled and respectful, all of a sudden she was bouncy and outgoing, and bubbling over with enthusiasm.

"Hi, Stacie! It's great to meet you at last. When we heard that Master Cameron was making his first visit in months, and what's more, bringing a new sub with him, we all wondered what you'd be like. Welcome to Aegis!"

"Thanks." Stacie managed a shaky smile. "This place is just…" She waved her hand around the room, trying to find the right words.

"Isn't it just? I've been to a couple of other clubs, and although the facilities for the subs are good, they're nothing like this."

The changing room was more like a relaxing salon, beautifully furnished and decorated, with mirrors on the walls and comfortable seating all around. There were lockers in a separate room, with cubicles for privacy, and bathroom facilities, including space-age showers, that were downright decadent.

"Your belongings will be safe here," Emma told her. "It's an honour system. Sub outfits don't tend to have much room for pockets, so carrying a locker key around usually isn't feasible. I'm sure Master Cameron's told you all about the club and expected standards of behaviour."

"He has." It had been a highly informative lecture with questions afterwards—not that it had put her off wanting to visit the place.

"And now you're wondering what you've let yourself in for. Every sub does. Trust your Dom, Stacie. It's a Dom's role to look after their sub, and with Master Cameron, you've got one of the best.

"Now, I'll leave you to get ready—we've already used nearly half your time as it is. When you're ready for a locker, you'll see a little panel on the front, with a sliding cover. Move the cover one way, and it shows green—move it the other way, and it's red. Green means it's available for use, but if the panel's red, it means the locker's being used and is therefore out of bounds. When you're ready, just go back the way we came—out of the door, turn left and keep going. It'll take you straight to the lobby and reception."

And with that Emma was gone, before Stacie had a chance to ask any of the gazillion questions suddenly buzzing around in her head.

She looked in the mirror and took a deep breath—not that she really had time for that particular luxury. She didn't want to get off on the wrong foot on her first outing as Cam's—her Master's sub, even if it was just to spend an hour or two at the club, finding out what it was all about.

Focus. Stacie found a locker for her belongings. There was a hanger in it for her jacket and plenty of room for the other items she would be leaving in there—bag, shoes, thigh-highs… and thong. Cam had had a change of heart regarding her clothes, so while she got to keep the skirt, she had to lose the thong. At least the corset stayed in place, although Stacie had the rather unnerving suspicion that it was a concession to this being her first visit to Aegis. When and if she returned, she had the distinct feeling that she'd be wearing something not unlike Emma's outfit… if it could even be called an outfit at all. That would be like calling a sandwich a seven-course banquet.

Hoping that she hadn't overstayed in the changing room, Stacie braced herself to go out to the public area where she was to meet Cam—her Dom. Emma had referred to him as *Master Cameron*—although he'd signed her birthday card as Master C, a title that she'd heard others use, he still hadn't said anything to her about calling him simply *Master*—a form of address, according to her research, that tended to be reserved for the special relationship between a Dom and sub who were intimately, emotionally involved. Even if she couldn't use the word aloud, it didn't stop her thinking of him that way.

Especially when she laid eyes on the man at reception—and boy, was he all man. One look at him, and her pussy was sobbing in complete and utter surrender. It wasn't just on its metaphorical knees—it was prostrate in front of him.

He'd changed too, and was now wearing the boots, leather trousers and leather waistcoat-style vest that she'd already seen him in on several occasions. In this setting, however, he wore them in such a way that made him seem so much more the Dom. The whole look of him made her skin prickle with needy arousal. Mouth dry, she walked towards him. Nerves made her forget her manners for a moment, and then her mouth snapped shut. She didn't have permission to speak, so she waited until he finished talking with another man—another Dom, judging by his dress.

Stacie didn't dare look Cam in the face, but she felt his eyes on her, and when he spoke—a single word—she felt pleasure bloom within her.

"Beautiful."

A finger under her chin lifted her head, giving her the opportunity to look at him properly. All she could think was that she could say exactly the same about him. It was like seeing him in high definition—he was all Dom and then some.

"Give me your wrist, honey."

The narrow band was red, and after he'd put it on her wrist, Cam held up his hand—on his wrist was a blue band, which, he explained, indicated that he was a Dom who wasn't looking for someone to scene with.

"And now this."

Stacie lifted her hair to one side to allow her Dom to fasten the collar around her neck. The feel of it against her skin was enough to have juices flooding her pussy anew.

"Tonight I'll be with you every moment, Stacie, so you have no need to worry—no one else will approach you, unless it's through me. In the future, though, if you're happy to come back again, you may find yourself alone.

"If that happens, and anyone approaches you who makes you feel uncomfortable, simply telling them *no* should be enough to make them leave you alone. However, if you do have any trouble, you'll see various people wearing armbands with DM on them. Go to one of them. They're the Dungeon Monitors and it's their job to make sure there's no trouble."

Cam looked at her for a moment, and then arranged her hair around her face and shoulders to his satisfaction. "Ready, honey?"

With one last glimpse of his sternly handsome face, Stacie lowered her eyes.

"Yes, Sir."

A couple of hours later, Cam was sitting in a leather armchair in the lounge, two glasses of fresh orange juice on the low table in front of him and his sub curled up on his lap. She was relaxed and happy, just the way a sub should be, especially with his hand under her skirt so he could play with her clit. That she was prepared to let him do that in public had momentarily left him dumbstruck. But then again, he could say the same about much of the evening.

It had been a surprising success. They'd watched a couple of displays in the main play area, where Stacie had been particularly interested in the demonstration of the use of the flogger on a sub bound to a St. Andrew's Cross. The hot-wax play had made her wince, while she'd avidly watched the spanking, as he'd suspected she might.

They'd then retired to the bar area, where Cam had taken the opportunity to catch up with friends with Stacie kneeling quietly on a cushion at his feet, until he'd lifted her onto his lap a short while ago.

Her behaviour during the entire evening had been exemplary—she hadn't put a foot wrong. He'd kept a watchful eye on her throughout, and while she'd come close to making a couple of entirely forgivable mistakes, she'd stopped herself just in time. Like any Dom, he had the utmost respect for all subs, but tonight *his* sub had been living, breathing perfection.

"Everything okay?" he murmured, his lips brushing a gentle kiss over her forehead.

"Yes, Sir. Very okay."

She sounded as contented as she looked. They'd talk about the evening tomorrow, once she'd had a chance to sleep on it, but he was cautiously confident that she'd want to come back to explore more, and possibly to experience more. She'd been *very* interested when he showed her a couple of the private rooms, set up for different scenarios.

He'd known it would be a lot for her to take in, so when they had the opportunity to take a step back and relax for a while, he took it—as much for his own sake as his sub's, if he were to be honest. Over the years, Cam had enjoyed most of the activities that went on in the club. Now, though, he was looking at them with fresh eyes, because he had to look at them in relation to the woman who felt so right on his lap. He'd test her limits, she knew that as well as he did, but he wanted to ensure that she knew nothing but pleasure.

"Well, well, well—fancy seeing you here, boss."

Cam looked up to see two senior members of his team standing in front of him, a house sub sandwiched firmly between them. He rolled his eyes and shook his head. "You're not tag-teaming the subs again, are you?"

Always working together, Dylan "Bax" Baxter and Conor Devlin were two of his best people, as heterosexual as it was possible to be but with a predilection for sharing a submissive. The two men had been out of the country on assignment for the last six months, and on their first evening back in the UK, where else would they be but at Aegis?

"Pixie here has no complaints, do you, love?"

Pixie giggled. "No, Master Dylan."

For once, Conor looked a little more serious than usual. "Why don't you go and find your friends now, sweets?"

A small pout put in a brief appearance. "Yes, Master Conor." And with that, Pixie almost skipped away to join a cluster of subs standing near the bar.

"Mind if we join you, boss?"

Cam gave silent consent and the men installed themselves in two of the remaining three armchairs grouped around the table. A male sub brought two more glasses of juice.

"Okay, guys, what gives?"

Bax was the first to speak. "Aren't you going to introduce us?"

"Aren't you going to get to the point?"

Conor laughed. "That kind of is the point, Cam. We've been wondering who's been getting you hot and bothered, and now we think we can see who."

"And why," Bax added with a grin. "She's a sweet one, boss."

And didn't Cam know it. "For fuck's sake, will you stop calling me that?" They both knew he hated it, and they both did it deliberately to bug the shit out of him.

It was at that point that a slender finger sneakily dug him in the ribs. Bax didn't catch it, but Conor did, and the smirk on the man's face told Cam that he was going to be in for a rough ride at work in the not-too-distant future.

"Stacie, these two jokers like to think they're the best in their field—I have it on my to-do list to set them straight at some point, but the ugly sod on the left is Dylan Baxter—"

"And I'm Conor Devlin, and I'm very pleased to meet you, Stacie."

Objectively, Stacie had to admit that in spite of what her Dom had said about one of them, they were two gorgeous hunks of manhood, very much in the same mould as the man who held her so securely but lacking that unique quality that drew her to Cam and only Cam. She greeted them as she would any other Dom, accepted their compliments graciously, and then settled back into Cam's arms while they continued to talk business—something to do with bringing Alex Lombard back into the organisation.

With the conversation going on around her, Stacie was content to carry on taking in her surroundings. Or she would have been, had Cam not continued to ramp up her arousal with his expert manipulation of her clit. He hadn't moved his hand from between her thighs—and Masters Conor and Dylan knew it, by the way their eyes occasionally flicked towards her skirt.

Stacie turned her face more into Cam's neck—not that she was embarrassed by what was going on, she was just desperate to stifle the giggle that clogged her throat at the thought of just how wanton she was becoming. A few weeks ago, the very idea of being here, like this, would have absolutely horrified her.

Cam and Alex, and now Conor and Dylan. Or Bax—whatever. All of them Doms, and these two—she risked another glance at each of them—every bit as attractive as Cam and Alex. No wonder Pixie had looked so… satisfied.

Finding that satisfaction with two men was not for her though, Stacie decided. One man—this man—was quite enough. End of. Still… a girl could look, couldn't she?

Her first impression was that Conor was the marginally more serious-minded of the two. While he and Dylan Baxter had been standing up, he'd looked to be of a similar height and build to Cam. His hair was dark and fairly short, thick and tousled, the exact colour of his eyes indeterminate in the subdued lighting, but his features… now they were striking. It was a face that could be capable of great kindness… but also great cruelty, she thought. For the right woman, Conor Devlin looked like a man who could kill, for all that he was cheerful and laughing now.

And if he was the dark side, then his companion was the light—definitely a born joker, but again, Stacie sensed there were hidden depths to the man. His hair was light brown—too brown to be blond—and his eyes were lighter than Conor's as well. He was every inch the easy-going, affable charmer on the surface, but when he'd been standing there, with his arm curved protectively around Pixie—a woman with whom he wasn't even romantically involved, judging by what had been said—Stacie realised that he too was a natural defender of the vulnerable.

Both of them were wearing street clothes—casual on the surface, but there was something about the cut and finish of their shirts and jeans that screamed quality. They certainly knew how to dress. Stacie smiled to herself—it had to be a Dom thing. A few weeks ago she'd thought men like this only existed in the pages of novels like Beth's—now she'd met four of them, and a quick scan of the immediate vicinity would seem to indicate there were quite a lot more. And that was just the ones who were members of this club. What of the other clubs Cam had told her about, not to mention the Doms—and Dommes—who kept their activities strictly private?

With her thoughts returning to the here-and-now, Stacie realised that she felt completely at ease among this trio of blatantly alpha males. There was an undeniable bond between them—she guessed because of their work, as well as their shared interest in BDSM and their membership of Aegis—and because she belonged to Cam, she would be treated with the same respect by these men because of that bond.

"Anyway, we'll pick this up on Monday," Cam was saying. "I know you two are on leave for the next four weeks, but something's come up and I could do with both of you at the conference on the seventeenth.

"Right now, though, I have to get my sub home for a good night's sleep. This is her first visit to Aegis, and I suspect she has a lot to think about."

No, she doesn't. Stacie had done all the thinking she needed to do, if he was referring to what she thought of the club and what she'd seen during the evening… not to mention which parts of it she wanted to sample firsthand. What she did want to do was talk about it, and when they returned to Cam's apartment, he gave her the opportunity.

"It was… incredible," she began, snuggling into his embrace as they lay in bed. Her hand was developing a fascination with the planes and dips of his chest and abdomen. "I loved it. I never realised clubs like that actually do exist until Beth, and then you, told me about them."

"Be more specific, honey. Tell me what you loved."

She'd been thinking about it on the drive back. "It wasn't so much the activities themselves as the connection between some of the Doms and their subs. You watch them, and you forget to breathe. It was almost… magical."

His hand covered hers. "It can be magic, when it's right. Really right."

Stacie waited, but the moment passed in silence. He wasn't going to say the words she wanted to hear—words that would tell her, or at least give her some indication of how he felt about her.

She shouldn't really have expected any sort of declaration—there was no reason to. It hadn't stopped her hoping that the evening would prove to be a catalyst, though. Was that the reason why she suddenly felt a hard knot of desolation in her stomach?

CHAPTER THIRTEEN

Stacie stirred the second mug of coffee, and had just taken the first sip from her own cup when Jen joined her in the office kitchen. She pushed the other mug towards her friend.

"So what's on your mind?" Jen asked without preamble. "You've been on a different plane of existence all morning."

She had—Stacie couldn't deny it. And she did have something on her mind. Something big. "It's Cam."

"Ah." Jen clasped her drink in both hands. "Cam-in-general or Cam-specific?"

In spite of her preoccupation, Stacie grinned. Jen had such a way with words. "Cam-specific."

Cam-very-specific, in fact. It was something she'd been mulling over for a few days now, debating the sanity of it, and she already knew that Jen thought her stark, staring bonkers for considering it.

The fact of it was, she was hopelessly in love with the man—as if there'd been any doubt. She had been for a while, and she wanted to tell him. She was *going* to tell him, because a little voice at the back of her mind insisted that it was imperative for her to do so.

"I know we've had this conversation before, Jen. I know what your views on the matter are, and I completely respect that, but my gut is telling me that I really need to do this."

Jen tilted her head to one side. "You're going to tell him how you feel, aren't you? And he still hasn't said anything to you?"

Stacie nodded. "I know you think I should let him take the first step, be the first to say something, but I'm really struggling with this now. I nearly told him twice over the weekend, and it's getting to the stage where I need to say the words, no matter what the consequences might be. If I scare him off..."

She swallowed hard. That was something she didn't dare contemplate... or hadn't until now. Now she was reaching the point where she had to take the gamble—all or nothing.

What Jen said next took her completely by surprise.

"You have to do what you feel's right, Stacie. Now that I've met Cam, seen the way he is with you..." She sighed. "I've never experienced that, and I'm too scared to take the chance again with anyone else, so I never will—"

"Jen, don't say that. You never know what's around

the corner. Look, it's going to be Christmas soon, and then there's New Year—"

"That's not the point I was trying to make," Jen said with a wry grin. "Before I went off on that detour to the land of self-pity—which is *so* not me—I was going to say, don't let my cynicism get in the way of your happiness. Tell him how you feel, Stacie—even I can accept he's not your average man. And I don't think he'll scare that easily."

Average was not an adjective that could ever be applied to Cam Fraser. Stacie tried not to compare the men around her to him, but she couldn't help it. When she thought about Cam… the thoughts gave her such wonderful, crazy feelings inside. She didn't just love the things they did together—she loved just being with him. One of her favourite activities, other than getting up close and personal, was as simple as it could get—an evening with him, a bottle of wine and a good movie on television.

Thoughts like that, though, made the afternoon pass painfully slowly—a state of affairs that was exacerbated by the knowledge that she wasn't getting to spend time with the man in question until later in the week, due to the demands of his business. Putting together the odd comments he'd made, she'd deduced that he was involved in some capacity with providing security at a high-profile international conference. A quick canter through the business and politics pages of a couple of broadsheets had told her all she needed to know.

Back to reality, and what continued to prey on her

mind was their conversations since that first visit to Aegis, and all the things that hadn't been said. The more she thought about it, the more Stacie felt that her relationship with Cam was reaching a critical juncture, where things might easily be *break* rather than *make*. Stacie's instincts told her repeatedly her that this was a relationship worth fighting for—worth taking risks for.

So she had to decide—what was she going to do and when was she going to do it? Maybe surprising him would be a good option—telling him what she wanted him to know when he least expected it.

Thursday… the conference on Thursday. He wouldn't expect her to go to the venue, and since she'd have no other reason to be there, she couldn't chicken out at the last minute—she'd have to tell him. It was a slightly crazy plan, admittedly, but she could be there to meet him when he finished, they could go for a meal somewhere… and that was when she'd tell him.

Almost growling with frustration, Cam raked a hand through his hair. Celebrities, foreign diplomats, other dignitaries and VIPs visiting London were the bread and butter of his home market operation, but sometimes he could do without all the politics. What he needed right now was Stacie—what he had was the thorny problem of organising his available people around the additional requirements posed by the increase in size of his client's delegation to the international conference.

He swore under his breath. He'd had everything planned down to the last detail for weeks now. Movements had been rehearsed and timed pretty much to the second. Then, a few days ago, they'd dropped the little bombshell that they were sending more people, who would be flying into Heathrow and would need escorting directly to the conference from there. This was in addition to the existing group who were being transported from their embassy, and it had turned a relatively simple job into a logistical nightmare.

He'd figure something out—he always did.

Leaving his plans and his laptop on the dining table, Cam went out onto the private terrace for a breath of fresh air—the advantages of working from home rather than hauling his arse to an office every day. In the beginning it had been just Alex and him, and a handful of their former comrades; they'd all been out in the Middle East together, so there'd been no point in having a fancy, expensive office in London. Over time it had become apparent that having a physical office wasn't a necessity, thanks to modern technology.

All of which meant that Cam could work from home when in the UK, although it did leave him with the disadvantage of being surrounded by memories of time spent here with his woman—a distraction he could do without, but one he very much welcomed. He'd not seen her since the weekend, and God, he was missing her. So was his cock.

Sunshine in December was always a bonus. Cam liked

sunshine. He liked it even more when he thought of spending time somewhere warm, with Stacie by his side. He flirted briefly with the thought of taking her away for Christmas, but then remembered that she'd said something about going home for the holiday.

The words she'd used made him ache. He knew why—it was the realisation that she didn't connect him with *home*. But then again, why should she? He'd known for weeks that he was in love with her, yet he'd still said nothing. He closed his eyes and pinched the bridge of his nose. Get Thursday out of the way, and then he'd tell her. The weekend would be ideal. He had plans for where he was going to take her—a place where he could attend to his sub's needs, the way every good Dom should.

Now that triggered a whole bunch of much happier memories of the recent past and anticipatory thoughts for the future—he even found himself smiling. *Stacie on the St. Andrew's Cross.* It made him hard just to imagine her bound to the saltire, her skin creamy and soft, waiting for the loving lash of her Master's flogger.

Given the way she'd enjoyed their visit to the club, the cross was one of the things he intended to use to show her how good things could be between them. What they had was right—better than right—and he needed to build on that now. He needed to tell her how he felt, and hope to God that she felt the same way about him—then they could talk about a future together, where he could take care of her properly. It was entirely self-indulgent, he knew, but for a few moments he allowed himself to imagine what it would be like, to find that house in the country with room enough for a family—not to mention a fully equipped playroom.

Ah well, he'd take time to grab a coffee, then get back to the grindstone. With Baxter and Devlin agreeing to make themselves available when they should have been on a well-deserved leave—a favour for which they would no doubt take great delight in making him pay through the nose in some way in the not-too-distant future—he was starting to get a glimmer of an idea about how to make Thursday work.

What he really needed was to get Alex back in harness. His friend had gone through years of living hell until Beth Harrison, as she'd been until their marriage, had become more to him than a much-valued assistant. She'd done for Alex what he, Cam, hadn't been able to, and that was to get the stubborn idiot to agree to therapy. It had been a tough road, but it had brought him out of the shadows that had claimed him and held him in thrall for so long.

A few hours and several phone calls later, Cam was satisfied that he had everything in place. Like any complex event, it could all go tits-up in a heartbeat, but all the elements that were under his control were just that—under control. His risk assessment was nothing if not thorough.

Shit, is that really the time? Cam stretched, easing the kinks out of his shoulders. He'd been at it for longer than he'd thought… it was too late to call Stacie now, and he sure as hell wasn't going to just text her about his plans for the weekend. He'd make time to speak to her in the morning, ensure that she understood that while he'd love to see her in the evening, he had to conduct a final run-through with his people, ready for Thursday, and that he'd make it up to her in a couple of days' time.

Oh yeah—the weekend. Now those were plans he was *really* looking forward to carrying out…

The crowd was making him nervous.

Cam had an uncomfortable feeling in the pit of his stomach. His eyes scanned the area immediately outside the front entrance to the convention centre. He saw the security cordon, representatives of the world's media, hordes of sightseers in search of a glimpse of the great and the good, a group of protesters—all the usual elements for a gathering such as this, and nothing that should have been making him so leery.

So far, everything had gone reasonably smoothly and according to plan. Delegates were arriving in an efficiently progressing convoy; the people he had inside the building were in position and had nothing untoward to report. He had two more limos en route, one from the embassy and one from the airport, and no reason to suspect that they might not arrive as scheduled, yet that uneasy feeling persisted.

Still, he'd be glad when the job was done in its entirety and his charges were safely delivered to their post-conference destinations. One day of talking, nothing accomplished, millions spent—it seemed to be the way of the world these days, but it wasn't in his job description to have an opinion on the matter.

More limos came and went, a luxurious conveyor belt delivering delegates to talk about putting the world to rights. Cam greeted the first of his clients to arrive and escorted them into the conference centre, where Dylan Baxter took over. Respectful and suavely charming, Dylan was their escort to the anteroom where refreshments were available before the conference proper started. Cam returned to his position outside, a disembodied voice in his earpiece informing him that the last vehicle was about ten minutes away.

A squeal of tortured rubber yanked his gaze to the approach to the convention centre and sent a burst of adrenaline through his veins—a white van had crashed through the security cordon and was careering towards the main entrance. Training and instinct drove him to start herding people away… and then his eyes locked onto the last face he expected to see here, a face that almost made his heart stop. For a half-second he froze, but then he started running towards her as if his life depended on it.

Her life depended on it.

The blast was deafening, the wave of blistering heat so powerful that Cam was flung across the forecourt of the conference centre. A hard, awkward landing drove the breath from his lungs. On his hands and knees, with his ears ringing and the smell of burning in his nostrils, he shook his head and then lurched drunkenly to his feet.

Confusion reigned all around him. Victims of the blast were everywhere, some staggering in slow motion, while others remained where they fell, bloody, broken and burned. The tinnitus muffled the cries, but as the sensation began to die down, the screaming became clearer. His senses returning to normality, Cam stumbled towards the supine form of the blonde woman he'd seen scant seconds ago, before all hell erupted around them.

He fell to the ground beside her, the trained medic suddenly at war with the distraught man in love faced with the sight of his woman unconscious and bleeding, just inches away from him.

Amid the roaring cacophony of wailing alarms, shouting voices and hysterical crying, with the blazing vehicle behind him, he didn't even recognise the voice screaming for an ambulance as his own.

"Alex."

He looked up to see his wife at the door of the office, her troubled face deathly white. "Beth? What is it? What's wrong? Are you all right?" He shot to his feet and went straight to her.

"I'm fine. That was Cam on the phone. There's been an explosion at the conference. He's at St. Thomas'—he said he's okay, just some cuts and bruises, but it's Stacie."

Alex frowned. "Stacie? What about her?"

"She was there. He said she just appeared, moments

before the explosion."

"What the hell was she doing there?"

Beth shook her head. "He doesn't know. He hadn't arranged to meet her there. As far as he was aware, she wouldn't even have known he was going to be there—she just appeared in the crowd. He was running towards her, and then all hell broke loose. Alex, we've got to go to the hospital, be there for him."

Her husband swore under his breath. "I'll bring the car around. Call Cam and tell him we're on our way, and get your coat."

"It's all right—I told him we're leaving now."

For a moment Alex had forgotten that his woman could read him like a book. Given the closeness the three of them shared, it was hardly surprising that she'd already given Cam that message.

Alex drove as fast as was legally possible, but once they got to London, the snarled-up traffic had him cursing under his breath. It was only the calming influence of Beth by his side, her hand resting on his thigh, that prevented him from slamming his hand down on the horn every thirty seconds. Thankfully the gods were on his side, letting him park reasonably close to the hospital, and then he and his wife headed for the Accident and Emergency Department. All they could do was hope that when they got there, Cam would be able to tell them that the news wasn't as bad as they feared.

They found him in the waiting area for A&E, looking like a man who'd been through hell. His face was bruised and battered—minor injuries given the event that had taken him there—but his suit, the jacket draped over one arm, was beyond all redemption, with streaks of dirt and grease amid the assortment of rips and tears. What was most important, though, was the fact that he was there and not injured badly enough to be considered an urgent case for treatment.

"Cam!"

His heart aching with love for her, Alex watched his wife run to his friend's side. Compassion was there in her eyes, and in the gentle touch with which she combed Cam's hair away from his face. Alex, on the other hand, was a touch more pragmatic.

"Cam, you look like shit. What the hell happened?"

Cam glanced at his old friend as the other man took the empty seat beside him.

"Car bomb. Christ, she was only yards away when the bloody thing went off. We were there on diplomatic close protection. The guys are all okay, no injuries at all, but Stacie..." His voice tailed off. "I hadn't told her where we'd be, but she must have pieced it together from things I'd said. She's too bloody smart for her own good. I caught sight of her just as the van was approaching. I knew something was wrong, but I couldn't get to her in time. She looked so beautiful... so happy. And then... the van blew up, she was unconscious on the ground and I was thinking the worst."

Beth's arms wrapped around him, giving him the hug

he badly needed. "Thanks, angel." He kissed her cheek.

"Have you seen a doctor yet?"

He shook his head in response to her question. "I've been talking to the police. Look, I'm okay. My hearing's coming back, and I've had worse than this," he waved in the vague direction of his face, "beating the crap out of him," he jerked his thumb in Alex's direction, "on training exercises."

He scrubbed a hand over his face. "Where the hell's that bloody doctor? I need to know what's happening to Stacie."

"Stay here." Alex's tone was all commanding officer. "I'll see what I can find out."

"Miss Matheson." The doctor looked up from her notes and smiled. "How do you feel?"

Stacie shifted uncomfortably in the bed. "Apart from being stiff and sore and having the headache from hell, you mean? I feel okay."

"Good. The cuts and bruises you sustained were only superficial, and will heal without leaving any scars, but more importantly, you'll be glad to know that the results of the tests have come back, and you and your baby are both fine."

The wind was rushing in her ears. No, she couldn't possibly have heard…

"Excuse me, doctor, what did you say?"

The doctor, an older woman, looked at her with a sympathetic smile. "You didn't know? I do apologise,

Miss Matheson. We carried out a pregnancy test as a precaution, and indications are that you're in the very early stages, maybe six weeks or so. Since you weren't aware, I assume that you haven't been to see your GP?" She nodded when Stacie confirmed that her assumption was correct. "Then I would recommend that you make an appointment as soon as possible. There's nothing to worry about, but it's important that you start your antenatal care at the earliest opportunity.

"Now, I'm going to get you admitted—I want to keep you in for a minimum of twenty-four hours, just to make sure that you don't suffer any ill effects from the concussion. And don't worry about your baby—I see no reason why you shouldn't go to full term without any problems. We'll get you up to an observation ward as soon as we can, and in the meantime, I'll let the nurse know that your partner can come and see you."

"Thank you, doctor. Er, you won't say anything to him about the baby, will you? It's just that…"

"I quite understand, Miss Matheson—it's only natural that you'll want to tell him the good news yourself."

Good news? Would Cam see it that way? Reeling from the shock, Stacie's mind was going around in circles, trying to piece everything together. It must have been just after she'd had the flu… after she'd spent three days throwing up. How could she have been so stupid? She'd never given a thought to additional precautions in the days after, when she and Cam…

A myriad *what ifs* tumbled around in her mind, each

one demanding that she think through the consequences of possible decisions—keep the baby or not, tell Cam or not, stay with him or not… Stacie covered her face with her hands in an attempt to shut out the screaming whirlwind of thoughts going through her head.

The only thing she was certain of was that she couldn't tell him—not yet. She needed time to deal with the idea of being pregnant before she could even think of how best to tell Cam, never mind actually telling him and coping with his reaction to the news.

"Stacie, honey?"

The mattress moved—she looked up to see Cam sitting there, worry written all over his face. From the look of him, he'd been patched up—since that was the case, they clearly didn't see any need to admit him for further treatment. With that thought, she managed a relieved if somewhat wobbly smile. Suddenly very tired, she let her head fall back against the pillow.

"I'm okay," she said. "Just a bit of a bump on the head—that's why they're keeping me in overnight."

His expression darkened. "It was more than a bit of a bump on the head, beautiful—you were unconscious for a while. And would you like to tell me what was going through your mind when I came in?"

She couldn't tell him—not yet. "Nothing. Just… whatever goes through a person's mind when they get caught in something like that, it was so… How many casualties were there?"

"A few dozen, some of them serious, but no fatalities

as yet… and stop trying to avoid the question. It wasn't nothing, I could see it in your face, and you *will* tell me, Stacie. I'll let this go for the time being, but we will be discussing it later. And talking of something like that," he continued, referring to the explosion, "what the *hell* were you doing there?"

He wasn't shouting, but Stacie knew that he was furious. And if he was furious with her just for being there, what would his reaction be to the news of the baby? "I… I wanted to surprise you," she managed to stammer. "I took the day off work. I was going to wait until you'd finished, but I didn't know when that would be. I knew it wouldn't be the surprise I intended, but all I was going to do was ask you when you'd be done. Please don't be mad at me."

He'd be mad enough when she told him that her birth control had failed.

"Beautiful? I'm not mad at you—I'm mad at myself for giving you enough clues to work out where I was going to be. I should have known better, considering the way you connected the three of us with Beth's book. I'm slipping in my old age." He leaned forward to touch a gentle kiss to her lips. "But please… don't do anything like this again. I aged ten years when I saw you out cold."

She managed a half-smile. He may have said *please*, but she knew an order when she heard one. "I won't."

It was close to midnight. Having spent yet another day with the team investigating the explosion, Cam was back in his apartment, dog-tired and unable to sleep. With every breath, the band of iron around his heart tightened a little more. Recent events had been a harsh and long overdue wake-up call, exposing his time with Stacie as nothing more than a dream… reminding him of the festering reality that was his chosen way of life. Reminding him that that way of life had room for only one person—not two.

He refilled his whisky glass. It was tempting to get rip-roaring drunk, but that was no way to remove the weight that was currently resting on his shoulders.

What the hell had he done? Been foolish enough to believe that he could have it all, that was what. He was meant to be alone—he'd always been meant to be alone, his life couldn't be any other way. His childhood had made him damaged goods and now he was in danger of inflicting a different kind of damage on the woman who was everything he wanted… the woman whom he could now never call his own.

She'd been hurt because of him. Stacie's safety was the only thing that mattered to him now and the only way he could keep her safe was to remove himself from her life. He remembered only too well what had happened to Beth Lombard the previous year, all because Alex wouldn't send her away from him. And that was a one-off situation linked to a specific incident in Alex's past, whereas this… this was his way of life and all he knew. As long as his work put him in danger, then she would be at risk too.

And if he gave up his work, what then? His identity would be gone, the man he was would be gone, the man to whom Stacie was drawn would be… gone. *She* would be gone.

Christ, it was a mess… and he could see only one way out of it, a way that would give Stacie a chance to be safe—and happy with someone else who could give her a better life. One that included children.

Pain lanced through him, the physical manifestation of grief for what could now never be. He remembered the occasion all too well. They'd been walking in the park, a young family a short distance ahead of them. The mother had been pushing an empty buggy while the father was holding the hand of their son, toddling along on unsteady legs. Stacie hadn't said anything, but he'd seen the look on her face, her expression one of unfulfilled love and wonder. In that moment he'd wanted to share a future like that with her.

He wasn't right for her—he never had been and he'd been a fool ever to think otherwise. The dream was over… now he had to wake up to the truth and do the right thing for the only woman who had ever really mattered to him. It wouldn't take long—a week would do it, and then he'd be ready to go.

In the end, it didn't even take that long. Just a couple of days later, everything was arranged. Cam swallowed another mouthful of Scotch. It was his third glass, but he was still sober enough to feel the pain of what he was about to do.

Pushing aside thoughts of the phone call he was about to make, he forced himself to consider the one he'd made a few hours ago. He hadn't wanted to go back to the Middle East again, not so soon, and most certainly not for a stay of six months, but it was the only way he could avoid going down on his knees and begging Stacie for forgiveness—and potentially putting her life in danger all over again.

In the days since he'd picked her up from the hospital, he'd focused on work and kept contact with her down to a minimum, figuring that distancing himself from her would be the best way to sow the seeds for their parting. It was working too—the last text she'd sent him, a couple of hours earlier, had very politely asked him to let her know when it would be convenient for her to call him, as she thought they needed to talk. The text also had a sense of apprehension about it that made him ache to take her in his arms and put everything right.

Of course, that entirely depended on whichever definition of *right* one wanted to use.

Instead, he resigned himself to a one-way journey to the hell of spending the rest of his life alone. He couldn't be with Stacie because of the risks his work posed to her safety. Any other woman he got involved with beyond a superficial extent would be subject to the same risks… not that he would ever be interested in any other woman that way. If he couldn't have Stacie, he didn't want anyone.

This was not what he'd been expecting to be doing just a couple of days before Christmas. The call he was about to make was going to be the hardest thing he'd ever done in his life, harder even than seeing his oldest friend more dead than alive. His bag was packed and by the door—the car would be picking him up to take him to the airport in about ten minutes. After take-off, he'd have seven or eight hours to finish what he'd started and get shit-faced drunk—then he couldn't think about Stacie and remember what he was about to do to her.

He picked up the phone, knowing it was the last time he'd dial the number that was branded on his heart as much as his memory. He'd rehearsed this moment until he'd almost been physically sick with self-hatred, but there was no other way—he had to protect her and the only way he could be sure of doing that was to make her hate him as much as he hated himself.

Her voice. She called it her telephone voice, so sweet and clear. He swallowed hard. He was about to lose the only thing that would ever mean anything to him—no, not lose, *reject*.

He had to protect her and this was the only way—by destroying her hopes and her dreams, along with his own. She'd call him a bastard and he'd deserve it. She'd hate him for a while—he deserved that too—and then she'd move on, to some lucky sod who could give her the happiness *she* deserved.

She was everything he'd fought against wanting for as long as he could remember. She was the woman he would always love, the future he could never have, the family that would never be his. It was time to say goodbye.

"It's over, Stacie. We're done. I don't want to see you again."

CHAPTER FOURTEEN

Three months later

Beth Lombard stepped out into the sunshine and took a deep breath—maybe not such a good idea, given that she was in the heart of London. Still, the meeting with her editor had been a good one. Her second novel was performing well, even better than anticipated, and the idea she'd pitched for her next endeavour had been well-received—just as well, since she'd been unable to resist the temptation to make a start on the first volume in the series.

The sunshine was a welcome change and a sign that spring was struggling into life. Beth felt a twinge of sadness—it was also a reminder of just how long Cam had been out of the country. His sudden departure just before Christmas was, she knew, linked to the shock break-up of his relationship with Stacie Matheson, the reasons for which remained a mystery. Cam had never spoken about it in his occasional emails and infrequent phone calls—determined to respect his privacy, in spite of her concern, Beth had never asked.

The fact that Stacie herself had apparently disappeared from the face of the earth also seemed to indicate an irretrievable breakdown. Beth hadn't seen the younger woman since she and Cam had parted company, but had often thought about her. She didn't even have a number for Stacie—not anymore. A couple of days after Cam's departure for the Middle East Beth had tried calling Stacie's mobile phone, only to discover that it had been disconnected. Since she had no choice but to respect Stacie's privacy as well, Beth had turned down her husband's offer to use his connections to find her. After all, Stacie had Beth's number and she knew where Beth and Alex lived, so if she decided to get in touch again, there was no reason why she couldn't.

Beth, however, had other things on her mind, things of a more personal nature. Another month had gone by, another month of failure, another month older, another month of waiting. When she left the house early that morning to take the train to London, she'd avoided sharing with her husband the disappointment of yet another negative pregnancy test.

Telling herself that they hadn't been trying long enough to justify this level of distress was getting old fast.

What hurt even more, though, was the knowledge of how Alex would react—the same way he always did, soothing her pain without giving her the opportunity to do the same for him, as if he didn't think that his feelings mattered. Her blood still ran cold at the memory of the time he'd blamed himself, the haunted look that returned briefly to his beautiful dark eyes when he spoke of the things he'd suffered in the past and their possible impact on his ability to create a baby with her.

She couldn't face getting the train home—not yet.

Beth turned the corner, her intention to catch a cab and pay a visit to her favourite chocolatier, when her eye was caught by a familiar curtain of honey-coloured waves, on the opposite side of the road. *Stacie?*

It took Beth all of three seconds to act—the first to make the decision, the second to check the traffic, and the third to start running.

"Stacie!"

The voice was one Stacie had never really expected to hear again. When Cam had told her so abruptly that their relationship was over, she'd made a decision to also sever all ties with the people who were his friends—the risk of her path crossing his at some point in the future would otherwise have been too great. So much for her grand plan.

Her steps faltered only slightly as she continued walking. If she could pretend that she hadn't heard Beth Lombard's voice, she could pretend that she didn't want to greet the other woman with a warm hug and a million questions about Cam Fraser. When she felt the hand on her arm, she had only a fraction of a second to school her features so that they didn't betray her thoughts and her foolish feelings.

"Stacie, I thought it was you! We've missed you! How are you?"

She should pull away from the warm hug, but the truth of it was, she couldn't. The friendship she'd shared with the other woman, though brief, was too deep to be pushed to one side, and she found herself wishing that she could have had a hug like this almost five weeks earlier, when she'd really needed it.

She'd missed Beth—Alex too, scary though he could be—almost as much as she was still missing Cam. Jen had been a wonderful friend through that awful time, but she didn't really know Cam, knew nothing of the dynamic of their relationship, and consequently Stacie hadn't felt able to share everything she'd gone through with her friend. As for telling her parents… she still didn't want to think too much about how that had gone.

"I'm all right," Stacie replied, even though she wasn't—not yet. "How are you? What brings you to London?"

"Oh, I'm fine, thank you. I've just been in a meeting with my editor." Beth's smile became a self-conscious grin. "Do you know, I still can't believe people want to read what I write, much less pay for it." She glanced at her watch. "It's nearly lunchtime. I don't suppose you'd like to join me for a bite to eat? On me—I feel like celebrating."

For a moment, Stacie was taken back to the night she met Cam, and the weekend of the party to celebrate the publication of Beth's second novel. Yep, it still hurt. Three months, give or take, since he'd turned his back on her, and it still hurt. Like hell.

"So what are we celebrating?"

Beth looked delighted. "I'll take that as a yes. We're celebrating the fact that my second book is doing pretty well, and my editor loves the idea for a series that I've just pitched to her. And last but not least, the fact that completely by accident, I've bumped into a dear friend I haven't seen for far too long. I've missed you, Stacie—and I've been worried about you. You disconnected your number."

She'd thought it best, at the time. All part of her plan to cut herself off from everything and everyone connected with Cam. Everyone except for…

"It seemed like a good idea at the time," Stacie said ruefully, "and if I'm honest, the way things ended between us, part of it was that I didn't think you and Alex would want to stay in touch. A clean break seemed to be the least awful option at the time."

Fifteen minutes later she was sitting across the table from Beth in a smart café restaurant, waiting for the salad she'd ordered. Against her better judgment she'd rung the office as well, to ask for the afternoon off. The truth of it was, though, that she'd missed talking to Beth, and although she was determined not to ask about Cam, she was kind of hoping that he might crop up during the conversation.

She didn't have to wait long.

"You do know that Cam went out to the Middle East again, right after you and he split up?" Beth said, after the waiter had served their food. "It was all very sudden."

No, she hadn't known that and now Stacie wished that were still the case. Not only had he not wanted to see her again, he couldn't even bear to be in the same country. How much worse was it going to get? What had she done that was so wrong? He'd never even known about the pregnancy. In that moment, she wished she'd ordered something stronger than mineral water to drink. "How is he?"

"Busy," Beth said as she buttered a roll. "I don't know how he does it. Eighteen-hour days and one day off every other week, if he's lucky. It's no wonder he's trying to get Alex back into the business."

Something he'd been trying to do that first weekend, if Stacie recalled correctly. "Alex still hasn't decided?"

Beth's smile faded a little. "It's my fault, I think. I'm fairly certain he wants to go back. He didn't at first, but after Cam spoke to him, he started talking about what would be involved and I think it's really fired his imagination—ways he can see the business developing for the future, but…" A troubled look met Stacie's eyes. "We're trying to start a family and it's just not happening. And I'm pretty sure that that's the reason for him holding back from making a commitment to the business. It's as if he sees it as one or the other, but I want him to have both, if that's what he really wants.

"I'm sorry." Beth forced a brighter smile. "I didn't ask you to lunch for you to hear me moan on and on. How have you been? Are you really all right?"

Debating whether or not to tell Beth Lombard the truth, Stacie hesitated just a fraction too long. It didn't take much pressure from Beth for her to cave in.

"Beth, please… promise me you won't say anything to Alex or Cam about what I'm about to tell you."

The euphoria of a successful meeting with her editor was long gone as Beth sat on the train, heading for home. What Stacie had told her had left her in a state of shock. If only she hadn't made a promise to her friend that she wouldn't share what she'd been told with her husband. How she was going to keep this from him, she had no idea.

Beth stared blankly out of the window at countryside that she just didn't see. Her mind was fully absorbed elsewhere. Silent tears occasionally fell, for Stacie and the child she'd lost, and for herself and the child she seemed destined never to have. Why did it all have to be such a mess?

Still, there was one positive thing that she'd accomplished, even if she had been sneaky and underhanded about it. When Stacie had disappeared to the powder room, she'd inadvertently left her mobile phone on the table… and Beth had taken advantage by using it to call her own phone, to get the number. At least she now had a line of communication, even a means of finding Stacie if necessary.

For once Beth was glad that Alex wasn't meeting her at the station—it would give her an extra twenty minutes to compose herself. She certainly needed it, especially since she was going to have to keep something from him. The problem she had was that her husband had an uncanny knack for knowing when she was hiding something, and no compunction whatsoever about doing whatever it took to get her to unhide it.

As she turned off the road and proceeded down the drive that led to her home, Beth concentrated on the result of the meeting with her editor—the original reason for her visit to London. She would at least be able to share that with Alex, and not only that, it was a good outcome too.

She saw him before she even stopped the car. Her heart skipped a beat. Alex never stood at the door like that—*never*. The expression on his face was frighteningly grave.

"Alex? What is it? What's wrong?"

The last time Alex had gone through anything remotely like this, it had been more than a decade and a half earlier, while on deployment in the Middle East. The intervening years had not made it any easier to deal with.

The call a couple of hours earlier had been totally unforeseen. He'd picked the phone up, glanced at the caller display and on seeing the international number had expected to hear Cam's voice greeting him with the usual friendly abuse. As soon as he'd heard Conor Devlin's voice, he'd known something bad had happened. Devlin's message had made Alex's blood run cold.

Cam was missing in action.

Years of training ingrained in every cell in his body had enabled Alex to listen to the cold facts of the report. His old friend had been on a rescue mission—a small group of consultants, employees of the international conglomerate that had retained Cam's company, among other security specialists, had been abducted some seventeen days earlier, and were being held hostage.

Although his people hadn't been responsible for the protection of the kidnap victims, Cam had been tasked with retrieving them. The authorities hadn't been informed of the kidnapping—a decision made by the senior representatives of the company that employed the hostages. The motive behind the decision was simple—it was in the best interests of the corporation not to appear incompetent in the eyes of their client, the government of the country. Instead, they had dismissed the security contractor that had bungled the protection assignment and asked Cam to mount a covert rescue mission.

Conor Devlin had been a member of the team Cam put together, along with Dylan Baxter. The rescue had gone according to plan, but it was at the extraction that the mission had gone horribly wrong. Cam had been covering their escape and would be the last one to head for the helicopter, but the enemy had got lucky… unlike Cam.

"He saw them setting up the rocket launcher before we did. He was yelling at us get out of there, Alex. I had no choice—I had to order the pilot to take off before they could hit us with an RPG. The last I saw of him, he was going down under half a dozen of them and then they were dragging him off—and he was still *fucking telling us to go."*

Stupid bastard. If Cam had gone and got himself killed… Alex didn't want to contemplate the possibility. As far as he was concerned, it wasn't an option.

Having taken the hostages to safety, Conor had taken the team back to the extraction point to search for Cam, but so far, they'd come up with nothing. Cam had now been missing for almost a week and their client was now disclaiming all knowledge of the incident. They'd been hung out to dry.

Having some idea of what had happened to Alex the last time he was in that part of the world, Conor had called him to request assistance as a last resort. He knew Alex had contacts that might be able to help, although Conor had been reluctant to drag Alex back into a world he'd left years earlier for those very personal reasons. A week of so far fruitless searching had left him with no choice. Time was running out for Cam.

Since the call, Alex had been fighting the urge to drop everything and head for the Middle East—his instinctive reaction to his friend being in trouble. However, even if he were in a position to do that, at the present time he couldn't add any value to what was already being done on the ground to find the blasted idiot.

The best-case scenario was that Cam had somehow already made good his escape and would be found soon. The worst-case scenario was that he was already dead and they'd never find his body—that wasn't going to happen. One way or another, Cam was coming home.

Alex just hoped to God that it wasn't in a body bag.

Realistically, though, the truth was likely to be somewhere between the two extremes—whatever it was, Cam was going to need help. Wherever he was being held, the chances were there would be a lot of guards. Until he had more solid information, Alex couldn't come up with a detailed strategy for getting his old friend out and home, but he could look at the bigger picture—mainly logistics and weapons, the kind of weapons to which Cam's team on the ground wouldn't necessarily have ready access. Now *those* he could start working on immediately. He still had the contacts he'd need to get things moving.

Alex pulled up a map of the region on his laptop. It wasn't going to be easy, but there was one saving grace—he'd known the country's ruler for years, ever since they'd gone through officer training together. Alex didn't give a damn about the reputation of the company that had got Cam into this predicament, and once he knew what kind of backup he'd need, he'd have no qualms about asking the prince for assistance or explaining why he needed it.

Hell, if they didn't find Cam soon, he'd be more than

happy to call the prince to request support in the search, and he didn't give a damn about dropping Cam's client in the shit in the process.

His most immediate worry, though, was his wife. Beth was due back from her meeting in London soon, and then he'd have to break the news about Cam to her. Knowing how much she was missing their friend anyway, Alex was deeply concerned about how she'd take it—on top of the repeated disappointments she'd had over the last few months. If he could take away that pain, he would—each time, the haunted look in her eyes almost killed him and for her sake he wanted it to stop.

And that was why he was waiting for her at the front door, to take her in his arms and tell her what had happened to Cam as gently as he could. He couldn't stop the distress of not being able to start their family from hurting her, but he'd do all he could to lessen the anguish that would come when he told her that Cam had been missing for a week.

The day was turning into one of the worst days of her life. Just when she thought it couldn't possibly get any worse, Beth sat in stunned, aching silence as she listened to her husband relate the details of the phone call he'd received that afternoon. On top of everything else, she felt too beaten down even to cry. Stacie's loss, Cam missing…

"What can we do, Alex?"

"Beth, sweetheart, his team's working on finding him

right now, they've been hard at it since he went missing. Conor's taken the lead, he's damn good at his job, and he's doing everything I'd be doing if I were out there. One way or another, we'll find out where he is, and when we do, I'll have a plan in place to get him back. It's what I do, love."

Her hero. He'd been that for so long… never more so than when he'd let down his guard and allowed her to see him vulnerable and hurting… allowed her to be strong for him. She could do that now. She cradled his cheek with a gentle hand.

"It's what *we* do, Master. Together. And I think there's someone else who needs to know what's happening." She paused, searching his face for the strength to tell him what was going through her mind. "I saw Stacie today."

"Stacie?"

"I didn't plan it. I'd just left the meeting and… well, I was going to do some shopping before getting the train back, and I just happened to see her. We ended up having lunch together."

His expression one of deep thought, her husband nodded, taking in everything she'd told him. "How is she?"

This was it. She'd tell him the truth—just not all of it. A promise was a promise. "She didn't admit it, but it was obvious—she misses him. And she still loves him. I believe he still loves her."

A sceptical eyebrow slowly rose. "And what gives you *that* idea? He never talks about her."

"Exactly—he never talks about her. *Never.* But more

than that, it's the *way* he dumped her. Over the phone? The *phone*, for God's sake! Cam is one of the most honourable men I know, and he would *never* do that, any more than you would. Not to mention the fact that he left the country the same night and he's not been back since. I'm sure he was trying to make her hate him. I may not know why he wanted to do that, I may not have known him as long as you have, I may not know him the way you do… but I know him the way *I* do. He still loves her, I'm sure of it."

"Beth, this isn't one of your books. Real life doesn't always have a happily ever after."

She looked at her husband—her stubborn, frustrating, brave, beautiful man. "We have our happily ever after. Cam and Stacie deserve to have theirs too." She could be just as obstinate.

"What if you're wrong?"

"I'm not. I know I'm not. But when I call her, I'm going to be in serious trouble."

A certain expression developed on Alex's face—an expression she knew only too well. "And you think you're not already?"

A short time later, Beth sat staring at her mobile phone, trying to summon up the courage to make the call. Her backside was still smarting. It wasn't just that she hadn't told him the whole story—Alex didn't like her to worry about anything, and she'd let her worry over Cam get the better of her. Alex's answer to that had been to take her to the playroom, and with a sound spanking had reiterated the fact that, while Cam was missing, everything was being done to pinpoint his location and by the time they had the co-ordinates, Alex would be ready to mount a rescue mission.

This phone call was going to require some finesse, Beth decided. It would be very easy for Stacie to cut her off before she had a chance to apologise and explain. The apology was going to be crucial in making this work. Stacie had made it clear that she didn't want or expect anything from Cam or her or Alex, and the way she'd said goodbye, gracious though it was, was a clear indication that she never expected to hear from Beth again.

Thumb poised over the call button, Beth experienced a moment of doubt as to whether she was doing the right thing. The doubt was all in her mind—her heart was utterly convinced that she should go ahead. *Cam and Stacie belong together.*

"Stacie? It's Beth—*please* don't be angry with me…"

This time, Stacie knew exactly where she was going. This time, she was going there in a new car that wasn't going to break down… which was just as well, because her knight in shining armour wouldn't be there to rescue her. She was on her way to rescue him.

A fanciful notion certainly, but having heard the awful news from Beth, she'd gratefully accepted the invitation to go and stay with her and Alex at Winterleigh. She'd felt this inexplicable need to be with them, no matter how stupid and irrational it might be. It wasn't as if she could actually do anything, but waiting on her own in London just wasn't an option.

She hadn't wasted any time either. Even though it was after hours, she'd left a message for her manager to let her know that she was taking a few days off due to a family emergency, then she'd thrown some clothes into a couple of bags and set off for Hampshire. Cam probably wouldn't want her involved, she knew that, but he wasn't there to object. She'd also told Jen what had happened, and that she'd be absent from work for a few days.

Winterleigh was just as impressive as she remembered. She'd barely stopped the car and got out when Beth came running out of the house. The two women hugged, and then they were both brushing away a few tears.

"Come on in," Beth said, linking arms with Stacie. "Alex will get your luggage. You *are* staying, aren't you?"

Stacie managed a watery smile. "For as long as you'll have me," she replied. "I've missed you both so much."

Beth's husband appeared at the door. Stacie's steps faltered as a bolt of trepidation flashed through her. She'd seen Alex Lombard in full-on Dom mode once or twice and found him positively scary. Given the way things had ended between herself and Cam, she was almost expecting him to be stiff and distant, but his darkly handsome face broke into a warm, hospitable smile as he greeted her with another hug.

"Stacie, welcome back," he said kindly. "I just wish it

were in better circumstances. Give me your keys and I'll bring your bags in. You go with Beth and make yourself at home."

She followed Beth into the house, surprised by the other woman's chuckle. "What are you laughing at?"

"Your face! You looked absolutely terrified when you saw Alex." Then Beth became a little more serious. "Stacie, no matter what happens between you and Cam, no matter how this turns out, there's one thing that won't change, and that's the respect Alex—any Dom—will have for you as a submissive. They all have this crazy, over-the-top instinct to protect. When I couldn't get in touch with you, back when you and Cam… Alex offered to use his contacts to try to find you, so we could get in touch with you again. He was worried about you—we both were—but I thought we should respect your privacy. I'm sorry."

Recalling how she'd felt at the time, Stacie knew she wouldn't have been receptive to any approaches—after all, she'd needed to keep a very big secret, and contact with Beth and Alex would have made that impossible. "Beth, it's all right. If you'd tried to contact me back then—"

"I understand. Did you never consider telling Cam?"

"I was still struggling to come to terms with it when he called me to tell me it was all over between us—it had only been a few days and…" Her voice trailed off into memory.

"Well, you're here now, and that's what matters. I'll

take you up to your room."

Stacie expected Beth to take her to the blue bedroom again, but instead she stopped outside the door of what had been Cam's room. "If it helps, you can stay in here."

"I'd like to—thank you."

"Good. Now, you take as long as you need to freshen up. We'll be in the family room—you remember the way? We can talk then. In the meantime, I'll go and put the kettle on—unless you'd prefer something stronger?"

"I'll open a bottle of wine. Here you go, Stacie—excuse me, ladies."

It was Alex, of course, with Stacie's bags. He took them into the room for her, and then she watched her hosts leave, trying to beat down the pang of envy… to have something like that with Cam was an impossible dream now.

Cam. Oh God, Cam. After Beth had told her he was missing, she'd had to make a dash for the bathroom to throw up. What on earth had happened to him?

There was one more question lurking at the back of her mind… one that she didn't want to acknowledge, yet couldn't avoid.

Was Cam still alive?

CHAPTER FIFTEEN

"I'm not who you fucking think I am!"

Cam Fraser's voice was hoarse with yelling—and hoarse with cursing as his hands made a grab for the chains shackling him to the wall, trying to lift his body up and out of the way of the vicious crack of the single-tail whip across his shoulder blades. Another expletive exploded from his lips at the ensuing trickle of blood that joined the others trailing down his naked back.

He had to endure another half-dozen painfully amateurish strokes before they released him from his bonds and dragged him back to the cell, where once again they chained him by the ankle to the wall. For long minutes he lay there, breathing through the pain, distantly aware of the plate of rice and unidentifiable slop that was left for him along with a couple of bottles of water.

Hell would freeze over before he'd eat that rancid crap. Unfortunately, the cuisine at this exclusive resort sucked in general, and he had the weight loss to prove it. His camouflage pants were now hanging off his hips and without a reliable source of nutrition, it was getting more difficult to maintain muscle tone and mass.

This unexpected free vacation had lasted about eighteen days now—or so he thought. He'd made the rookie mistake of losing track of time just after he'd been taken to the first cell he'd occupied. That he'd been unconscious at the time didn't cut any ice with him.

Ice. Scotch on the rocks. The chink of cubes in the glass, condensation dewing the outside, and he was ready to take his first sip...

Pushing aside the thought and all the painful reminders of home that came with it, Cam tugged ineffectively at the chain—one end was well and truly anchored in the wall, while the other was connected to the iron band around his ankle. Why the hell did he bother? All the straining did was pull open the wounds on his back that were trying to heal. He needed the key for the lock on the shackle or even a half-decent lock pick would suffice. Failing that, an oxy-acetylene torch to cut through the chain would do nicely, but oddly enough he had a feeling that he wasn't going to see any of those items any time soon.

Then there was the cell door to get through, his captors to get past, transport to hijack... whether he died trying to escape or died from the punishment being inflicted on his body, it didn't matter—the end result was still the same.

Alone again. For a little while he could relax—as much as it was possible to relax while being held prisoner and periodically subjected to what could only be described as torture. Cam knew they'd be back before long, though, to take him back to that room and ask him more questions about matters of which he was in total ignorance. Their language was one of the more obscure regional dialects—Cam recognised just enough to deny all knowledge and then the beatings would start again. It was only a matter of time before they moved onto more refined forms of administering pain, in an attempt to extract information he simply did not have. And even if he did have it, he'd see the bastards in hell first.

The fundamental flaw in their thinking was their assumption that he was closely allied to the prince and was a military adviser to the pro-Western government. They believed he was working alongside the armed forces, and wouldn't be told that he was a security contractor in the private sector.

Cam rubbed his eyes with the heels of his hands. He should have known better than to agree to clear up the mess left by one of his business rivals. Hell, if it was him, he'd have cleared up his own… strike that, he'd never have made the fucking mess in the first place. His subjects sure as hell stayed protected—they didn't get kidnapped by radical fundamentalists.

He stared at his bare, bloody feet, using the focus to block out the pain raging across his back. Years of training had given him other techniques to deal with the questioning—not to mention torture techniques that were far more sophisticated and painful than the methods these dilettantes were using. What he couldn't block out—at least not as easily as he'd been able to at first—was the sense of foreboding that his life was going to end in this place.

He had to face facts. They'd moved him three times already, always at night, always blindfolded and in the back of a death trap of a truck—he had no idea where he was now, and he doubted that anyone else would know his location either. The chances were that they'd long since assumed he was dead. He was on his own, and the odds weren't looking good.

Cam had had a hunch from the start that taking on the job of rescuing the consultants would be a poisoned chalice. As he'd laid down covering fire for his team to get the group of civilians to the extraction point, his gut had told him repeatedly that he was in deep shit. He'd signalled to them to head for the incoming helicopter, knowing that someone would have to take the rear to cover their escape—knowing that that someone would have to be him.

The plan had worked too, until his men and the civilians had boarded the chopper. At that point, his men should have been providing covering fire for him to make the sprint to join them, but some of the civilians had panicked and got in the way. Those vital seconds were all the rebels had needed to overpower him and take him captive. At the same time as he was going down under the weight of at least four, maybe even six of his adversaries, he'd seen another group setting up a rocket launcher. Cam's last thoughts had been to get everyone out of there and that he'd figure something out—he always did.

Except this time, maybe he wouldn't…

Waiting was the worst part. Days of it, waiting for a call from Conor or Bax with news of Cam's whereabouts. Alex used the time to go through various possible scenarios, until he reached the point where he could do no more—not until he got something more definite to go on. He was seriously tempted to fly out there and assist with the search himself.

Every time the phone rang, it elicited the same reaction—adrenaline would course through his veins, readying him for the mission to start in earnest, while Beth and Stacie would immediately seek each other out, anticipating that the call would be the start of the process of getting Cam back where he belonged.

When *the* call finally came, Alex took it in his office, knowing that when he eventually emerged, the ball would have started rolling—and once started, it would only stop when they had Cam back safe and sound. He listened intently to what Conor had to say. At the same time, he assessed the potential plans he'd come up and discarded those that were not feasible. Fine details would need to be ironed out but by the time the call with Conor ended, Alex had a high-level plan in mind and a mental list of the resources required to implement it.

The first phone call he needed to make was one about which he had grave reservations. He would be asking a lot of the recipient of the call, but for Cam's sake, he had to try. Given the terrain they would be traversing on the rescue mission, Ros Edwards' expert driving skills could mean the difference between total success and deadly failure. Ros, however, was still on active service, and if the mission failed, the resulting complications could be anything up to and including a major diplomatic nightmare. That being the case, Alex couldn't blame her if she declined to offer her assistance.

"Ros? It's Alex Lombard."

"I've been waiting for your call, Alex. What's the word on Cam?"

Alex wasn't surprised that news had reached her about his old friend's predicament—the bonds of military service transcended the distinction between the public and private sectors. He gave her a concise rundown on the latest intel. "It's a big ask, Ros, but given the location, I could really use your expertise on the ground. I know that if we got caught it would be—"

"Can anyone say *career-limiting*?" She gave a short laugh, devoid of humour. "Hell, who needs a bloody Government pension anyway? You don't have to ask, Alex. I'll tell Guy I'm taking a couple of weeks' leave—he's always on at me to go and spend some time in the sun. I'll just tell him I'm doing exactly that, and I won't be contactable. He doesn't need to know *exactly* what I'll be doing in the sun. We'll just have to make damn sure we don't get caught—we don't need an international incident on our hands, on top of everything else."

"I think the chances of our getting out in one piece just increased exponentially. Thanks, Ros. I owe you. We'll be deploying in the next twenty-four to forty-eight hours—I'll be in touch."

Alex put the phone down. That call had been more successful than he'd dared to hope, but there was one more to make—one upon which everything else depended. He picked the phone up again. He hadn't called the number in years, but if ever there was a time he needed to, it was now.

"Your Highness? *As-salamu alaykum.* It's Alex Lombard. How are you? I know, sir, a very long time. You remember my partner, Cam Fraser? I need your help…"

At the end of the conversation, Alex let his breath out slowly. The prince had promised that one of his business jets and its crew would be at Alex's disposal and available for departure from 20:00 the next day—not only that, his personal physician and a trained medic would meet them when they landed, prepared to accompany them back to the UK, if necessary.

Significantly, the prince was also going to make available all the portable firepower they'd need. It seemed that—for once—fate was on their side.

With Conor and Bax already in transit back to the UK, Ros Edwards on board, and further members of Cam's team with whom they would meet in country, Alex allowed himself the luxury of believing that his plan might just work. The initial rendezvous would be at a private airport almost thirty miles away, where they would board the prince's jet. The outbound flight would give Alex the opportunity to brief all three on his plan to rescue Cam Fraser.

When they landed at the prince's personal airstrip, there would be three armoured Land Rovers, courtesy of the prince but not traceable to him, waiting for them, along with the rest of the hand-picked team, ready to make the journey to the location where Cam was being held captive. Once there, they would effect his release—using whatever means necessary—and then he and Ros would bring Cam back to the airstrip in one vehicle, while the remaining members of the team would disperse, to return to their original assignments.

If everything went according to plan, a few days from now Cam would be safe and sound, back in the UK.

All that was left was the most difficult task of all—breaking the news to Beth that he was going back into the field. When he'd first talked to her about the possibility of returning to the security arena, he'd given her his word that he'd be going back purely as a consultant, and the riskiest thing he'd be doing would be sitting behind a desk all day. She was not going to be happy, but since it was Cam who was in trouble, she'd understand. He hoped.

He found her in the family room with Stacie. Both women looked at him expectantly. He wasn't going to insult their intelligence by beating around the bush.

"They've found Cam. He's still alive, but we need to get him out quickly. I've got the team on standby—we're flying out tomorrow night."

"What do you mean, *we*?"

Alex looked at his wife, took in the open fear and denial in her eyes, the tension in her stance as she stood to face him. She knew exactly what he meant.

"Sweetheart, we have to get him out. I can't just give them a plan and send them on their way. There are a million things that could go wrong—I have to be there. And I owe Cam my life too many times over." He wrapped his arms around Beth, gaining as much comfort from the embrace as he was giving to her. "I need both of you to stay here—"

"No." Stacie stood up then, a look of determination on her face. "He's there because of me, so I'm going with you. I won't get in the way, I promise."

"And if she's going for Cam," Beth joined in, "I'm going too—for you."

"*Neither of you is going!*" Alex thundered. He could barely believe what he'd just heard. "What the *hell* are you thinking?"

His wife glanced at the instigator of this insurrection, and then looked squarely back at him. "We're thinking that we want to be there to support the men we love and care about," she said, with that stubborn tilt to her chin that he loved so much. "We've already discussed this between us, just in case the opportunity arose, and we're going!"

"This is going to be fucking dangerous, and you are *both* staying home, where you'll be safe! The op has no official backing, and having to keep an eye on you two is the last thing I need!"

"You won't need to keep an eye on us!" Beth flung back at her husband and then instantly calmed down. "We're not stupid, Alex. In the wrong place, we know we'd only be in the way, but Stacie and I have already come up with a plan. We both agree that we could fly out there with you. I mean, you're going to have to fly to that area, aren't you? Even we worked that one out. We could wait at the airport, make ourselves useful if you need extra pairs of hands to take care of the small stuff that doesn't need your experience and expertise."

Heaven save him from scheming women. It served him right for marrying a smart sub. It seemed like she was already halfway through planning the fine details of the mission for him.

"That's the prince's *small* jet?"

Alex couldn't help but chuckle at his wife's reaction to the Boeing 737 waiting for them on the tarmac. It was evident that she'd imagined something considerably smaller, and he hadn't disabused her of the idea. "You're forgetting, love—his title may be *prince*, but in his small but very, very rich country, that makes him the absolute monarch. He's both the head of state and head of government—at least until he can introduce the reforms he wants to make, to make his country more democratic."

And that was the background against which Cam had been captured. The prince was trying to modernise his country; however, a not insignificant group of traditionalists were doing all they could—not to retain the status quo, but to regress to an almost feudal society. They were responsible for kidnapping the group of consultants Cam had been tasked to rescue. The consultants had been hired to make a study of how the country's modernisation might best be accomplished—that had made them a prime target.

Formalities complete, they boarded the jet. While the exterior was fairly anonymous, the interior was a study in opulence and comfort. It was clear that no expense had been spared in fitting it out. The large seats in the main cabin were upholstered in buttery-soft cream leather, and were as comfortable as a feather bed. Highly polished light wood shone and marble gleamed in the bright lights, and the light-coloured carpets were woven with the prince's personal insignia. The overall impression was one of immaculate taste and the wealth to indulge it.

After a brief meeting with the captain, Alex made sure that Beth and Stacie were safely installed in their chosen seats, then went to have a quick word with Ros, Conor and Bax, who had already been waiting at the ultra-modern air terminal when the three of them arrived. Once the plane had taken off, the real work would begin.

When they were in the air and well on their way, Stacie unfastened her seatbelt. "How does Alex come to know the prince?"

"They met at Sandhurst."

"The Royal Military Academy?" That would make sense, given Alex's bearing and natural air of command.

Beth nodded. "They went through officer training together." She looked across the cabin to her husband, who was already deep in conversation with Ros, Bax and Conor. There was a map spread out on the table between them—Alex was briefing them on his plan to rescue Cam.

"A good few years ago, before he started the business where I worked for him, Alex was in partnership with Cam in Spectrum Security. The prince's brother was one of their clients," Beth explained. "He was a diplomat in a neighbouring and somewhat less peaceful country, and Spectrum provided an escort for his son—to take him to and from school, among other things.

"I'll spare you the details," she continued, "but the prince's nephew and Alex were kidnapped and held for ransom. While he was held captive, Alex was very badly hurt. I wanted to be here in case… well, in case it brings back some old memories for him." She shifted slightly in her seat and visibly winced.

"Are you all right?"

Beth gave her a smile—the kind one sub gave another. "Shall we just say that before we left, he tried to tell me again that I wasn't coming on this trip? When I insisted I was, he made his feelings on the subject known in no uncertain terms."

"You mean he…?" Stacie sent a meaningful glance in the direction of Beth's seat.

Beth nodded. "And that's only part of it. After he spanked me, he told me I still wasn't coming… for a month! He said that orgasm denial is the only real punishment that works with me. He's right, of course.

"Try not to worry too much, Stacie—if anyone can get Cam out of there, it's Alex. He knows what he's doing, and he knows the region. Now, why don't you and I prove we're not just here to improve the scenery, and work out how best we can help when they get back to the plane with Cam?"

Alex looked over at his wife—she was engrossed in what appeared to be a fairly serious conversation with Stacie. From the gestures she was making, his best guess was that she was working out a strategy for what the two women would do once he and his team returned to the plane, hopefully with Cam, and hopefully with him still alive and kicking. Bloody woman—he loved her so fucking much. A wry grin turned up one side of his mouth as a thought occurred to him… if this op turned up in one of her damn novels, he'd give her a session in the playroom he'd make sure she never forgot.

He turned his attention back to the three people who would be his team leaders.

"Okay," he said, "Let's get started. The good news is that Cam hasn't been moved since we last confirmed his location, so the mission plan is good to go. Ros, we're going to need your off-road skills…"

During the next couple of hours, Alex went through

every detail of his plan, over and over again, until the three people who would be accompanying him knew it as well as he did. When the plane landed, they'd be met by the other members of the team, who would then also be briefed on the mission plan.

Those individuals were responsible for liaising with the prince's people with regard to transport and weapons. Although Alex hoped that it wouldn't come down to a firefight, they needed to be prepared for the worst—there was no telling what might await them, but they were all professional enough to adapt and deal with any change in the operation.

Once the briefing was done, all they could do was try to rest and relax for the remainder of the flight—make the most of the downtime before they had to hit the ground running. Alex's attention turned to his wife. Beth was asleep in one of the large, comfortable seats. She'd sent Stacie to sleep in the luxurious bedroom. When the prince's personal physician, accompanied by a member of his medical team, boarded as soon as the plane landed, that bedroom would be transformed into a temporary sickbay.

The gnawing sensation returned to his gut, that Beth and Stacie shouldn't have accompanied them, but at the same time he was glad his wife was there. Sight of her kept him grounded in reality, in what really mattered. With a brief acknowledgement to the others, he went over to where she was curled up—she barely stirred when he lifted her into his arms and then sat down with her on his lap, this woman who was the other half of his soul.

Ros, Conor and Bax spread themselves out around the cabin, each of them settling down to get some much-needed rest in preparation for what lay ahead. The flight attendant dimmed the lighting and one by one, in quick succession they all fell asleep, until Alex was the only one left awake, with only his thoughts and fears for company.

The last time he'd been in this part of the world—not their destination country, but another close by—it had left him with memories that had haunted him for years. The woman he cradled so tenderly in his arms had been with him on every step out of that hellish nightmare, and without fail had given him her strength when he'd needed it.

His plan to get Cam out had to work—it had to. They'd been friends and comrades for so long; they were closer than brothers, and he was damned if he'd leave the stupid bastard to die alone in a foreign country.

If he wasn't dead already…

Alex closed his eyes. For now, his wife needed him to be strong and confident. She had faith in him and he would do his utmost to ensure that that faith wasn't misplaced.

Though he'd been the last to fall asleep, Alex was still the first to wake a handful of hours later. He took advantage of the calm before the storm to kiss his wife, momentarily regretful that the luxuriously equipped jet didn't have a second bedroom to which he could have taken her.

Still, out of all of them, Stacie was the one who would have gained most benefit from being able to sleep—it would stop her fretting her way through the flight. He, Ros, Conor and Bax, thanks to their military training, were all able to sleep whenever they could, wherever they could, and Beth would always sleep best wherever he was.

A soft sigh alerted him to Stacie's return to the main cabin—she was standing at the opening of the passage-way that led aft, and was looking at him with a longing that instinct told him wasn't directed at him.

Rather, it was a longing for the way he held Beth so close to him, a longing for Cam to hold her the same way. He didn't know what had gone wrong between the other couple any more than Beth did, but the look on Stacie's face confirmed that Cam was the instigator of the rift and also told him that, in spite of what Cam might think, the matter remained far from resolved. It seemed that Beth might be right after all.

"We'll get him out, Stacie," he assured her with quiet conviction.

She managed a small smile. "I know. I can't help but wonder, though, what if he's already—"

"He isn't," Alex cut in harshly, not wanting her thoughts to go where his had already been—it wasn't a good place. She had to have hope—they all did, otherwise they might as well head back home without even touching down.

A short time later the plane began losing altitude for its

final approach. The landing itself was smooth, and when the jet came to a gentle halt at the terminal, the door opened and there was an eruption of noise and activity.

Beth took Stacie to a corner of the cabin, well out of the way of the eight or ten men who had just boarded the plane. Like her husband, they were all dressed in desert camouflage battledress uniforms, devoid of any insignia or other identifying marks.

This was an Alex she'd never seen before—a man who was a virtual stranger to her. He was all military now, very much the commanding officer, with a presence that set him apart from the others, even Bax and Conor. She shook her head, trying to clear it of the thoughts that all of a sudden made her mouth dry.

"Are you all right?"

She looked at Stacie and managed a small uncertain smile. "I've never seen him quite like this before," she admitted quietly. "I knew he was a captain, on his way to being promoted to major when he resigned his commission, according to Cam, but that part of his life was over before we ever met. When he told me about his past, I never expected to see him have to relive it."

She continued to watch as Alex allocated assignments, telling each person what was expected of them. Several large canvas bags had been brought on board by the new arrivals. When they were opened, several facts hit Beth all at once. Weapons like those were something she'd only ever seen in the movies and on television, and had never imagined in her worst nightmares that she might see them in real life. Certainly never in Alex's hands, ready to be used with extreme prejudice. The knife he'd used in the fight with Ewan Underwood was one thing, but this was something else entirely.

Oh, she'd watched him shoot clay pigeons with his Purdey shotgun more times than she could remember, but that was a country gentleman's pursuit—not a matter of life and death. As she watched him check the vicious-looking military-standard firearms, it dawned on Beth that her husband, the man who made love to her so tenderly, the Dom who turned her into a quivering mass of sobbing sexual need on a regular basis, whose collar she wore with pride and at whose feet she would willingly kneel, was a trained killer. She'd known he was, of course she had, but to see it, really see it for the first time…

Cold and unable to breathe, she wrapped her arms around her body tightly, determined not to go to pieces.

"Beth."

She looked at Stacie again, felt the other woman's hand rubbing her back in a gesture of comfort.

"He's still Alex," Stacie went on quietly. "He's still your husband, the man you love. You already know what's he's capable of, what he had to do last year to protect both of you. This is no different. It's just clothes."

Just clothes. That was it. He'd been wearing normal clothes when he'd saved them both from Underwood's revenge, when he'd fought the man to the death. The only thing that was different was the way he was dressed.

Slowly Beth began to breathe normally again, regaining control over her respiration and her pounding heart. "I know. I'm sorry," she whispered. "I don't know what came over me. Having hysterics won't help anyone."

Out of the corner of his eye, Alex caught sight of the quiet drama being played out between the two subs. On seeing his wife's reaction to the array of firearms and other weapons, he wanted nothing more than to go to her and give her the reassurance she needed, but he'd then seen Stacie's lips move and her arms go around Beth. Maybe they should have remained in the UK, but the truth was that he needed to keep Beth close to him, he always had, and he was glad that Stacie was there to do what he could not.

Having assigned the teams and checked that the munitions they'd brought on board matched the list he'd given the prince, Alex strapped on the combat vest and began to assemble his gear—including his sidearm, spare ammunition and the all-important comms equipment. It was a long time since he'd last had to prep for a mission, but it seemed that muscle memory lasted forever. Just as well, given the circumstances. Even the combat boots had a comforting familiarity about them.

Satisfied that everyone knew exactly what they had to do, the urgency with which their goal had to be accomplished, and the stringent requirement not to create an international shitstorm for both the prince and the UK government in the process, Alex braced himself for what, for him personally, was the most difficult part of the mission—saying goodbye to his wife.

"Listen to me, love. Depending on how long this takes, there'll have to be crew changes but there will be a full complement on board the plane throughout, ready for take-off. The captain will let you know when we're on our way back and close to boarding. When he does that, I want you and Stacie to be in your seats, seatbelts fastened and ready to go by the time we board. I know you'll both want to know about Cam, but that has to wait till we're airborne. Will you do that for me?"

Her arms around him, Beth stood on tiptoe, so that she could whisper in his ear. "Yes, Master."

When he heard the words, Alex knew that he would have her complete obedience in the matter. Oh, she teased him, tested him and provoked him, but when the chips were down he could count on her to do what he needed her to do.

"Master?"

"Yes, sweetheart?"

"Bring him back. And please… be careful." She looked at him with eyes full of love, and the fear she was trying so hard not to show. "Stay safe. I don't know what I'd do—"

He placed a finger over her lips, silencing her immediately. "Don't even think it, love. Everything's going to be all right. Trust me."

She did—he could see it in the absolute devotion with which she looked at him. He always saw it. How had it taken so long for them to truly find each other?

"I do." She reached to touch a sweet, tender kiss to the corner of his mouth. "We'll be ready."

His eyes took in his sweet submissive, every detail of her from her glorious hair to her feet shod in practical boots, cataloguing her and committing her to memory for the hours that lay ahead. In all the time they'd been together, as employer and employee, Dom and submissive, husband and wife, she'd always had his back, just as he'd had hers. The fact that she was doing it now, under such testing circumstances, told him yet again how lucky he was to have such an incredible woman in his life.

"And don't think I don't know why you were so insistent on coming along on this jolly."

He saw the memories in her eyes, the pain she'd felt then because of the pain he'd been in, knew that whatever happened in the future, she would always stand by him. He knew he wasn't worthy, but he'd never stop trying to be.

"I couldn't let you be here alone, Alex. Not here."

He held her to him, awareness of her coursing through his body like a river in full flood. He had just one more thing to say, one more thing to do.

"Listen, Beth, and don't argue with me—not about this. You and Stacie should be perfectly safe here, but if the shit hits the fan and I think there's any danger to you, I'll get a message to the captain. He's under strict orders to get you out of here and back to England. No arguments, Beth."

He could see that she didn't like it, just as he expected, but he could also see that she accepted it. And that just left one more thing to do…

Alex looked at his left hand, at the wedding ring he'd never taken off since Beth had put it there—just months ago, but at that moment it felt like a lifetime, the lifetime he wanted with her. Slowly, reluctantly, not wanting to do it but knowing he had to, he removed it from his finger and pressed it into his wife's palm.

"Look after this for me," he told her, his voice husky with emotion. "I don't want to risk losing it out there."

CHAPTER SIXTEEN

More days had passed, one blurring into the next, always the same routine… until the day they shackled him to the wall and it wasn't a whip that streaked fire across his back but a baseball bat that slammed into his ribs. His only thought then, as he struggled to breathe, was to wonder how long he had before they graduated to something even harder.

And after that… Cam knew only too well what the possibilities were, just as he knew with ironclad certainty that his captors would have no reservations about using whatever they had access to. Metal, water and electricity could be a lethal combination.

There was only so much punishment that a body could take. When they returned him to his cell this time, Cam stretched out carefully on the straw-filled sacking that passed as a mattress. Every movement, every breath was agony now. His medical training, along with the previous firsthand experience of the aftermath of hand-to-hand combat, was telling him that he had a couple of cracked ribs to go with the lacerations, contusions and insect bites that peppered his body. Not that any of it mattered now.

The probability was that he was going to die in this hellhole, and it was going to be slow, bloody and painful. Their treatment of him was no longer about extracting information—they weren't even going through the pretence of asking him questions. No, it was now simply about using him as a means of venting their hatred of all things Western… he was certain of it. He hadn't been put in front of a video camera and ordered to read out a prepared piece of propaganda at gunpoint. There had been no ransom demand. He was there simply as their whipping boy, until they tired of their deadly game and took it to its inevitable conclusion.

And when he was finally released from this living hell—a release that would only come with death—it would be without seeing Stacie again, without making love to her again, without telling her how he felt about her and how much she meant to him. In spite of it all, though, he was still convinced he'd done the right thing in pushing her away—if he hadn't, she'd only be wondering and worrying about him now… grieving for him eventually… wasting the best years of her life on a man who didn't deserve her because he wasn't good enough for her.

He'd done the right thing.

Cam had spent most of his life alone in the darkness, apart from the all-too-brief time that Stacie had been a part of his life, the centre of his universe. The darkness had claimed him again, and soon it would keep him forever.

"Talk about overkill, Cam—you didn't have to go to these lengths to persuade me to come back."

Cam gave a half-hearted laugh. He was crazy, hallucinating or dying, and he didn't really care which one it was. If he had the choice, all things considered, he'd go for the last, then all this shit would be over and done with.

"Fuck off, Lombard—can't you let a man die in peace?" he muttered darkly. With an effort he turned away from the annoying voice and the background cacophony of more shouting and intermittent gunfire, with the odd explosion thrown in for good measure. For a delusion, it was entirely too realistic.

"No, he can't, numbnuts, and if you think I came all this way and put my career on the line to drag your sorry-arse *corpse* back to Blighty, you can damn well think again, Fraser. You die on me, and I'll bloody well kill you myself."

Ah, the barbed wit that was the business end of Ros Edwards. He was surely on the way to hell and no mistake—there was no way she'd be standing at the door, dressed in desert camouflage, providing cover with a lethal-looking assault rifle. Just as there was no way that Alex Lombard, in similar attire, was holstering his sidearm to deal with the shackle on Cam's ankle. "And I love you too, Edwards." He gave a short bark of humourless laughter that sent shards of agony through his chest. A man was liable to say anything when he was hallucinating.

Or dying.

"What the hell are you doing here, Alex?" He wondered if a hallucination would actually own up to being a hallucination.

"Rescuing you, you bloody idiot. It's time to go home, Cam."

Home. A stifled sob almost choked him. He'd had a home for a while. Her name was Stacie, but even if this delusion turned out to be reality and he really was going home, he still wouldn't deserve her. She was far better off without him.

When Alex pulled him to his feet, the flames across his back banished the maudlin self-pity. The pain from that and his protesting ribs drove him to his knees.

"Christ, Cam, what the hell have they done to you?"

"What does it fucking look like?" he snarled, his breath catching again. Physical agony and good manners did not make natural bedfellows.

The world swam around him in giddying circles as he found himself draped across Alex's shoulders in a somewhat inelegant but effective fireman's lift. More pain exploded in his torso.

"We're getting out of here right now." Alex's voice was harsh with determination.

"Then fucking well put me down, I can walk."

The assertion proved to be the cue for Ros to join in, with a selection of profanities colourful enough to make a squaddie blush. "That's great, Cam," she added, "but right now, we need to run!"

Breathing through the torment, Cam was only vaguely aware of his changing surroundings—the rubble-strewn corridor with stone walls that was the route to the room where he'd been tortured and to which memory every muscle in his body contracted in Pavlovian response, the sounds of gunfire and explosions, now getting louder and louder… the acrid stench of conflict that fired up memories best left in the distant past. Then they were outside in the night, lit up by the flashes of more deafening blasts. There were more voices he recognised too—Bax and Conor, and members of the team he'd last seen boarding a helicopter and never expected to see again. All yelling, all fighting to be heard above the madness of violent combat.

"This is going to hurt, Cam."

Not enough warning. Cam grunted sharply when, unprepared, he landed on his side in the back of one of three armoured Land Rovers. Pain from his grating ribs strafed his nervous system yet again, while the impact drove all the air from his lungs. Along with a couple of the other guys, Alex got in the back with him—he could only hope that Ros, being the miracle worker behind the wheel that she was, could get them out of there without any loss of life.

Oh God, if anyone had been hurt because of him…

The vehicle set off at speed, lurching roughly over the

uneven ground, each jolt putting his body through more suffering. As he lost consciousness, the last thing Cam felt was Alex examining his injuries and the last thing he heard was his old friend telling him to hold on…

"They're on their way."

Stacie looked towards the front of the plane. Beth had just emerged from the flight deck behind the doctor, and she wasn't smiling.

"Is everyone—"

"By some miracle they all got out. The team's all pretty much unharmed, no serious injuries, although they've been banged up a bit, but they're not out of the woods yet. It's going to take them a good few hours to get back here." Beth started towards her. "Stacie, Cam's been hurt. They didn't say how badly, just that he needs medical attention, and the sooner the better."

Emotions all over the place, Stacie sat down in a state of shock. The fact that Cam was still alive was a huge source of relief and she was duly grateful, but then the pendulum swung in the opposite direction when the full impact of Beth's words struck home. Her imagination went wild, and not in a good way.

All of a sudden, it was getting hard to breathe—Stacie closed her eyes and concentrated, breathing through the emotional pain as Cam had taught her to breathe through physical pain. She was not going to panic and get hysterical—that wasn't her, and even if it were, it was the last thing anyone needed right now. She felt Beth's arm go around her shoulders, giving support that she really needed at that point, just as she had comforted Beth before the team left.

"It's going to be all right, Stacie," Beth told her. "They'll be here before we know it, so I think the best thing we can do is help to make sure everything's ready."

They'd already done that and several times over, but Stacie knew Beth was right. With something else to focus on, it would be easier to deal with the next few hours, because heaven knew, the last few had been in danger of sending her stir crazy. She managed a hesitant smile. "Beth, next time we go on one of these rescue missions, remind me to bring a good book."

It felt good to laugh, even if only for a few moments.

On her way back from the bathroom, Stacie glanced through the bedroom door… and stopped dead in her tracks. The doctor—a handsome man of Middle Eastern appearance, who spoke impeccable English—and his assistant had finished setting the cabin up as a medical facility. Seeing it as such, knowing it would be needed for the man she loved, made Stacie's blood run cold.

No, I am not going to panic. One thing she'd learned during her relationship with Cam was the value of self-control. She'd learned from his example and from what he'd taught her about herself. She drew in a slow, steady breath and squared her shoulders. She could do this… she *would* do this. She had her pride, and she'd show Cam, even though he didn't want to see her again.

The time passed by painfully slowly. A new crew came on board for the return journey. The medical team moved around the cabin, talking quietly in Arabic, ensuring that access from the aircraft door to the bedroom was unimpeded.

Stacie and Beth tried not to think too much about what would soon happen. They tidied cushions that didn't need tidying, drank what seemed like gallons of coffee, courtesy of the members of the cabin crew who came and went, wandered aimlessly through the jet, looking out of the windows at a view that never changed. Sleep was impossible. Stacie decided that when she arrived back home, she was going to take up yoga or meditation… something that would help her to relax better.

"Excuse me, ladies." It was the captain. "Mr. Lombard left instructions that you were to be informed when their arrival was imminent. He and his party are approximately ten minutes away from the airfield."

Beth and Stacie looked at one another: this was it. Stacie took a firm hold on her self-control and moved to take her seat. She chose one that would give her a good view of the route from the plane's door through the cabin to the passageway that led to the rear of the jet. Beth sat next to her, and once they'd secured their seatbelts, she felt her friend cover her hand and give it a squeeze.

"Whatever you need," Beth said, "I'm here."

Stacie nodded, afraid to speak in case she betrayed too much of what she was feeling. It amazed her that Beth could be so concerned about her, when the other woman must surely be just as worried about her husband as Stacie was about Cam. She turned her hand palm uppermost and responded with a squeeze of her own.

A few minutes later, controlled chaos erupted through the door. Stacie's breath froze in her throat as she watched Alex stride through cabin, half-carrying, half-dragging another man. He had one arm around the man's waist, and was holding on to the arm that was draped limply around his neck.

Her brain was telling her it could only be Cam but she didn't want it to be him… it couldn't possibly be him. This man was barely conscious, had been to hell and beyond. No, Cam couldn't have been through whatever this man had gone through. Body beset with sympathetic pain, expression giving away nothing of the horror she felt, Stacie could only stare after the two men as they disappeared down the passageway. She was scarcely aware of the way Beth was squeezing her hand, as if she were trying to force every last drop of blood from Stacie's fingers.

The doctor was right behind Alex and Cam, followed closely by Ros. She looked as scruffy and unkempt as Alex did, with smears of dirt on her face and clothes, her hair—previously gathered up in a short practical style—was all over the place. It was plain to see that wherever they'd got to, whatever they'd done to get Cam out, it hadn't been a walk in the park.

The plane began to move.

The jet quickly reached its cruising altitude. As soon as she could, Stacie unfastened her seatbelt and dashed for the bedroom to which Cam had been taken, leaving Ros sound asleep, and Alex and Beth to their emotional reunion. She was just about over the initial shock of seeing the condition Cam was in when he was brought on board. Now all she wanted to do was help.

"Get her the fuck out of here!"

Stacie froze in the doorway, a deer in the headlights of Cam's undiluted anger and pain, his groan of agony and the sight of his dirty, bloodied chest and the cuts and bruises to his face and torso. Naked, he was lying on his side on the bed with the doctor and his assistant by his side, and what was abundantly clear was that he didn't want her there.

"Come with me."

Her steps were stiff and wooden as she followed the lead of Beth's quiet voice, the other woman's hands gentle but firm on her arms as she shepherded Stacie away from the door. Stacie was only dimly aware of Alex passing them in the aisle, heading towards his friend, and had no real recollection of how she came to be sitting in the lounge with Beth pressing a glass of cognac into hands that were as numb as her bludgeoned emotions.

"Drink this," Beth insisted. "Try not to let it get to you. He's been through a lot, things we can't imagine, he's in pain and he doesn't know what he's saying."

Stacie gulped down a mouthful of the fiery spirit. She barely felt the burn when it hit her stomach. "He knows," she countered bleakly. "Alex was right. I shouldn't have come. I just wanted to know… to be sure he was all right."

"He will be, Stacie. Cam's as tough as Alex—he wouldn't let them get the better of him. I know it looks bad now, but once he's been cleaned up and he's rested, he'll make a full recovery, I'm sure of it."

Tears she couldn't hold back began to fall down Stacie's cheeks. Now that the numbness was starting to wear off, the memory of what she saw of Cam's injuries was coming back. "What did they do to him? And why? What did they want?"

"I don't know, but you saw—the doctor's with him now. They'll give him something for the pain, get him cleaned up and patched up, and then he'll probably sleep for most of the flight. You should sleep too, try not to think about it."

"How can I not think about…?" Her voice tailed off to a whisper under the scramble of disjointed thoughts going through her mind. "The baby. You didn't tell Alex…?"

"No, I promised I wouldn't. He won't say anything to Cam because there's nothing he can say."

"I'm sorry, Beth." More stupid tears. "I should never have put you in that position—"

"Hush, it's all right. There are some things that the men don't need to know."

"Such as?"

Neither of them had noticed Alex's silent return to the main lounge—he'd gone to check on Cam but was now standing a few feet away, arms folded across his chest and with a face like thunder to accompany his glacial tone. Given the military-style dress and the evidence of the battle to rescue Cam, his appearance was all the more intimidating.

Beth stood up and faced her husband, her chin lifted in a show of stubbornness. "The relative merits of one designer handbag compared to another, of course. How's Cam?"

"Beth, don't. Don't even *think* you can divert my attention by asking about Cam. What don't I need to know?"

"Alex, this isn't the time or the place—"

"Perhaps so—for now. But if you think for one moment that I'm going to let this slide, sweetheart, you are sadly mistaken. We are not done with this conversation." Having made his position clear, Alex let his attitude ease up a little. "Dr. Nassar's working on Cam now. He's had some pain relief, they're getting him something to eat, and then he's going to sleep—the doctor's going to make sure of that. For now, though, there's nothing we can do apart from wait." He rubbed the back of his neck. "All I can suggest is that you take a leaf out of Ros' book and get some rest." He glanced towards the exhausted woman who was still asleep in one of the large comfortable seats.

Beth moved closer to her husband, lifted a hand to cradle his cheek. "You look like hell," she said without preamble. "Stacie, will you be all right for a few minutes, while I help Alex get cleaned up?"

"Of course. I'll be fine—you go."

Stacie watched them leave, realising belatedly, as she heard Beth asking her husband if he was all right, that she hadn't yet thanked him for what he'd done. Still, there was an eight-hour flight ahead of them—plenty of time to express her gratitude.

An hour or so later, the doctor came into the main cabin. Stacie instinctively reached for Beth's hand, while Alex went to meet him. Ros too was instantly awake.

"How is he, Dr. Nassar?"

"Better than he looks, Mr. Lombard. He's dehydrated and undernourished, as I'm sure you're aware. His visible injuries are not as bad as they look—they are mostly superficial, although he has sustained fractures to his ribs. With what they appear to have done to him, internal injuries are a possibility, but the indicators for that so far are negative. Were it otherwise, I'd recommend turning back for immediate hospitalisation. He's on a drip now to rehydrate him, with intravenous analgesia for the pain and antibiotics to counter any infection from his wounds and the insect bites.

"He's also had a little to eat, we've cleaned him up, and he's now sleeping, which frankly is the best thing for him at the present time. I would like him to be checked up in a hospital—x-rays and so forth. To that end, His Highness has arranged for an ambulance to meet us when we land, to convey Mr. Fraser to a private clinic. His Highness said that in the circumstances, it was the least he could do."

"*Shokran.* Thank you, Dr. Nassar."

"May I see him? Please?"

Coming to stand by the side of Alex, Stacie couldn't wait any longer. She'd listened intently to the doctor, but she wanted… no, *needed* to reassure herself that Cam was all right.

"As I said, Miss Matheson, he's asleep now, so he won't be able to talk to you."

Given the vitriol of his earlier outburst, it was probably better for her that he couldn't. "That doesn't matter. I'd just like to sit with him for a while, if I may?"

With a growing sense of trepidation, Stacie pushed the door open, trying to make as little noise as possible. The doctor's assistant, who had been sitting with Cam, rose and gave her an understanding smile. As he passed her on his way out, he whispered that he would be outside if she needed anything.

For all that it was like looking at a stranger, Stacie instinctively recognised the battered form of the man she still thought of as her Master—even though it was the last thing he wanted. His breathing was shallow and slightly raspy, possibly due to the damage to his ribs that the doctor had mentioned. His hair was scruffy and dishevelled and the three weeks' worth of beard made him look like a stranger, but it was his general condition that broke her heart. The weight loss was more than merely noticeable, not to mention the bruises, the patched-up cuts, and what looked like a multitude of insect bites. One thing was for sure—the doctor's definition of *superficial* differed vastly from hers.

It was all her fault. She'd done this to him. He'd gone to that place because of *her.*

"Oh Cam," she whispered, taking a seat beside the bed. "Would it have made any difference if I'd told you how I feel?"

She slipped one hand under his and began to stroke the back of his fingers. The nails were broken, the cuticles damaged and bloody… in spite of its condition, it was still the strong hand of her Master—a hand that had taught her of the pleasure to be found in pain, in giving up control, in trusting and loving a man such as Cam.

The memories, the feelings… all of it was overwhelming. On impulse, she raised his hand to kiss the back of it, and then touched her forehead gently to the scraped knuckles.

Please let him be all right.

If only things could have been different. She remembered his reaction to her presence at the conference centre, and the strict instruction not to do anything like that again. How the hell would he have reacted to her being here if they'd still been a couple? She probably would have needed a soft cushion to sit on for a month at least. She'd have given anything to have that, in place of the venomous words he'd spat at her a short time ago.

If they were still a couple, she'd have the right to be there and stay with him—she'd watch over him until the plane landed and she'd go to the hospital with him. When he was discharged, she'd drive him home and take care of him until he was fully recovered.

Reality, though, dictated otherwise. Although the doctor had said that he'd be unconscious for a while yet, she couldn't risk staying much longer in case he woke up unexpectedly. She'd taken his rejection twice already—she didn't want to be on the receiving end a third time.

Having stayed for as long as she dared, very slowly Stacie stood up, her eyes fixed on Cam as she did so, drinking him in for what felt like the last time. Her heart ached to take care of him as he'd taken care of her when she had the flu, but that just wasn't going to happen. In a few short hours, the plane would land, he'd be whisked off to hospital… and she'd never see him again. At least she'd had this, though the circumstances couldn't be much worse. She bent to kiss his cheek.

"Goodbye, Master."

Two words—that was all it took to shatter her heart into a million razor-sharp fragments. It would never be whole again. A few steps took her to the door. She opened it, and walked away from everything she'd ever wanted.

Had she stayed a little longer, she might have heard the low groan that Cam gave in his sleep. She might even have imagined that the single word he moaned was her name.

By the time the plane landed, Alex and Ros had cleaned up properly and changed back into civilian clothes. Apart from a few visible cuts and bruises, no one would have suspected that they'd been doing anything other than making a brief business trip out of the country.

The Customs and Immigration formalities were, of necessity, brief—the ambulance was waiting to take Cam to the private clinic. Alex accompanied him, which left Beth and Stacie to make their way back to Winterleigh in the Range Rover. On arriving there, Stacie saw no reason to delay her own departure for London and home.

"I need to go back to work anyway," she explained to Beth as she stowed her bags in her own car. "Please, would you do something for me?"

"Of course, anything. Are you sure you won't stay another few days?"

She shook her head. "I can't, Beth. I know you think he didn't mean what he said on the plane, but I believe he did. Please… would you just let me know how he's doing—when he's all right?"

Beth gave her a hug. "You know I will. And Stacie, you're always welcome here, no matter what."

Yes, she knew that, just as she knew that it was highly unlikely she'd ever again see the beautiful house and the people who owned it. This time, it really was goodbye.

CHAPTER SEVENTEEN

"What the *hell* were you thinking?"

Alex looked up from the papers he was reading, to see Cam standing in the doorway to his office. The other man had been staying at Winterleigh since his discharge from the clinic a few days ago. He had to admit that his friend was looking a lot better already, although the man could still stand to regain a little more weight.

It didn't stop him spoiling for a fight, though. This sounded like it was going to be the confrontation Alex had been expecting. He very carefully set the document down on his desk. "What the hell was I thinking about what?"

"Beth and Stacie—on the plane. *Especially* Stacie. You *know* we're no longer involved."

"Yes, I know," Alex acknowledged calmly. He indicated the chair on the opposite side of the desk. "Do you want to sit down before you fall down?"

"I'm fine." In spite of his declaration, Cam pushed himself away from the doorframe and took up the invitation. "So?"

Alex gave a humourless bark of laughter and sighed. "They were safe—they stayed on the plane throughout."

"They shouldn't have been there in the first place!"

"You try telling that to your sub, Cam—"

"She's not my bloody sub. Will you get that through your thick skull?"

Unruffled by his friend's outburst, Alex quirked an eyebrow. "Are you sure about that?"

"Yes, I'm fucking sure. She was hurt because of me. She's safer without me in her life. I had no choice."

The statement took Alex back almost a year and a half, when Cam had urged him to send Beth away for her own safety while they resolved the situation with the late—*very* late—Ewan Underwood. The man was nothing if not consistent, Alex had to grant him that.

"Anyway, I didn't come here for a therapy session, Alex." Even though he'd only just sat down, Cam stood up again. "Thanks for putting me up, but I need to get back to London and back on the job."

Alex knew it was no good arguing—all he could do was try to make it a little easier for his friend. "Stay for lunch and I'll give you a ride back to town," he offered.

Cam shook his head. "Thanks, Alex, but I need to get going. I've called a cab to take me to the station—with luck I can be at Waterloo before one."

"Cam—"

"It's okay, Alex… I'm okay."

Beth frowned. "He's gone back to London already? Without saying goodbye?"

"He's a grown man, sweetheart. He doesn't have to answer to anyone."

She flopped onto the seat vacated half an hour earlier by the man about whom they were talking. Her mouth compressed into a thin line, and then she gave a strangled squeal of frustration.

"What's the matter now? Plot not going well?"

She gave her husband one of her looks. "The plot in my book is going fine, thank you very much—at least there, people do what I want them to do!"

Alex sat back with a long-suffering sigh. "You're doing the fairy godmother thing again—put the wand down and back away slowly. You can't fix the world."

"But this is Cam and Stacie!"

He stood up and held out his hand. "Come with me—I think we'd better discuss this somewhere more comfortable."

With her hand enclosed in her husband's, Beth accompanied him to the family room, where he sat down on the sofa and pulled her down beside him.

"Beth, don't interfere. You have to let them work it out for themselves."

"And if they never work it out? Alex, they belong together!"

"Don't interfere!"

She looked at Alex as if he were a complete stranger. "And if that mugger hadn't *interfered*? If I hadn't been attacked… would we be here, now, like this?"

"That's different—"

Beth slowly shook her head. "It's not so different, Alex. I'd been working for you for three years, and in all that time I had no idea that you viewed me as anything other than your assistant—and even if I had, I couldn't have done anything about it because I'd have been scared of being wrong and having to leave my job… and you. But you… you could have done something but you didn't, not until I needed help. Cam and Stacie need help, Alex, otherwise they'll never—"

"Beth, they have to find their own way. Leave it!"

She pressed her lips together. What she was about to do went against everything that she believed in. "I can't, Alex," she said quietly. She closed her eyes briefly, trying to marshal her thoughts. "You already know I've been keeping something from you. Stacie swore me to secrecy, but I can't just stand by while they throw everything away. Not after what they've both gone through."

Alex's silence drew her gaze back to him.

"Both? Is this to do with the conversation I interrupted aboard the plane?" His expression was as grave as the tone of his voice.

She'd known he wouldn't miss that—he never missed anything. "Both," Beth confirmed softly, "and yes, it is. When I bumped into Stacie and we had lunch together—

the day we found out about Cam—I got the feeling, while we were talking, that there was something wrong. Although she was reluctant to tell me, she didn't take much persuading either, and then she made me promise not to say anything to you or Cam about it."

Alex wrapped his arms around her. "I knew something was going on."

And he'd been giving her a chance to come clean about it. "I'm sorry, Alex. I wanted to tell you, but I couldn't break my word, not then, and then we got word about Cam. While we were waiting for you to bring him back to us, I tried to convince her to tell him but she won't."

"So what is this big secret? Tell me, Beth."

Why did Doms all have that certain tone, the one that a sub could never resist? Beth had heard Cam use it on more than one occasion, but it was her husband's voice that had the greatest impact. Even so, she still struggled to find the right words. Were there any right words? Would it affect Alex as much as it had affected her? Beth leaned her head against her husband's shoulder, needing his strength as much as she wanted to give him hers, for what she was about to tell him.

"Stacie was pregnant, Master," she whispered. "She found out when she was caught in the car bomb. It was a complete surprise, but Cam ended their relationship before she had a chance to tell him… and then a few weeks ago, she lost the baby."

Her heart ached when Alex's arms tightened around

her… giving comfort, not asking for it… *again.* She heard him curse under his breath.

"Christ, I had no idea. Is she all right?"

"She says she is, physically, but if it were me… I'd need more time to recover emotionally as well. I think she does, too. She doesn't even have Cam to share it with. Alex, wouldn't you want to know if it was me? If that happened to us?"

She felt him move, knew that he was kissing the top of her head. His voice was unusually gruff when he spoke. "Yes—but then I wouldn't be the stupid prick who pushed the woman he loved out of his life."

A few days later, Beth was on the train to London again. She had it on good authority that Cam, still recovering from the injuries to his ribs, would be at his apartment, so that was where she was heading. Amazingly, her husband hadn't tried to dissuade her from this course of action, so now she was determined to do her utmost to give one of her closest friends and the woman he loved—no matter what he said—the happy ending they deserved. *Together.*

She sighed. Doing this for characters in her books was so much easier.

A cab took her to Cam's riverside apartment. She'd been there more times than she could remember, and as Cam had a set of keys for Winterleigh, so she and Alex had the same for his place. She let herself in the main entrance and made her way up to his apartment.

The building reminded her a lot of the place Alex used to keep in the city. It was in a prime location by the river, came with a seven-figure price tag, and had all the welcoming comfort of an upmarket hotel chain. Cam really needed to find that house close to Winterleigh. He was the nearest thing to family that she and Alex had, and it would be good to have him living nearby—preferably with Stacie.

Beth glared at the door to Cam's apartment. Although she had the key, she chose instead to ring the bell.

Battle was about to commence.

"What the—Beth! Come on in, I just made coffee."

After giving him a careful hug, she followed Cam into the apartment and made herself comfortable on the sofa, while he prepared a second mug. When he came back with the drinks, she patted the seat beside her. "Come and sit down here, with me."

"Okay." Cam made himself comfortable, leaning back in the corner of the sofa with one arm resting along the back of it and his right ankle resting on his left thigh. "Something tells me you have something on your mind, angel." He sipped his coffee. "Everything okay?"

"Everything's fine, thanks, and I do have something on my mind." Beth decided to get straight to the point. It never did to prevaricate with a Dom. "It's about Stacie."

And bang, up went the man's defences. Beth felt almost physically rebuffed, but she wasn't about to let it put her off. She was a sub, and she was made of sterner stuff than that.

"Angel, I don't need to hear about Stacie. We had a brief fling, we split up—end of story."

He wasn't fooling anyone. If he no longer had any feelings for her, his reaction would have been one of indifference—if Beth had harboured any doubts that she was doing the right thing, they would have been dispelled in that moment. "Cam, you don't believe that any more than I do—so just shut up and listen. Stacie made me promise not to say anything about this to either you or Alex. I've already broken that promise in relation to my husband, and since it's something that affects *you*, I have even more reason to break it where you're concerned."

"Beth—"

"Please, Cam! Just listen to what I have to say. *Please.*" The tears were frighteningly close to the surface again. So much for thinking she'd managed to get rid of them all. "Cam, I wish there were a way to say this without hurting you, but there's something you really need to know. About Stacie."

Beth sought refuge in her coffee, trying to find the right words. She didn't want to hurt this man any more than she had to. And what she had to tell him would hurt.

"Angel, if you're trying to work out how to spare my feelings, don't—just tell me. Whatever it is, I can handle it—I'm a big boy now. What about Stacie?"

He had no idea. Beth felt a glimmer of the pain she knew was heading his way. Cam's feelings in general ran far deeper than the image he projected might suggest. She'd seen him and Stacie together, knew just how much she'd meant to him even if he'd never faced up to the fact himself. His body language now verged on the defensive, as if he were bracing himself to hear something he really didn't want to hear.

"She never had a chance to tell you, because she only found out when she was in hospital after the explosion at the conference. She needed time to deal with it herself before she spoke to you about it—to work out how best to tell you." She pressed her lips together, the words forming in her mind. Well, he said he was a big boy…

"Cam, she was pregnant. She had no idea until they told her in the hospital, and then about six weeks after you left, she had a miscarriage. She wasn't going to tell me, but I pushed her into it."

Stacie. Pregnant. Miscarriage.

Each word felt like a roundhouse punch a heavyweight boxer would have been proud of. Christ, what had he done?

An arctic chill struck through Cam's body. "Why the hell didn't she say something?" He looked at Beth's face, searching for answers.

"Think about it, Cam. She'd assured you she was on birth control—but then she got the flu and was sick, and for that period it was less effective. A few weeks later, she's told that she's pregnant, and it's the last thing she expects to hear. The news was devastating for her. She needed time to come to terms with it herself before she told you, because she had no idea how you'd react. Then you got the idea into your thick head—"

"Excuse me?"

"Alex told me what you said. You got the idea into your *thick* head that she needed protecting and the only way you could do it was by leaving her. You didn't discuss it with her, you never gave her a chance to make her own decision about it. You decided you knew best, and she had no say in the matter."

The rush of memories was overwhelming. He'd got her hurt, and then blithely made his arrangements to leave the country—got all the ducks in a row, then in cold blood he'd called the woman he loved and told her it was all over. He'd been so sure he was doing the right thing, but all he'd done was leave her at her most vulnerable.

He tried to put himself in her place. Being caught in the explosion was bad enough, but then she'd had an unplanned pregnancy thrown into her lap. She had no way of knowing how he'd react; she'd be wondering if she should have the baby, and if she did, should she keep the child? How would she cope on her own?

And then the miscarriage—weeks later. She must have decided to have the baby… and then she lost it. He couldn't even begin to imagine…

Holy shit, he'd been the biggest bastard in creation.

"Cam, I know you blame yourself for her getting hurt," Beth continued, her voice soft and full of compassion, "but it wasn't your fault. It wasn't her fault either. If you want to blame someone, blame the terrorists. Are you all right?"

Beth's gentle hand on his arm brought him back to the present… to reality. "No, I'm not all right," he admitted heavily, guilt making it difficult to speak normally. He felt like he'd never be all right again. "Do you know how far…?"

"Twelve weeks, give or take. A girl, Stacie said."

A daughter. Oh Christ, he'd had a daughter. With Stacie. "I don't deserve her, but I have to go to her, Beth—I need… *we* need to talk about this, and get everything out into the open."

"Don't be angry with her, Cam."

He took in Beth's worried expression. "It's all right, angel. There's only one person I'm angry with—it's not Stacie, and before you ask, it's not you either. It's me." He shook his head. "I should have said something. It's long overdue."

It had taken every shred of willpower Cam possessed to wait until his ribs were fully healed before he went to face his sub. For the mission that lay ahead, he needed to be at the top of his game.

Stacie was at work, still in the same job—a phone call to her office from one of his people had confirmed that. Cam could have met her there, maybe taken her out for lunch… if what they had to talk about hadn't been so important, so emotional, so personal… so painful. Instead, he'd chosen to sit in his car, fifty yards down the road from her apartment building, and wait for her to come home. Then they could talk.

If she'd let him in to talk to her.

It was a hell of a big fucking if.

He checked the time again—the fifth time in the last fifteen minutes. Her office would have closed about twenty minutes ago—if she'd left on time and not taken any detours, she'd probably be arriving soon.

Cam forced his hands to relax—the stretch of his fingers, after they'd been clenched tightly for so long, made his knuckles ache. This was going to be the most important conversation of his life, and he had no idea where the hell he was going to start. He'd been wrong, so wrong, to end things between them. Stacie had haunted his thoughts every day while he'd been away. And he didn't even want to think about the way he'd rejected her on the plane back to the UK. He'd been a complete bastard towards her and he didn't deserve to have even a chance to make things right.

Movement down the road caught his eye—someone was walking from the direction of the Tube station. Even at that distance, he knew it was her—he recognised her walk. She had a bag over one shoulder and a carrier of groceries in the other hand. When she reached the steps in front of her building she ran up them, towards the main entrance.

Christ, she was a sight for sore eyes. Young and pretty and all the good things, the best things he'd ever had in his life. And the mother of his lost child, his shame reminded him. Would she ever forgive him? Did he even have the right to ask? He closed his eyes. He was a fool to ask, the answer was a foregone conclusion, but he had to try, he had to find out if there was any chance that she might let him back into her life.

Who dares wins, *right?*

The door closed behind her. Now he had to wait for another resident to arrive, so that he could slip into the building behind them. Announcing his presence via the intercom would only give her the opportunity to marshal her defences. Of course she could still deny him entrance once he reached her front door.

I have to try.

He let three people go in before he decided he was ready. He looked at the flowers laid on the seat beside him—no, they were too obvious, but the other item, the one that was small enough for him to conceal it in his pocket… if the conversation went in such a way that it became evident that she wouldn't want it, she'd never know he had it. With a deep breath, he got out of the car and pulled on his jacket—she'd always liked the charcoal-grey suit, black shirt and black silk tie. Finally out of reasons to procrastinate any further, he started the longest walk of his life.

I have to try.

Ascending the stairs to her apartment was almost like an out-of-body experience for Cam, as if someone else was in control of his actions and he was looking down from above. Someone else lifted his hand… someone else's finger pressed the doorbell.

And if she looked through the spy hole in the door, she'd never let him in.

I have to try.

A chain, a bolt, the click of a secure lock. Cam heard them all and tried not to think of the time he'd added those security measures. The door slowly opened. In the widening gap, he saw a shoulder, an arm, a fall of honey-gold waves… and storm-grey eyes that quickly hid whatever emotions were going through her, as the woman he loved beyond all reason stepped back, opening the door wider.

"Beth's talked to you, hasn't she?" she said quietly. "You'd better come in."

I have to try.

It was only a matter of time. Realistically, Stacie knew that Cam would find out the truth sooner or later—it was simply too big a secret for it not to come out at some point. She blamed herself for telling Beth in the first place—if she couldn't keep her own secret from Beth, how could she expect Beth to keep it from a man like her husband… a man like Cam? Stacie wondered exactly how much Cam knew.

"Please, sit down," she invited, extending a hand towards one of the large sofas. "Would you like a drink? I was just about to make some coffee, but I have wine if you'd prefer that."

He cleared his throat. "Coffee will be fine, thanks. White, one sugar."

"I remember," she said without emotion. "I won't be long."

The kettle had just boiled, so it only took her seconds to make the drinks. When she returned from the kitchen, he was still standing by the coffee table, where she'd left him.

A rush of heat overwhelmed Stacie at the sight of her Master. She'd never imagined she'd ever see him there again… and looking handsome enough to send any woman weak at the knees. The suit was one of her favourites and fitted him to perfection, not that she would have expected anything less. She had a feeling that he was wearing it like a suit of armour—as if he were about to go into battle. Battle for what, though—that was the question.

He was standing with his hand in his trouser pocket, fidgeting with something—not his car keys, as they were on the coffee table. He was all potent male animal… and to anyone who didn't know him as Stacie did, he would have looked completely in control.

Still his sub at heart, Stacie was so tuned in to him that she couldn't help but pick up on the air of uncertainty, something she'd never seen in him before. By default, then, she had the upper hand—and found that around Cam, it was the last thing she wanted.

Remember what he did. Remember what he said.

She did remember… and she'd forgive him in a heartbeat if he asked her to, but that was one thing a man like Cam would never do. At least, not of a woman whom he didn't love.

Stacie put a mug down on the coffee table, close to where he was standing, then took the other one to the opposite side, to put as much distance between them as she could. She couldn't even begin to imagine what he was here to say, but she figured that having that space there couldn't be a bad thing. And if the worst came to the worst, from where she was sitting, she could be in her bedroom and behind a locked door before he could get to her. Not that she thought it would come to that for one moment—Cam, like any Dom, was all about control.

She sipped her coffee and waited.

After a few moments, Cam unfastened his jacket and sat down. He reached for the coffee but drew back, wiped his hand over his face and the back of his neck. "Stacie, there's so much I need to say to you, but I'm damned if I know where to begin." He looked at her as if he were searching for inspiration.

"Why don't you just start? I'm sure the order won't matter, so long as you say everything you came here to say. Then you won't need to come back."

And where the hell had that come from? Stupid question, she thought—the answer was obvious. It came from the part of her that was still raw and bleeding, the part that had listened to him tell her that their relationship was over, the part that had listened to the doctor tell her that she'd lost her baby… the little girl who was the last part of the man she loved that she would ever have.

She should have been pleased when that particular

barb struck home, but strangely it hurt even more when, for an unguarded instant, she caught the flash of pain that crossed his face. Her foolish heart. Even now, after everything that had happened, she still had feelings for him.

What an idiotic understatement! You love him and you always will.

All things considered, she hadn't known Cam that long, but in all the time she'd known him, she'd never seen him lost for words. Until now.

The seconds ticked by, until finally he spoke.

"First of all, don't get mad at Beth—she had the best of intentions when she came to see me. And I'm glad she did. I know about the baby, Stacie," he admitted heavily. "I'm sorry. So sorry."

So that was it. That was what he came to say. Whatever she'd thought he might say first it wasn't that, but there was no doubting his sincerity. It was almost as if he aged visibly as he said the words. But sorry for what?

"Don't worry—I like Beth too much to be mad at her. I should never have asked her to keep it from Alex. I should never have told her in the first place. Why are you sorry, Cam? That I lost her, or that I got pregnant in the first place?"

This time he looked directly at her, his expression one of complete horror, then his eyes fell again, focusing on the hands clasped between his knees.

"You have every right to ask that," he said raggedly. "I'm sorry you lost our daughter. I'm sorry I wasn't here for you when it happened. I'm sorry I lost sight of the most important thing of all."

"And what's that?"

"That we belonged together. That I loved you."

Belonged. Loved. Past tense, no longer in the present. Stacie's heart cracked. Just when she thought she was starting to get over the pain of losing the man she loved and the life they'd created together, he had to come back into her life, only to disappear from it again just as quickly, as he surely would after this visit.

"Why are you here, Cam? What's the real reason? Wasn't hurting me over the phone enough for you? You had to come here, put me through that all over again, so you could see for yourself just how much you hurt me?"

If that was all he'd come for, then he could leave right now.

"Stacie, I can't tell you how much I regret that—"

"Then why did you do it?"

Her tone was more aggressive than she intended it to be but it struck home, judging by the sudden pallor of his face… as if in that instant, he realised that she wasn't going to be a pushover. Whatever she might have thought his response would be, the response she got surprised her again.

"To keep you safe. You were hurt because of me, Stacie, because of what I do. It's the only thing I'm any good at, the only thing I know how to do… I had no choice. It was the only way I could protect you."

Was he really saying what she thought he was saying? That he'd dumped her because of his *job*?

It would be easy to accuse him of choosing his work over her and their relationship, but something was telling her that that thought had never entered his head. He was an honourable man—his actions the night they first met told her that—and his point of view was exactly as he'd said… that she was hurt because of the job that was such an intrinsic part of him that it was impossible to tell where the job ended and the man began. And the only way he could protect her from being hurt again was to remove himself from her life. Yes, she could quite see his way of thinking leading him to that conclusion.

He repeated the statement. "I had no choice, Stacie. I thought about giving up my work so we could be together, but I knew that would change me into someone you wouldn't want and you'd walk away from me anyway."

As if she'd ever not want him. The way his mind was working was making her head spin. Male logic was decidedly one of life's great mysteries. "Would you excuse me a moment, please? I won't be long."

Stacie headed for the bathroom, her mind in turmoil. She so wanted to believe everything that Cam had said, but her sense of self-preservation dictated otherwise. As she splashed cold water over her face, she acknowledged that she was just trying to buy herself a little extra time.

The love she had for Cam Fraser had diminished not one iota in the time they'd been apart. It never would, and she would be deluding herself if she were to think otherwise. She wanted to be with him, spend the rest of her life with him, have a real family with him. She wanted to give him her love and her trust again, give both of them a chance to be loved and to be happy.

So what was she to do? Behave like a prima donna, haul him over the coals, carry on extracting her pound of flesh? Or just face up to the fact that the stupid arsehole had made a mistake, he'd come clean about it, and all that stood between them and happily ever after was her ability to forgive him?

He'd done what he'd done for the best of reasons, it was as simple and as misguided as that—he was a strong man who wanted to protect what was most precious to him, someone he loved. How could she not forgive him for that? He'd just gone about it in entirely the wrong way. He was an idiot male who thought he knew best.

Don't they all?

She loved Cam for the man he was… and his work was a large part of what made him the man he was.

Reject the job and you reject the man. Accept the man and you accept the job.

She loved him, and with that love came understanding and compassion… and the ability to forgive.

However, one niggle remained—the fact that he'd said he loved her in a way that might be interpreted to mean he no longer felt the same way. On the other hand, it might just be a clumsy expression of his feelings—then and now. She could make all the guesses and assumptions she wanted but they wouldn't help—only the truth could do that, and if the truth was that he no longer loved her, then she could be strong enough to deal with it.

She knew what she had to do. Heart and mind at one and at peace, she returned to the living area… and what she saw almost stopped her heart in her chest.

Cam knew there was only one thing he could do to convince the woman he loved that he'd told her nothing but the truth. For her, he'd do anything. She could be back any minute, but if fate were with him—and it appeared to have been, so far—he'd have enough time to carry out his plan. He yanked off his jacket and tie, toed off his shoes, rolled up his shirt sleeves, and moved around to the other side of the coffee table, so that he'd be the first thing she saw when she came back.

Then, uncaring of the effect it would have on his Savile Row suit, Cam Fraser sank to his knees, placed his hands palm upwards on his thighs, assumed perfect slave position… and waited. If getting her back took letting her flay the skin off his back and walk all over the bloody remains, he'd do it.

Whatever it took, he'd do it.

He heard the sharp intake of breath at the same moment as he saw the feet, shod in elegant heels, stumble to a halt a few feet away from him.

"Cam?"

"For someone who keeps harping on about the importance of clear communication, I've made a piss-poor job of it so far. I love you, Stacie, and I'll do whatever it takes for us to be together." He bit out the words. "Pushing you away was the single most asinine thing I've ever done in my life. I'm begging you to give us—give *me*—another chance, and I'll do whatever it takes to prove how much you mean to me. I'll give up my work—whatever you want.

"Except for one thing—I'll never ask you to forgive me for not being here when you lost our daughter. I can never forgive myself for that and I can never expect you to forgive me."

He fixed his gaze on the feet in front of him, watched them take a couple of steps towards him. They stopped, and as the pencil skirt was pulled up over the knees, the feet stepped out of the shoes, and all of a sudden Stacie was kneeling in front of him, sitting back on her heels, just out of reach.

"Ask me," she said, her voice clear and strong. "Ask me to forgive you for not being there when our daughter died. Say the words."

She was looking directly at him, her face betraying no emotion. Cam felt as if she were waiting to drive a knife straight into his heart.

"I'm sorry, Stacie," he began, dread filling him as he embarked on what was starting to feel like the last conversation he would ever have with the woman he loved. "I'm sorry I pushed you away. I'm sorry, sorrier than I can ever express, that I wasn't with you when our daughter died. I'm sorry I made you go through all of that alone. I should have been here, with you. Please…" His voice faltered on a rising tide of turbulent emotion. "Please, can you forgive me?"

Her expression didn't change, not one iota—she simply looked at him as if she were looking into the depths of what passed for his soul. Then she rose to her knees, laid her hands palm down on his, and with silent tears running down her face, she leaned towards him and kissed his mouth, before sitting on her heels again.

"I love you, Master," she said simply. "How can I not forgive you? You thought you were protecting me, I understand that now. But it doesn't mean that what you did, how you went about it, was the *right* thing to do. Staying with you—or not—for reasons of *my* personal safety was *my* choice to make, not yours. You took that choice away from me."

It was then that Cam realised just how badly he'd underestimated his brave sub. He thought of all the things she'd done for him since they met, all the times she could have safeworded out of their relationship and hadn't. Sometimes she'd been knocked back a step, but only a step. Her core of quiet resilience had always enabled her to come back, and stronger than before.

The woman he saw before him now had strength, grit and determination—she'd proved that when she'd insisted on accompanying Alex on the rescue mission. Submissive though she might be, she wouldn't submit to just any man. It would only be to the man she deemed worthy. For better or worse, she had chosen him to be that man.

"I'll never do that again, beautiful," he promised. "You have my word."

Her mouth turned upwards, forming that bewitching

smile of hers. "You're forgetting something, Master."

She let her gaze fall to their hands, still resting palms together on his thighs. With the gentle touch he'd missed so much, she turned his hands over, then lifted them and lowered her head, to touch her forehead to his knuckles. When she remained in that position of obeisance, Cam felt the gift of her power, her control, flow to him.

"Stacie, look at me."

He didn't think he'd ever have his fill of looking into her beautiful eyes. Her cheek was soft beneath the back of his fingers, and when she moved to kiss them, he couldn't hold back any longer. With gentle hands he framed her face, and then lowered his head to kiss her.

"I've been a fool, honey," he began, eyes closed, forehead resting against hers. "I can't be without you, not now. I'll make it right, I promise. I'll give up my work, there must be something else—"

She drew back slowly, her gaze making him feel as if he were under a microscope. Her finger lay gently on his lips.

"You don't need to give up anything. Master, I told you that I forgive you—and it already *is* right… almost."

"Almost?"

Here it comes. Cam braced himself for the worst.

Her hands were gentle on his face, tracing the line of his brow, his cheek, his upper lip… learning his features by touch. "There's one thing missing. I know a sub isn't supposed to ask for anything, Master—"

Her eyes were telling him what she needed, and it

wasn't what was in the small box that he withdrew from his trouser pocket. That was the furthest thing from her mind—he knew it even before he saw her stunned expression on seeing the white-gold ring set with three brilliant diamonds for the first time. With a solemnity befitting the occasion, he lifted her left hand and held the ring at the tip of her third finger.

"Stacie, I ask you to take this ring and do me the honour of becoming my wife, and as your Master, I offer you my collar. You are free to accept one, both or neither."

Cam exhaled slowly, subconsciously matching the rate of his respiration to the movement of Stacie's hand as she slipped her finger into the ring.

"Master, I accept both… with all my heart."

EPILOGUE

Cam let his breath go on a peaceful sigh. After the whirlwind of activity that had filled the last few days, it felt good to unwind at last. A vacation in the sun was long overdue. The added bonus was the beautiful young woman currently sleeping in his arms, her deliciously curvaceous body draped partially over him as they relaxed together in the balmy tropical evening.

A whole month of pure relaxation lay ahead of them. They'd arrived on the private Caribbean island by boat just a few hours ago. After taking the time to unpack and shower, they'd walked along the beach to watch the sun go down and run through the crystal-clear waters that lapped at the shore, before returning to the luxurious bungalow that would be home for the next few weeks. Although they were both tired, neither had wanted the day to end just yet.

The double lounger on the sun deck had proven irresistible. From there, during the day, they would be able to see the beach and the blue Caribbean beyond, the curving shoreline with its white sand and fringe of palm trees. For now, though, with the sun well below the horizon, they had the stars for company, along with the odd call of the island's nocturnal wildlife, and the gentle wash of the waves over the sand that had finally lulled Stacie to sleep.

Cam was about ready to join her. Part of the pre-vacation craziness had been tying up loose ends at work, but knowing that he'd left the business in the safe hands of Alex Lombard was going a long way towards helping him to relax. It was good to have his old friend well and truly back on board, and their plans to revamp the company were already going well.

One of the first suggestions Alex had made was to expand the business into other related fields, but to provide a service that was more strategic than operational, to act as advisers rather than boots on the ground. Risk assessments were something they carried out as a matter of course for all their own operations, so providing the same for clients was a natural extension. And if Cam's recent experience in the Middle East was a taste of how crisis management could go wrong, then crisis prevention had to be the better option for any potential client. Cam was as sure as hell that he could have prevented *that* crisis... unlike the business competitor on whose watch the hostages had been taken.

Since they were examining the possibility of expanding on a consultancy basis, Alex had also proposed extending an invitation to Sir Guy Somerton to join them. The man had extensive and highly valuable experience in the field of security, and an air of gravitas that would lend even more weight to their already formidable professional credibility. According to conversations they'd had with his niece, Ros Edwards, he'd been growing increasingly frustrated with his role as a "glorified civil servant", so they'd dangled the carrot of a new challenge, one where he could get his hands dirty again.

Guy wasn't the only recipient of an invitation to join Spectrum. Their approach to the recently married Ryan Quinn, another member of Aegis, whose expertise lay in the field of maritime security, had been favourably received, to the extent that plans were already under way for a three-way partnership. Quinn was a former Royal Navy officer who'd also served with the Special Boat Service for a number of years. Widening the scope of the services they could offer their clients—who included high-net-worth individuals with the money to spend on luxury motor yachts and the like—could only be a sound operational move.

But that was business, and Cam really didn't want to think about that on the first day of what was not just a vacation, but a honeymoon. The wedding, organised as quickly as was legally possible, had been deliberately low-key, just Beth and Alex Lombard in attendance, along with Stacie's friend Jen as the chief—and only—bridesmaid.

Stacie's parents had also been there. After their initial

meeting, they'd happily accepted that Cam was the man with whom their only daughter had chosen to spend the rest of her life and welcomed him into their family with open arms.

He'd met them for the first time just a couple of weeks after he'd proposed to their daughter and expected them to give him a rough ride—after all, he *was* the man who'd got their daughter pregnant and left her to go through a miscarriage alone. However, her father had asked him just a couple of questions—did he, Cam, love his daughter, and would he look after her? Cam had looked the other man squarely in the eye and told him the truth—that Stacie was the most important thing in his life and he'd give up his life to protect her. Whatever Stacie had told her father about him before that meeting, she'd clearly convinced him that Cam was good enough to be his daughter's man.

Now, for the first time in his life, Cam Fraser had a real family. It was a concept that was taking quite some getting used to.

Having attended the wedding ceremony—where Alex had been his best man—Beth and Alex had also been present at the collaring ceremony at Aegis, where Stacie had proudly given him the gift of her submission before all their friends in the community. And most surprisingly, one of those witnesses had been Jen Peterson—slightly bemused by what was playing out before her… and the focus of covert attention from both Dylan Baxter and Conor Devlin. Cam had the feeling that interesting times lay ahead for the petite, raven-haired beauty.

Their soon-to-be business partner Ryan had also been there, standing protectively at the side of the lovely Fiona, his wife and Mistress. They were both relatively new to the scene, learning about it and each other. Ryan was finding peace and freedom in his submissive role, while Fiona still occasionally struggled with reconciling the new-found dominant side of her nature with the person she'd always perceived herself to be.

Cam was among those who were helping her to understand that by embracing Ryan's gift of sexual submission, she was giving her sub what he needed. What was abundantly clear through it all, though, was her love for her husband—her respect and admiration for him, and her dedication to his care. Cam had seen Ryan at work on joint ops, knew exactly how tough he was and would be willing to go into any life-or-death situation with the man at his side—Ryan Quinn was lethal when it came to unarmed combat, yet Cam had seen him kneel before his Mistress, a slave collar around his neck to match the cuffs at his wrists, and submit to her every desire.

Ros Edwards, an alpha Domme if ever there was one, had been of most assistance to the Mistress-in-training—it was just a pity, Cam reflected, that Ros' preference for alpha male subs was such a tall order. The available male subs at Aegis tended to throw themselves at her feet, but she had little patience with any of them—they simply weren't a sufficient challenge for the former military police officer. Ros needed a sub she could get her teeth into—figuratively, if not literally.

And Ros had been the only one of their close friends absent from the ceremony. Her uncle had asked her to take on a special assignment that was strictly off the record as far as his organisation was concerned, and in the latest development, it had unfortunately taken her unexpectedly to France a few days earlier. When she'd called to offer apologies, it had been apparent that she had rather mixed feelings about the trip itself, in addition to being mightily pissed off about missing the ceremony.

For the event, Stacie had been a barefoot vision in white, with the honey of her hair a cascade around her shoulders, the dress a simple affair in silk as pure as snow in colour, V-necked front and back, though not too revealing, with a full skirt that swirled from her hips and fell to mid-calf. Very modest for a BDSM club, but for this almost sacred occasion, that was how he'd wanted her to be. Her wrists loosely, symbolically bound behind her back with a gold-coloured silk rope, she'd knelt before him and vowed to love, serve and care for her Master for the rest of her life. He hadn't known exactly what she was going to say—the words she chose left him in no doubt as to the depth of her love for him.

As he'd locked the ornate white-gold collar around her neck, Cam had recited the words he'd chosen to express his love and declare his commitment. He'd kept his plans a secret from his precious sub. At the end, when he'd tilted her chin up to look into her eyes, they'd been shining with unshed tears, but what had spoken to him most clearly was the love behind the tears and the smile on her face. He would take that vision of her with him to the grave.

His gaze gentle with all the love he felt for her, Cam looked down at his wife, still sleeping peacefully, trustingly in his arms. She'd been through so much, with the car bomb, losing their daughter, not to mention flying out to the Middle East on the mission to save his worthless hide. She might have forgiven him, but Cam would still never forgive himself for letting her suffer alone. If only he'd known…

We can still have children, Cam.

He'd discovered that that was the one thing she'd really worried about. So long as he had Stacie, he wouldn't have cared, but right now, being father to a little girl with her mother's eyes and spirit was his idea of heaven.

Cam closed his eyes in a silent prayer of thanks, for all the good that filled his life. Alex, Ros, Conor and Bax, all of them more than just friends and colleagues—without them, and all the other comrades whom he'd resigned himself to never seeing again while he was held captive, he wouldn't be here now. And without Beth, he wouldn't have the woman who was the centre of his world. They'd never given up on him, even when he'd all but given up on himself. Those were debts he could never repay.

And above all else, there was Stacie—his beloved wife, and a future with her that far surpassed anything he could have imagined. He'd been given more than he deserved, but as he kissed her hair, he made one more vow—to devote the rest of his life to this incredible woman and prove himself worthy of her love every day.

ABOUT THE AUTHOR

When Christie Adams, author of contemporary steamy romance, isn't completely absorbed in the writing process, she's probably thinking about it—either the book she's currently working on, or one of the dozen other stories she'll have percolating away at the back of her mind.

In addition to writing, she also loves investing time in reading a good book, or browsing the internet in search of cute videos of puppies, a pastime that often helps with writer's block—or so she claims. On those rare occasions when she can tear herself away from the computer, she has a weakness for James Bond movies and romantic comedies.

Good chocolate is also one of her passions in life, often accompanied by a glass of her favourite tipple, English sparkling wine. And if she can be persuaded to abandon her writing for a while, she finds that chocolate, wine and a good movie on TV is an excellent way to pass a winter's evening.

To find out more about Christie and her books, please visit her website—http://christieadamsauthor.com

Printed in Great Britain
by Amazon

38140681R00212